M000237737

SOAR: A Soul's Quest

Ketan Kulkarni, Christopher Morris, Francis Yoo

HARP Publishing: The People's Press
Clydesdale, Nova Scotia, Canada

HARP Publishing: The People's Press
216 Clydesdale Road
Clydesdale, Nova Scotia
CANADA B2G 2K9
www.harppublishing.ca

SOAR ©2023 Ketan Kulkarni

All rights reserved. No part of this book may be used or reproduced
in any manner without written permission from the publishers.
Information about purchasing copies of this book
can be obtained from the publishers.

harppeoplespress@gmail.com

Catalogue-in-Publication data is on file with the Library & Archives
Canada ISBN: 978-1-990137-39-6

Cover Design and Editing: Lauren Squillino
Cover Art: Ketan Kulkarni
Interior Artwork: Reeva Kulkarni, Grade 3
Book Layout: Greg Walsh

David Suzuki Foundation (one nature): https://davidsuzuki.org ;
The Circle of Abundance Indigenous Program,
Coady International Institute,
St. Francis Xavier University: https://coady.stfx.ca/circle of abundance,
receive 20% of sales distributed equally

Artwork

Cover art was created by **Ketan Kulkarni.** The painting: **Soar** was first displayed at the 68th Dalhousie Student, Staff, Faculty and Alumni Art Exhibition

The illustrations at the start of each chapter were all created by **Reeva Kulkarni**

Reeva is a grade 3 student at Halifax Grammar School. She loves science, mathematics, art, reading, and writing. Outside of school she enjoys Lego, sewing, painting, puzzles, piano, skating, and swimming. She enjoys leadership, critical thinking and problem-solving.

Testimonials

Soar is an inspiring story with which I deeply resonated. Always feeling that I myself never truly fit in with the status quo, or with society's standards and rules, for me *Soar* is a wonderful story of finding oneself and truly finding joy and happiness as you follow Soar's journey. I believe most people will relate to the struggles, the lessons, the relationships, and the emotional challenges along the way. As you read the book, it forces you to really look back at your own life—to reflect, learn, and grow. **I believe that *Soar* will be an international bestseller,** as anyone will be able to pick up this book and see themselves in *Soar*. I highly recommend it.

Warren Barry spent 30 years as an entrepreneur in medicine and specialized in myofascial release. Warren is a human resources business consultant and coach. He is the creator of The Flying V @ Work, and helps organizations fly in the metaphorical V formation by understanding and utilizing the cognitive and instinctual aspects of the mind. He is also the creator and host of the Better the Pond—Pondcast. He can be reached at warren@instinctivesolutions.ca

Soar is an inspirational and insightful work, colored by vivid description and wonderful writing. I found it to be powerful and utterly compelling.

Mark Manduca is a Number 1 ranked Wall Street analyst. His career as a top-ranked analyst spans senior positions with leading investment banks, including Citigroup in London, where he served as Managing Director in Equity Research and led multiple industrial-based research activities. Earlier, he spent eight years with Bank of America Merrill Lynch, where he led the business services and transport research teams.

Prior to GXO, Manduca consistently led the top-ranked European transport research teams for close to a decade, as determined by Institutional Investor. In 2021, he received the most votes individually across all sectors and regions in the European Institutional Investor survey and was named the No. 1 European Transport Research Analyst for the tenth consecutive year.

I know Ketan as a skilled clinician, researcher, and caring colleague. Our work in pediatric oncology invariably leads to contemplation of the meaning of life and how we can make the best use of our time on earth. *Soar* is a heartfelt exploration of that quest and will be of interest to anyone who is on their own personal journey towards meaning.

Katrina MacDonald is a career pediatric oncology nurse and is passionate about lifelong learning and growth. One of the great privileges of her life and career is to work alongside exceptionally thoughtful, caring, and collaborative healthcare professionals.

Soar is a reminder of the traditional power of the allegorical tale to instruct us on how to deal with life's most profound challenges. As a result, the book resonates with universal myth. On one level, it is an expression of the Hero's Journey, on another, an examination of the transformation of learner into teacher. The story also raises issues of contemporary relevance. These include how we as individuals must reconcile personal growth with family expectations, and how that growth, once achieved, can return to enrich our culture of origin. This is a book not to be read quickly but to be contemplated thoughtfully.

Barbara Emodi has worked as an editor, writer, and journalist. Currently, she is a political commentator on CBC (Halifax, Nova Scotia). She has also taught communications at several universities and was the director of communication for a senior political figure.

Soar is a beautiful, flowing narrative about a young eagle who sets out on the journey of his life. The writing is lyrical, with many unusual and vivid descriptions that contribute to the fresh quality of the story. This is a great book for anyone to read who is seeking a sense of reflective calm during or after a period of being 'too busy'.

Kathleen W. Smith, PhD, enjoyed a long career with the Canadian Public Service as an inspector/investigator. In her retirement, she obtained Master's and PhD degrees in Psychology, holding a Postdoctoral Fellowship in England for three years. She has finally returned to her first passion: the serious practice of classical piano. Kathleen's personal website is https://kathleenwaltonsmith.ca/

Soar is a finely written book that takes the reader on an incredible journey, with extraordinary life lessons being shared along the way. *Soar* is a unique continuation of the deep explorations towards authentic living which were originally provided by authors Drs. Ketan Kulkarni and Francis Yoo in *The Legendary Quest*. I thoroughly enjoyed the opportunity to travel with *Soar* as he learns what it means to live a life true to himself and teaches others to do the same. Soar challenges the life lessons that he learned while he was young, in order to work towards a life that is in true alignment with his desires. The book therefore offers several thought-provoking concepts that may be applied to our own lives. The ending packs true punch, prompting us to reclaim our lives from societal expectations that may no longer be serving us on our quest for deeper, more meaningful lives. I am inspired to make changes in my own life thanks to *Soar*! Highly recommended!

Jillian Rigert, DMD, MD, is an Oral Medicine Physician, head and neck cancer researcher, and Life and Professional Leadership coach devoted to improving the quality of life of patients and clients. Dr. Rigert has a YouTube channel with a mission to support people as they learn to live the life that they truly desire—in alignment with Soar *and* The Legendary Quest! *With a shared mission, Dr. Rigert has partnered with authors, Drs. Kulkarni and Yoo to develop a YouTube series dedicated to supporting people on their Legendary Quest, seeking authentic fulfillment in their lives as they reconnect with their true selves and peel away from the societal expectations that are no longer serving them.*

Resonate? Join the community here:
https://www.youtube.com/c/JillianRigertDMDMD

Soar is a beautifully written story chronicling in its various phases the process of self-discovery, fulfillment, and happiness. Its use of metaphor reminds me of the bestselling book, *"Who Moved My Cheese?"*

Christopher H. Loo, MD-PhD, is a physician who became financially free at the age of 29, and retired at the age of 38, after making strategic investments following the 2008 financial crisis. He is passionate about the intersection of social media, Web3, Bitcoin, metaverse, and AI for thought leaders and influencers. He is a graduate of the MD-PhD programs at Baylor College of Medicine and Rice University Department of Bioengineering. He is founder and CEO of the Financial Freedom for Physicians Podcast. He can be reached at chris@drchrisloomdphd.com

A captivating story about pushing past boundaries and living a purposeful life aligned with your core values. I highly recommend *Soar* to anyone on a quest for self-improvement.

Dr. Yatin Chadha is an early-career radiologist practicing in Toronto. He created the "Beyond MD" podcast with the aim of striving for deep learning in all facets of life, and of bringing something useful to the world, especially to his colleagues. His podcast covers financial topics highly relevant to Canadian healthcare professionals, and has reached as high as #23 on the Canadian business podcast rankings. Yatin believes in pursuing life's endeavours with full intent, networking, and creating lasting memories with his wife Sima and his two boys, Rohin and Zian. He is happy to mentor others on their journey, and can be reached at beyondmdpodcast@gmail.com

In addition, there were twelve other beta readers who contributed to the book, and many other editors and advisory members who preferred to remain anonymous. We thank them all from the bottom of our hearts.

Foreword

I would first like to thank Ketan, Chris, and Francis for giving me the opportunity to contribute this foreword to a book that I greatly value.

When I first spoke to Ketan a few years ago, I knew he was searching for more. I even felt the drive within him that was going to open the doors he approached, not necessarily with ease, but with persistence and determination. This wasn't a common conversation that I had with my fellow physicians, but it was familiar from my own personal experience.

I hadn't met Chris or Francis at that time, but by the time their first book, *The Legendary Quest*, was released, it became evident that all three had been investing diligently in themselves in so many ways. This began from a place of curiosity, learning from adversity, and driving forward toward progress; and it has since encompassed many, many fields and facets. This includes becoming coaches, starting an art gallery, becoming advocates of diversity, equality, and social change, sustaining efforts to spread self-awareness and international advocacy, building courses to help physicians and professionals battle burnout, and compiling a prolific writing portfolio. The journeys of the three co-authors have overlapped in many ways, while they have all brought their diverse qualities and backgrounds to the project.

One day I received an email asking me to write a foreword for this book. Although I felt honored, I wanted to ensure that I could add something of value. I went straight to thinking: Will I like this book? Will I relate to this book? For me to write, it needs to come from the heart, and my heart needs to connect with the subject. Authenticity is everything, and that stems from the heart. So I told the authors that I wanted to dig in and take my time before I committed to anything.

I started reading *Soar* with an open mind. I say this because I usually focus on topics, such as leadership and personal development, as discussed in traditional non-fiction books. I began reading it one morning, as part of my routine to invest in myself. I found myself becoming immediately engaged. Early in this book, I started to recognize the common threads and fabric of the story. This is not the usual fictional narrative that doesn't relate directly to me. It is rather a transformative journey that emphasizes growth and the expansion of our mindset. It also offers ways to connect with others, to acknowledge and respect others with kindness and empathy, and to continue to live and teach in this way to anyone with whom we interact. It is written in a skillful way that provides extensive detail, while still keeping the reader thoroughly engaged.

This book was inspiring not only to myself. I have shared the story with my wife and my daughters, and I plan on sharing it with anyone who feels "stuck." Soar's story is everyone's story—everyone, that is, who needs a reminder that there is more out there to explore, understand, and experience.

In line with my current beliefs, as so eloquently expressed in this book, we don't have to escape a place to grow. Sometimes we merely need to change our position and perspective to understand ourselves and others. A continuous journey of learning, success, happiness, and fulfillment is what most of us seek, and it is what I have committed my life to achieve. This book strongly aligns with how I see my time in this life, and I believe that it will stir emotion and inspiration in all of you.

I want to continue to support and share content that is educational, inspiring, and entertaining, because we can all use more of this for our own growth and development. This book also has a particularly valuable message for those young readers among us. Here's to reading more, to doing more for ourselves and others, and to being kind and empathetic along the way. I sincerely hope that you enjoy this book as much as I did, and realize that both the obstacles and the opportunities that we encounter in life are often manifested by ourselves.

Thank you, Ketan, Chris, and Francis for combining beauty and inspiration into what is a narrative that will resonate with so many.

Dr. Navin Goyal

Navin Goyal, M.D., is a physician and entrepreneur who serves as CEO of LOUD Capital, an early-stage venture capital and alternative investment firm leveraging capital, entrepreneurship, and education to grow impactful companies across the globe. Bringing his physician training to do good for people, Navin strives to make venture capital more purpose-driven, inclusive, and accessible. Before co-founding LOUD Capital, Navin practiced anesthesiology in a large hospital-based setting and was for several years Medical Director of a community hospital.

The beginning of his entrepreneurial journey was the co-founding of OFFOR Health (formerly SmileMD)—a venture-backed mobile healthcare company that expands access to care, with a dedicated focus on lower-income and rural communities. His story, his experience, and what he sees as an opportunity for physicians to have a broader impact on themselves and society is the focus of his book, Physician Underdog.

Preface

We three students of life met in 2019, and soon realized that we were all on similar quests for excellence! It also became evident that we had diverse, yet overlapping, backgrounds, life experiences and perspectives, that emanated from three different continents.

In working together, we envisioned creating a body of work that reflected our views and collective philosophy on life, which we believe is rarely reflected in the prevailing media and cultural messages that people tend to receive.

Thus, in *The Legendary Quest*, we espoused a methodology that will help anyone achieve a happy and successful life, on their *own* terms, and in accordance with their *own* values.

In this second book, we have created what we intend as a magical and inspirational fable that illustrates and builds on the themes of *The Legendary Quest*.

We believe that everyone has, in some form and capacity, a *Soar* within them. We are not expanding on this too greatly here, as we hope that our story speaks for itself and resonates deeply within you. But one thing that has become abundantly clear to all three of us, and that we hope this story acutely reflects, is that life is a journey, but the journey is as important as the destination, if not more so.

Soar's story is, we believe, broadly applicable to human experience across the globe, regardless of any demographic or social factors. This story is for everyone, regardless of age, race, gender, or any other identifier. The story is equally applicable for, and to, any preferred pronoun.

Finally, we should say that we also intend this book to be food for thought regarding the issue of how we, as humans, interact with the animal kingdom, and indeed what our place is within that wider ecosystem.

We hope you truly enjoy accompanying Soar, an eagle with anthropomorphic qualities, on his journey.

1. The Hunt

Soar tilted his head attentively to one side, focusing his eyes on the undergrowth. He sensed some movement in the bushes, and years of experience told him that there was a rodent fumbling around in the shrubbery. His talons gripped the branch with anticipation, as he prepared to swoop down and surprise his prey. Soar's sinewy body was as tense as a coiled spring, every aspect of his being focused on this single promising location. Soar calculated that it was approximately 200 yards away; the creature would never see him coming. He would pounce as silently as snowflakes falling on the winter earth.

However, just as quickly as his senses heightened, the moment passed. What seemed to be the rustling of a mouse or rabbit turned out to be nothing more than a gusty breeze, sweeping through the lush pastures of his surroundings. Soar relaxed his posture, relieving his grip on the branch. He contemplated that it was turning out to be an unsuccessful afternoon. Two no-shows and one gray hare that managed to scurry into its burrow before he could complete his elegant descent. Oh well, there was plenty of food back at the lodge. But nothing beats the thrill of the hunt.

Soar sighed and stretched out his powerful wings, beginning the ascent that would take him home. It was a chilly March evening in Aquilana, far chillier than usual. Soar immediately sensed this; his internal systems were attuned to the seasons with the accuracy of a barometer. The wind even whipped up beneath him at one point, momentarily blowing him off course. He narrowed his beady eyes and quickly corrected his trajectory, reducing his altitude somewhat to avoid the unexpected disturbance. Sometimes you encounter these bursts of thermals, particularly around sunset, as the air cools, and the end of the day approaches. Hunt high in the morning, hunt low in the evening; Soar mentally chastised himself for his rookie error.

As Soar approached the familiar territory of Long-Tail Lodge, the final vestige of the golden sun was disappearing steadily behind the horizon, like a giant coin sliding inexorably into a vending machine. The sky blushed bright crimson—its distinctive blood-red facade interrupted only by grouplets of wispy clouds. The final furlongs to home were punctuated by immense sloped valleys, which created the impression of a canyon. A crystal-clear river flowed between the vast peaks, although the lack of visible light made it seem inky black at this time of night, even with Soar's compelling eyesight. He reflected nostalgically on the many times that he'd drunk from these often icy waters, as he raised his wings precipitously and began his final descent.

Life was pretty good in Aquilana, Soar reflected. We're a group of apex predators; what's not to like? Food was plentiful, the natural world was beautiful and life-affirming, the community was united and supportive. There was a profound sense of comfort in knowing that your basic needs have been met. He had rapidly climbed the ladder to become one of the community's most respected hunters, regularly receiving respect and admiration from both males and females within the tribe.

Yet somehow something was missing. There was an inner itch; a persistent hunger at the core of Soar's soul that had never quite been satiated. From his earliest memories, he always had the intrinsic sense that there was more to life than he learned from his peers and authority figures. This was usually dismissed as youthful impudence. And, sure enough, Soar had eventually settled into a routine existence with the other residents of Aquilana. He hadn't rocked the boat as much as his youthful idealism had demanded.

But the spark within him had never stopped burning. His movements were more measured and purposeful now, but his heart was no less pure. Surely it was normal to seek adventure beyond your immediate environment;

we're eagles after all, right? There is so much more that we could experience and contribute beyond the confines of our routine existence. We don't need to limit ourselves. Indeed, we need to invest every drop of blood and passion in seeking our true potential. That is normal. I am the normal one, Soar told himself, no matter what they say!

His chain of thought was interrupted as the mountains over which he was flying parted, and the familiar burnished oak of Long-Tail Lodge loomed into view. Soar straightened out his prodigious wingspan until it was parallel to the ground and began the maneuver that would take him home. His altitude began to rapidly decline, but it was all perfectly under control—his descent as poised as the spin of a Bolshoi ballet dancer.

The final pathway to the lodge was decorated with an array of elaborate oil lamps, ornately hung alongside the extent of the landing area, with much the same purpose as the lights on an airport runway. Soar could perceive this illumination from hundreds of yards away, and it informed him as he made his descent.

Soar slowed as he made the final preparations to land, his eyes centered with laser-like precision on one particular worn patch of ground. This was one of the designated safe spaces for landing; used with such frequency that a sizable area had been completely denuded of grass, until it resembled the pitcher's mound at a baseball stadium. Soar landed safely, with little more than a bump, simultaneously rotating his neck around 180-degrees to check for signs of life. Never let your guard down; that was one of the first lessons that you were taught in Aquilana. Soar had rebelled against many of the more dubious teachings, but he had taken that one well under his wings.

The lodge building itself featured a sloping roof with slanted timber. Rows of symmetrically arranged arched windows, tall and narrow in design, enabled natural beams of light to seep in. There was nothing and no one outside, but emanating from the golden glow inside Soar perceived several familiar figures, silhouetted against the failing sun of late evening. As he approached the lodge, Soar heard laughter; there was an evident atmosphere of joy and joviality. He really wasn't in the mood for socializing but nonetheless Soar steeled himself, preparing to step inside.

*   *   *

The wrought iron fireplace, as black as coal, gleamed against the gloomy evening light. An occasional errant flame leapt flickering above the height of the others to break the uniformity of the fire, while a persistent crackling of smoldering wood adorned the ambience of the room. The sitting room of Long-Tail Lodge was characterized by its traditional stone floor; the graphite gray limestone that formed the ornate tiling had existed for many centuries. Vast oak beams ran symmetrically along the ceiling, while the room's leather furnishings were luxurious yet comfortable. The sofa and chairs had been softened by a myriad of sitting sessions over the years, becoming yielding and accommodating in the process.

There was an underlying but perceptible feeling of permanence embedded in the room, as if it had always been here and always would be here. This contributed to the comforting nature of the lodge; the family had come to rely on its opulence, along with the supportive community that resided in the surrounding area. They wished for nothing, they wanted for nothing—all except one member of the family...

Solomon furrowed his imposing brow grumpily as he sipped his brandy. "Is it necessary for us to use so much fuel at this time of year? It's nearly Spring! We don't have unlimited resources."

His wife, Jemima, accustomed to his outbursts and miserly behavior, tried to stop herself from smiling. She couldn't, however, entirely prevent a slight upward movement in her facial expression. "Yes, it's necessary," she explained patiently, "because it's, you know, really cold!" There was no malice behind her mild sarcasm.

Solomon shifted slightly in his grand armchair. "Well, don't say I didn't warn you when we run out. It's not me who suffers in the cold or feels the constant need to live in tropical temperatures. I won't be the one complaining if more snow arrives, and we don't have any fuel." Satisfied that he'd closed the subject, Solomon afforded himself a more voluminous slurp of his drink, enjoying the way the potent liquid warmed, almost burnished, his tongue.

"No, you're never the one to complain!", his daughter Carrie perked up. And despite the slight tension of the argument, or perhaps because of it, all of the family burst out laughing. At first, Solomon was annoyed with the mild mocking of his character. But eventually he surrendered to the teasing from his nearest and dearest, and the jocularity of the situation. He leant back and chuckled: "Okay, point taken, but let's at least try to be sensible! We don't know how long this winter will last; we equally don't know when the next winter will come. We are well provided for here, we all know that we're fortunate, but we must cope with what we have. We can't magic food, fuel, or fortune out of thin air."

There was a general murmuring of agreement and acceptance, and the family reached a comfortable point of synthesis. They *were* fortunate, but it was also true that they had to be realistic in their expectations. Since settling and colonizing Aquilana, it had become an oasis of calm and contentment. The residents of Aquilana were unfamiliar with the uncertainty that lay beyond this amenable territory. And they didn't wish to familiarize themselves with it. A fearless and reckless attitude was to be discouraged.

Sitting in the middle of the spacious expanse of the sitting room was an enormous mahogany dining table. So thick was the magnificent wood of this dominant feature, the table had to weigh a ton. As the family sat talking, the sumptuous aroma of meat roasting in the wood-burning oven wafted in from the kitchen. The flavorful fragrance was so seductive that it was almost possible to taste the juices.

"Where is that boy?", Solomon asked impatiently. "He's never on time!" The relationship between Soar and his formidable father was not quite turbulent, but not quite tranquil either. Although their interactions were never unduly disrespectful, they had nonetheless clashed on a regular basis during Soar's childhood. Soar considered his father to be unnecessarily authoritarian; Solomon thought himself not authoritarian enough! Solomon reflected on the stern guardianship of his own father and concluded that he allowed Soar to get away with murder! Another sore point was the unevenness of familial discipline. Soar observed the way that Solomon dealt with Carrie and felt that it was fundamentally different to the way he was treated. Carrie was handled with kid gloves, at least from Soar's perspective.

But their relationship wasn't entirely founded on discord. Soar was grateful for the life skills that his father had taught him; Solomon could be an unforgivingly hard taskmaster, but also proffered praise generously when it was merited. This meant that when Soar did receive approval or validation, he knew that it was deserved. It wasn't his father buttering him up; he had truly earned it. Consequently, Soar developed a profound faith in his own ability from the tenderest age; his father's gruff guardianship had instilled an acceptance of the travails of life. Whereas other eaglets in the convocation could be hesitant and tentative, reluctant to venture out from the protective bubble of their parents, this had never applied to Soar. He had been toughened like a callus; hardened to tolerate the friction and pressure of what could be an unforgiving world.

Solomon had intended for his guidance to induce responsibility in Soar, whereas it had, in fact, prompted a sense of fearlessness and adventure. This was the root cause of the tension between them. Solomon emphasized the value of community and obligation; Soar longed for unexplored horizons beyond the confines of the familiar Aquilana. The community could be suffocating for Soar, with everyone knowing everybody else, and seemingly everything about everybody else! This jarred with the free-spirited independence at the core of Soar's soul. He accepted his duties in the community, but still longed for a broader canvas to decorate, for vibrant new environs to explore and conquer.

At that moment, Soar sailed through the front door of Long-Tail Lodge. "Look what, the cat dragged in!", Solomon scolded, a slightly playful expression belying his apparent dismay.

"Yeah, yeah, I know I'm slightly late. I am aware of this! But I spied a few hunting opportunities on my way back," Soar explained.

"Have you got anything to show us then?", his mother asked expectantly.

"No," Soar replied sullenly. "Nothing worked out today."

"Well, you can't win every day," Jemima said encouragingly. "You've been prolific this year, no one doubts the contribution that you've made to the tribe."

Soar acknowledged his mother with a nod, slumping down in one of the dining chairs. But having failed to capture his prey, the hunter was at least eagerly anticipating his evening meal.

"Dinner won't be ready for a few minutes," his mother explained composedly. "Why don't you tell us more about what you're been up to today, Soar?"

"Oh, nothing much," He replied dismissively. "Just a load of no-shows and false alarms. Nothing worth talking about."

No one spoke for several seconds. There was an undeniable atmosphere in the room; the air hung heavy like a numbing wine. Everyone shuffled around, staring at their feet, attempting to think of something to say. Then Carrie piped up with a cheerful comment about dinner. She had always been a ray of sunshine in Soar's life, and he often wished that he could be more like her—always on an apparent equilibrium. Soar's mood lived up to his name; it escalated, spiraled, and descended alarmingly, with neither warning nor regard for the consequences.

Nonetheless, once Carrie had broken the ice, Soar relaxed and began chatting away, savoring his imminent dinner. They had always been a close family, and it was perhaps this closeness that Soar found unsettling. It should have been a source of support in his life; a stanchion that provided leverage against the often cruel and menacing world. And it had been. But it was also restrictive for someone of Soar's mindset and character. He could never truly acclimate himself to the whole concept of responsibility and belonging, much as he had attempted to do so. And yet, naturally enough, he still felt an undeniable sense of attachment to those that had raised him. This conflict was omnipresent within him, pulling him one way and then the other like a particularly gusty breeze, ensuring that he could never feel truly settled. He was torn between the yearning desire for freedom, and the consoling feeling of the familiar.

As the family members chatted away, Soar's mother had slipped into the kitchen almost unnoticed, and soon the main dish of the day was being presented on the dining table. Roast grouse—an exemplary classic. As soon as she pierced the succulent flesh of the animal, its juices began oozing out steadily, followed shortly afterwards by a subtle stream of crimson blood that stained the translucent liquid, heightening the anticipation in the room.

Soon the family were all tucking into the main meal. For a couple of joyous minutes, the conversation slowed to a virtual standstill, as the four eagles fixed their attention on the spoils of previous hunts. Food was cosmically, spiritually associated with the hunt; something from which humans have become almost entirely dissociated. In Aquilana, a low-key contempt for humans tended to circulate, with their soulless little packages of plastic-adorned meat, as well as a haughty disregard for their claims of being the planet's superior being. "They don't know what it is to hunt, they don't know what it is to fly, they don't know what it is to live!" was a commonly repeated motto that reverberated around the community. And, rest assured, it's no accident that we shit on your windshields!

Even by the standards of eagle communities, Aquilana was phenomenally close-knit. There were only a small number of families residing in this privileged part of the world, and most of them had been there for generations. Consequently, they were meticulously protective of their own, while being extremely suspicious of outsiders. They deemed these conjoined attitudes to be a keystone in the smooth functioning of the region.

Eagles in Aquilana faced fewer direct threats from predators than many other animals, but their lives were not so serene as to be immune from hazard. Soar recalled one crafty fox taking the life of a neighboring eaglet just a few months ago. Indeed, the lives of the young were notoriously precarious. Juvenile eaglets had to contend with predation, accidental death, falling from their nests, and even fratricide—the killing of an infant eaglet by one of its siblings. Nonetheless, in Aquilana everything was done to protect against this; the closeness of the community being a conscious attempt to not only create an ideal environment for its residents to flourish, but to nurture its young. Soar remembered it being drilled into him that you must always have your wits about you. The infant eaglets of Aquilana were fed this dictum almost before they'd had their first taste of meat.

Although mealtime was considered important, conversation was not forbidden. Once the initial respectful silence had been observed, the conversation around the dinner table returned to matters of societal importance. Solomon observed that stocks of meat were running lower than usual, and that they needed to fortify themselves against any unanticipated factors, especially as wintery conditions were likely to endure well into springtime.

Soar again found himself squirming uncomfortably in his seat. "But father," he began, "we've never yet run out of anything! It's absolutely unheard-of for us to have anything approaching a famine."

"Yes, and that's precisely because we're careful," his father answered immediately, with the air of wisdom and authority that had been earned from decades as an Elder. "You always imagine that there's some promised land on the horizon that we don't know about; well, let me let you down gently—there isn't! You're living in it!"

Soar was frequently irritated by his father's know-it-all disposition. This was one occasion on which he was no more willing to let the matter go than he would be a flailing mouse that was fighting for its life.

"How would you know when you never venture more than five miles outside of Aquilana? You nearly had a heart attack last week when I picked up that mongoose near Crag's Creek! Anyway, if we get a little low, I can always hunt down some more food. I don't need to worry."

"What, like today?" his father asked inquisitively.

Soar went quiet for a second, nibbling on his grouse resentfully, as he considered his response. He was so right and his father was so wrong; how could he fail to see that? This was not a generational divide, it was a matter of principle.

"Well, I'm not exactly firing on all my hunting cylinders while being confined to a ten-mile radius! I'm top of the hunting charts for this year, what I've done is already a bloody miracle!", Soar retorted passionately.

"Please don't curse at the dinner table, Soar," his mother pleaded.

"No, I'm not going to say sorry this time," Soar responded. "It's just a word. The meat we've just eaten was bloody! We kill every day! I'm damned if I'm going to apologize over a bloody word!"

His father paused, before speaking calmly. "Soar, don't disrespect your mother. You're only eating because of her. You take her, us, Aquilana, and everything for granted. I know that you're young, and I also know that you're talented. I don't tell you that too often because I don't want to spoil you. I'm proud of how we raised you; it's made you the hunter and credit to the community that you are. But you always think you know best, whereas no one always knows best."

"That would equally apply to you," Soar replied quietly. He suddenly had no energy for this argument; it was already venturing in a direction that was all too familiar, and the ever-decreasing circles of this quarrel were tiresome. "Look, you know how I feel. I've made it clear countless times."

Before Solomon could respond further, Soar's mother interjected. "Come on, let's just leave it alone. It's been a long day, Soar. You're grouchy because your hunting didn't go as well as usual, let's all just chill out and sleep on it. We can finish our dinner, gather around the piano, and enjoy the rest of the evening."

Soar smiled as marginally as is possible, recognizing his mother's earnest role as peacemaker, while begrudgingly deciding to accept her proposal. And, sure enough, they all did indeed gather around the upright piano, its chocolate-colored exterior slightly fading from years of wear and many evenings of key-mashing frivolity. Carrie could always tinkle her way capably through an array of crowd-pleasers and was soon pouring herself into an upbeat number.

As the family relaxed, everyone was grateful that the moment of conflict had passed, including Soar. He didn't actively seek conflict, nor garner any pleasure from it, but his fearless nature dictated an unwillingness to back down whenever it crossed his path. There was no doubt that these moments of familial harmony were preferable to being at odds with one another. But it was equally doubtless that nothing had shifted inside him. His attachment to his feelings was as resolute as ever; his desire to explore undimmed and undiminished.

2. The Storm

oar awoke suddenly from his slumber. That wasn't unusual in itself; his razor-sharp senses were keenly attuned to the most minor indication of disturbance or danger. But this was different. The savage, yet unmistakable, sound of hurricane-force winds blustering menacingly through Aquilana was loud enough to easily penetrate the windowpanes. Soar had spent thousands of hours investigating, acclimatizing, familiarizing himself with every nook and nuance of weather and its overarching systems. It required merely the blink of any eye to assess this storm. It was serious. Life-threatening even.

By the time Soar swooped downstairs, his family were already waiting. They'd all awoken almost simultaneously and had rapidly drawn the same grave conclusion—this wasn't a situation that could be ignored. There was no time for pleasantries; instead, the most stilted yet urgent conversation took place.

"We need to get out of here," Solomon began.

"Agreed," Soar replied.

"Where are we going?", Jemima asked pointedly.

"Bailey's Barn?" Soar suggested. "That metal structure should make it through anything."

"But that's ten miles away, can we make it that far in these winds?" Carrie wondered.

"We can do it together. I know you can do it, Sis, I believe in you. Nothing can stop us," Soar replied with feeling.

"Right, let's roll. Let's get out of here," Carrie responded, encouraged by her brother's faith in her.

As they set foot outside, an imposing tornado at once towered over them. It whirled and twirled with an awesome power that gave it the appearance of a predatory funnel. Thankfully, it was far enough away to ensure that the family could begin their ascent undisturbed. Within seconds, the whole family had bowled into the darkening skies, with full faith that their physical capabilities would enable them to climb above the storm. Such was the barbarity of the weather conditions, it was barely possible to perceive the extent of this climatic upheaval, let alone the damage and destruction. Aside from the rampant corkscrewing winds, angular rain was battering down ferociously. Visibility was essentially zero, which was hugely disadvantageous for a family of eagles who were so reliant on their exceptional eyesight. They would have to rely on instinct instead.

They were well aware that, as eagles, they were extraordinary birds; the only feathered creature able to fly straight into the fiercest of storms. Even in typhoon conditions, they could use thermals to soar at heights that humans can only experience in an aircraft. Solomon, Jemima, Carrie and Soar quickly located a rising air current, and began a breakneck climb to thousands of feet above sea level, circling repeatedly as they did so. This was usually child's play, but the lashing precipitation meant that obstacles could not be easily identified, if at all. They were traveling at the speed of a sedan bombing down the highway. Anything could wipe them out.

But, almost as quickly as they entered the monsoon, the four intrepid eagles exceeded the upper extent of the stormy clouds, elegantly bursting through this encircling layer of doom. From a towering vantage point, the family once again experienced a feeling of safety and security, peering down with a sense of fascination at the darkness beneath them. All four realized that they were relatively safe at this height; they could glide for vast distances of thousands of yards with minimal effort, so riding out the storm should be quite feasible. Nonetheless, it had been a hazardous undertaking. It was far more usual to seek shelter in such circumstances, but that just had not been an option. They were all fully aware that their predominantly wooden home was vulnerable to high winds, and they'd had no choice but to bail out.

As their elongated wings enabled them to coast effortlessly above the raging storm, the air surrounding the family was more than just an ample current; it was filled with a tangible sense of relief. But Soar felt something else, quite distinct from relief. He felt exhilarated. Conversely, he scolded himself for failing to identify the signs of a storm brewing earlier in the day. It was sloppy and lazy. He expected better of himself. He would have to correct that when....

"Come on, Soar, keep up!"

Soar noticed that he'd fallen slightly behind the pack, as he turned these compelling observations over in his head. "See, I told you that you'd make it, sis!" he announced triumphantly.

"Yes, of course, obviously you would know best!", Carrie teased her older brother.

"That was me trying to pay you a compliment!", Soar replied.

As he traded good-natured barbs with his sister, the prolific hunter surveyed the magnificence of the planet. Soar was often overcome by the splendour of his surroundings, of the sheer scale and scope of experience. Very few of the millions of species and trillions of biological entities on the planet would ever experience what Soar was fortunate enough to experience. He never took this for granted. Even in this scenario, he felt no scorn towards the stupendous power of nature, no resentment of its destructive tendencies. No fear, no resentment, no anger. Just respect and wonder.

"We're so lucky, Carrie," Soar told his sister almost breathlessly.

Carrie turned and looked at her brother quizzically. "That's funny, I don't feel particularly lucky at the moment! We could have all been killed, we don't know where and when we can land, and we don't know if our home has even survived."

"Our home is everywhere, our home is nowhere," Soar replied cryptically.

Carrie sniggered. "It's been a hard day, but I do believe that you've lost your marbles, brother!"

Soar responded playfully. "You can't lose what you never had!" And he swooped off without warning, accelerating rapidly, ensuring that he had the last word in this conversation. Beneath him, Soar observed the omnipresent grayness being perforated by a flash, a sudden cosmic Polaroid! Bolts of lightning appeared without warning, creating jagged spears of illumination; captivating, yet ominous, like the tongue of a serpent. Again, Soar made no apology for feeling a profound sense of wonder at the beauty and magnitude of the world.

The ongoing storm meant that it would still be a few hours before they could land. But there was no hurry.

Bailey's Barn turned out to be the ideal place to ride out the storm. The descent proved to be far simpler than the ascent; they didn't so much outrun the storm as wait for the storm to outrun them. In time, a clearing appeared and the eagles needed no second invitation. They nosedived faster than Kamikaze pilots, before adroitly correcting their descents and landing right alongside their target.

Once the eagles nested inside the barn, its sloping, corrugated iron roof was sturdy and impermeable, meaning that they could snuggle up for the night within some alluring bales of hay. It was late by the time they arrived, and thus human intervention was no cause for concern. Finally they could relax.

Despite the vast amount of energy that they'd expended during the day, it wasn't the soundest night's sleep for any of them. The fate of Aquilana echoed around their restless minds; even Soar felt a deep concern for the community and its safe haven, though he recognized this apparent safety to be illusory. He also found himself ruminating on the day's events, the majesty of the physical world, and the incorrigible itch that he felt to explore it. But eventually physical necessity overcame mental fixation, and Soar felt himself drifting inexorably into a sleeping state of consciousness.

As is common with extreme weather, the storm passed by as quickly as it arrived. The morning vista that greeted them gave no indication of the barbarity that had preceded it. Starlings were already tweeting tunefully in the trees, by the time the golden sun had poked its elliptical head above the horizon. It was a clean, crisp Spring morning; still, peaceful and nourishing. A morning frost had pleasingly decorated some of the meadows that dominated this hilly region, as if the pastures were a verdant cake that had been liberally dusted with icing sugar.

The four eagles hardly spoke a word to one another that morning, partly due to tiredness, but far more pressing was the gravity of their situation. There was neither time to hunt nor eat, and it was barely even necessary for them to discuss what happened next. After the briefest of dialogue, they headed back to Aquilana, dreading the fate that awaited them. It should have been a spectacular journey home, spiraling through the arresting mountains whose emerald fields sprouted and undulated like bulging muscles. But the mood was dull; there was no need to voice the unspoken truth that none of them knew what the immediate future held for them. They glided determinedly through the bracing air as they approached the final rugged escarpment that hid their home from view.

As soon as they rounded the corner, Aquilana loomed into their eyeline. Except that it didn't. What loomed instead was sheer devastation. Where once there had stood an organized neighborhood of residential and community buildings, now there was little more than rubble. The violently rotating columns of air had swept through Aquilana, destroying everything in their path. Mighty trees that had stood for generations had been knotted, uprooted, summarily dismissed. The Town Hall, the food storage center, all of their reserves of water, the hunting practice arena for eaglets, an array of dwellings—they had all been dispatched across the countryside in innumerable directions. And although Long-Tail Lodge hadn't been completely leveled, it was immediately evident that it was damaged beyond reasonable repair. The roof had been swept away; the tornado had prised it clean off, as effortlessly as a butter knife slices open a boiled egg. Because of this, all four main walls had largely caved in. Some of the skeleton of the building remained, but there was little that could be realistically salvaged. What had seemed such an inseparable component of their lives and souls was gone for good.

Carrie sobbed at the sheer horror that they were witnessing. Soar moved to comfort her, but in truth he felt like crying himself. There was nothing truly consoling that could be said at a time like this. They could only move forward. The past is always the past, no matter how much we may cling to it. But it is only in moments like these when the scale of the reassurance that we garner from our collective memories becomes apparent. It was not merely that buildings had crumbled. Something that had seemed a permanent part of their collective psyche, from which so many happy memories had been derived, was far less enduring than it had appeared. This was every bit as disturbing as the mere practicalities and logistics of their future lives, whatever shape they were to take.

For some moments, all four members of the family stood and stared, once again not knowing what to say. It was impossible to put a positive spin on the situation; there were no platitudes that offered even the pretense of solace. Eventually, they began to move stiffly, their bodies beginning to absorb the physical impact of understanding that their collective existence had been permanently remolded.

Constantine Fazackerley peered over his half-moon reading glasses at the assembled throng. The togetherness of the community had been heart-warming, but he sincerely missed the grandeur of the old Town Hall. It was not in his nature to be too sentimental, but observing the townsfolk perching on some makeshift logs made him long for its former Victorian magnificence.

It was now 48 hours since the event that had come to be known as The Tragedy. While it was a tragedy, it was also—Constantine was determined—a temporary blip; a bump in the road that would ultimately be navigated without enduring incident. Aquilana had always been his home, it always would be his home, they could build back stronger. With him at the helm as the Head Elder, there was nothing that couldn't be achieved. It was simply a case of planning and commitment. Aquilana was lucky to have him, and with the benefit of his many years of experience, the community would gloriously rise from the ashes of The Tragedy to build a brighter future. This was, after all, their way of life, and their parents' way of life before them. There was no alternative.

Meetings chaired by the town Elders were often preceded by a respectfully subdued level of conversation. But the events of the last few days meant that such deference wasn't possible; a throbbing hum of chatter pervaded the atmosphere, as the eagles and eaglets present discussed the immediate future. Eventually, Constantine had to raise his voice to call the audience to order, indicating that he was ready to address them. They fell silent quickly; his reputation and status went before him. There were hundreds of beady eyes now gazing intently up at Constantine, and this prompted the purest sentiment of responsibility in him, as well as pricking his more impure sense of self-importance.

"Good afternoon, everyone. Thank you all for attending," Constantine began. "It's been a distressing time for the whole community of Aquilana. We're all still trying to process what has happened over the last 48 hours. Thankfully, our diligent planning has meant that the underground stores remained untouched and undisturbed, and that should see us through the next few weeks without difficulty."

Constantine scratched his beak self-consciously for a second. He was an accomplished public speaker but had never quite become accustomed to having hundreds of eyes and ears fixated on him, and only him. "We are also fortunate in our misfortune. The Tragedy has occurred at an ideal time of year. Winter is likely behind us, we now have months of blossoming Spring, replenishing Summer, and mild Autumn; plenty of time to begin The Great Rebuild. I'm confident that we can restore Aquilana to its former glory and more, while easily retaining enough food stocks to ensure that our standard of living is maintained."

The majority of the audience listened intently, understandably craving some hope and favorable news. But there was one notable skeptic present.

"Excuse me!" Soar interrupted, causing many of the townsfolk in front of him to crane their necks around to face him. It was certainly not normal practice for one of the Elders to be questioned so quickly, without invitation, and before he had even finished speaking. But Soar had already heard enough and was determined to share his particular perspective on the issue.

"How on God's green planet are we going to rebuild what was here before within a timeframe of a few months? This is completely unfeasible. It doesn't even make sense, you're simply not facing the reality of the situation!" Soar became aware of an air of hostility towards his comments, but continued unabashed. "I'd love to hear your masterplan for how this is going to be achieved, with some specific timeframes. What is going to happen is that the top hunters like myself are going to be forced to work their talons to the bone, in a vain attempt to bail everyone else out of the food shortages, while the Elders stumble around attempting to achieve something that is impossible."

Soar knew he was being contentious, controversial even, but believed in the rightness of his views, and certainly in his right to express them. "And then, six months down the line, we won't be any better off than we are now. In fact, we'll be worse off, because we will have effectively wasted those six months. We won't have massively increased our food stocks, and we will then face the reality of another cold, harsh winter." Soar finished his diatribe triumphantly. "It won't be a Great Rebuild, it will be a Massive Flop!"

Constantine surveyed the impertinent youth, his blood boiling inside his aged veins and arteries. "I'm speechless, Soar! You've always been the naysayer, and you've always been proved to be wrong! Time after time, the Elders have put plans in place that have seen Aquilana prosper, despite your continual interruptions, disrespect and protestations. And, I might say, your own life has flourished because of us. You don't know how lucky you are, yet you repeatedly peck at the hand that feeds you. You would be nobody without us and would have no identity outside of us. You wouldn't survive without what we have put in place!"

There was a general murmur of agreement among the assembled masses. "Look, Soar," Constantine tried to gather his composure, and continued his comments in a more conciliatory tone, "in a matter of days we will have finalized our plans for rebuilding Aquilana. I'm sure when you see them that you'll feel reassured, and you'll be ready to join with the rest of the community. We know that you mean well, but this constant questioning of the Elders undermines the togetherness that we must cultivate as a community."

The Head Elder raised his eyebrows meaningfully at Soar as he spoke. Although he was annoyed by the insolence of the interruption, he also recognized something of himself in the youngster. He was proud, headstrong, idealistic, driven by the rampaging testosterone of youth. We have all been that eagle at one time, Constantine reflected.

"Well, I don't agree! This is not going to work! I'm not going to see the plans because I'm not going to be here," Soar retorted. "You lot can do whatever you want, I've already made up my mind."

Constantine rolled his eyes, and aimed his response at the audience, rather than Soar. "Well, we've all heard that one before, haven't we?"

Chuckles of solidarity from the townsfolk were immediately audible, and Soar felt incandescent with rage. How dare they dismiss and diminish him in this way! A fury percolated inside him that was every bit as formidable as the typhoon that had prompted the meeting. Enough was enough. Now was the time for action.

"Well, this time I'm serious," Soar interjected.

"Then I challenge you to leave this bed of roses and fend for yourself! I guarantee that you will regret it within a day or two and return sheepishly. That's if you survive at all!" Soar was furious, but decided against challenging the patriarch any further, holding his tongue, as he simmered inside.

The rest of the meeting passed largely without incident. Although there was a genuine sense of community within the settlement, there was also an intrinsic deference to the processes, procedures, and perspectives of the community and its Elders. The prevailing wisdom was that the Elders were symbolic of the knowledge and understanding that were passed down from one generation to another, and that questioning this was misguided. The young and talented would eventually rise to the ranks of Elders themselves, and so the cycle would continue. In this way, Aquilana remained hermetically sealed, like an ant colony. Neither time nor energy was wasted in pursuing new knowledge. This was already the best life possible, and there was no point in yearning for something that didn't exist or challenging the way that things had always been done. Throughout his early life, Soar had repeatedly battered his head against this mentality, in the manner of a lumberjack obdurately chopping away at a particularly dense tree trunk. And he was still doing it to this day.

After the meeting was adjourned, the rest of the attendees breezed away rapidly, but Soar sat sullenly on his own, as a million dizzying fragments of historical memories buzzed around his mind. There was an instinct inside Soar that had made him question authority from the youngest age. It was never possible for him to simply accept the rules and regulations that came from above; he wanted to truly explore and understand all possibilities. Yet this tendency, this critical component of his makeup, that Soar considered to be a fundamental part of his identity, had never been encouraged.

It had begun in Preschool. The supervisor and teacher, Miss Brahms, had never really taken to Soar, nor humored his emerging inquisitiveness. His questions about the world beyond Aquilana, the automatic respect for Elders, and many other topics, were renounced, refuted and, sometimes, ridiculed. And then this process intensified at school. The whole education system was essentially an impenetrable barricade; unshifting and unyielding in nature. Wholly convinced of its righteousness, thoroughly hostile towards anyone who dared to question its orthodoxy.

Indeed, the simmering broth of his high school had bubbled over numerous times for Soar. His classmates had nicknamed him Soar the Bore, mocking his questioning of the teachers and their guidance. He got into quite a few scrapes as well, although there was no prospect of Soar being bullied. He was way too tough. It was only after he'd given a couple of young eaglets a severe pasting that the name-calling began; the ringleaders were far too cowardly to engage Soar physically.

What particularly stung was that his parents largely refused to offer backing. They didn't uncritically support the teachers and the system, but they also made it clear that they disapproved of Soar's attitude. Even when other students tried to fight him, his father suggested that this was a natural consequence of Soar's behavior, and that he should learn to live with it. And, in a way, this had served Soar well. If his father's counsel was intended to reinforce his sense of independence, then it had been an overwhelming success. But this kernel of self-reliance had also expanded and mutated in directions that his father had neither intended nor anticipated. It permeated Soar, suffusing him with an acute sense of his own self-worth and value.

And yet, even as one of the most revered and rampant hunters in the community, Soar's opinion was not truly respected. "How long do I have to wait before I'm allowed to have a say in anything?", Soar mused. Recollection is always imperfect, but still Soar had the overall impression that he'd been belittled and restrained by this community. And it had just happened once again, at the most important juncture that Aquilana had ever encountered. For years, the attachment that he felt to the community in which he'd grown up had been engaged in a see-saw struggle with the resentment that had been incubating in his gut. But now this tantalizing balance had finally tipped decisively in one direction.

At that moment, Soar noticed his family wandering towards him. He girded himself internally, realizing that he was about to have the hardest conversation of his life.

"Hey Soar. Don't take what happened at the meeting personally," Jemima began sympathetically, placing a consoling wing on her son's shoulder.

"I didn't. I'm used to it. It's been the same all of my life," Soar replied, calmly but pointedly.

It had been an emotional time for everyone in Aquilana, and none of them had any appetite for another quarrel. But Soar wasn't primarily tired because of the storm and its consequences. He was tired of authority. He was tired of limiting attitudes. He was tired of the small-mindedness and dogmatism that ultimately reigned supreme in this society. He was tired of being tied down. And he was particularly tired of being told that he was wrong for wanting to seek something better.

Soar turned to face his family. "I've got something that I need to tell you all," he began in a measured tone. "You're probably not going to like it, but it's something that I feel very strongly about, it's something that is deep within my heart and soul."

None of them knew quite what Soar was about to say, yet in a way they all also knew exactly what was about to unfold. There was a moment of silence and tension, as if they were all passengers in a looming, unavoidable car crash.

"Spill it then, son," Solomon said earnestly.

Soar cleared his throat. "I'm leaving Aquilana. I want to take on Constantine's challenge! I want to seek new pastures. I want to see the world. I want to pursue my full potential. I want you to come with me, but I know that you won't. I know that you see your future here, and you feel that you belong here. I respect that, and I respect and love all of you. I hope that you can respect me and my decision."

His father opened his mouth to reply, but before he could speak, Soar spoke quietly. "Please let me finish. I will listen to everything you have to say once I have finished."

His father looked at him with equanimity. "Okay, Soar. Please continue."

Soar felt surprisingly composed. "I also don't agree with the proposed plans of the Elders. In fact, I don't agree with so much here. But what was said in that meeting is wrong. I *do* appreciate how lucky I am, and I *do* appreciate having grown up here. But I can't grow any more if I stay here. I want to go on a voyage of discovery, and it's not just discovering the world around me. I want to discover myself and explore my purpose. That will never happen here."

Soar's mother paused for a second before responding, acknowledging the gravity of Soar's words. "Do you realize the danger involved in what you're about to do?", she asked compassionately.

"Of course, Mom. Of course, it would be safer and easier to stay. Of course, it would. But I have grown resentful of life here. I will always have fond memories of Aquilana, but it doesn't support or sustain me anymore. It feels more like a lead weight that I have to drag along with me." Emboldened, Soar decided to up the ante. "Anyway, we're supposed to be eagles! We do what other birds don't do—we fly straight into storms! We're supposed to laugh in the face of danger. We're not cowards, make-doers, mild-mannered malingerers! We're proud and fearless. We fly, we hunt, we live!"

Again, the three of them paused before Carrie broke the ice. "I'm really going to miss you, bro!"

"You're the best, Carrie. I'm super-proud of you."

"I don't want you to go, Soar," his mother began. "Your father and I have discussed you so many times. We always tried to be upfront with you and share all our feelings with you directly, but sometimes we had to talk about you in private. We only did it because we care." His mother smiled hesitantly as she spoke. "We have known for a long time that you weren't happy. We hoped it was a phase that you'd outgrow, but I can see now that it is you who have outgrown your life here." Jemima began to cry as she contemplated her son literally flying the nest. "When are you going to leave?"

It was impossible for Soar to bite back the tears any longer, and he began to weep as he responded. His sobbing made his response stilted and staccato. "Now. The longer I leave it, the harder it will be. I love all of you so much, and I want it to stay that way. I don't want to feel constrained and grow to resent you. I must go."

Finally, his father spoke. "Son, I want you to know that I really don't agree with you. Maybe I was too hard on you at times, but it was only because I wanted you to grow into someone that I was proud to have raised. However, I will support you today." Solomon paused, partly to regain composure, and partly for effect.

Soar was sobbing now. "I feel closer to you all now than I ever have. That's what makes this so hard." The four of them wrapped their wings around one another in a collective hug. "You will see me again sooner than you think."

None of them had dry eyes. Even his father shed a tear. And then, with a final wave, Soar began his ascent towards the heavens. The irony was that he was leaving Aquilana feeling more respected than he ever had. The conversation with his family had reached the most satisfactory conclusion possible. He finally felt accepted by them, and this could only strengthen their relationship in the future.

Soar had regrets about the timing of his departure. But the other inhabitants also had the same option. We can cling to the wreckage of a sinking ship, or we can spread our wings and fly. There were remnants of affection and nostalgia for Aquilana buried deep within him, but as he climbed majestically, the decision that Soar had made felt right. His radiant eyes spotted water buffalo herding in the distance, as the midday sun peeked proudly through the fluffy, cotton wool cover of cumulus clouds, creating a vivid raft of wafer-thin sunbeams that splayed out in multiple directions, like an immense solar protractor.

The future ahead of Soar was uncertain. But rather than daunting, this uncertain future was exciting.

3. The Journey

As he approached the formidable mountain range, Soar could appreciate its jagged beauty. The peak of each summit varied in height, meaning that the range took on the appearance of a fluctuating stock chart from a distance. Soar had climbed to a height that was close to the limit of his potential; drifting elegantly thousands of feet above sea level. Such a height in free flight is an achievement so scarce that only a few vultures, cranes, and geese are able to surpass it. Soar allowed himself a moment of self-satisfaction. His eyes drooped lazily as he watched the moderate wind whip up small sections of snowfall at the tips of the white-capped mountains. Then he suddenly focused his vision, as he noticed the breeze creating mini-snowstorms that startled a group of nesting marmots.

Soar knew that the mother of the family would be on the lookout for any predators, and he employed a time-honored eagle strategy; he played dumb. Pretending that he hadn't spotted the marmots, Soar deliberately craned his supple neck in the opposite direction. He gently, lazily allowed his wings to waft up and down, as if he hadn't a care in the world, steadily, almost imperceptibly, easing his altitude as he did so. And then, suddenly

Soar accelerated in a twisting motion, almost like a helter-skelter, launching a vicious, scything attack on the herbivores.

But before he even reached his target, Soar realized that he hadn't been quick enough. The distinctive grunting of the marmots was already audible, perhaps a little more frenzied than usual, and given that Soar's hearing was far from exceptional, this meant that the family would hear it too, and soon be able to seek safety. Sure enough, they ducked inside a tiny cave-like structure, where it was impossible for Soar to reach them. He made lingering eye contact with the mother, staring at her witheringly, as if to communicate to her how fortunate she was to be alive. Soar then swooped away once more, continuing on his journey, content that there would be more prey to hunt down in the imminent future.

It was harder on your own than with a community behind you, Soar was willing to admit. This was not a surprise, he reasoned, but this expectation didn't make the situation any easier to deal with. As with many fantasies, the opportunity to pursue them preoccupies you, consumes you, until every fiber of your being seems to ache with desire for them. Then you're plunged into them, and the bracing reality hits you like a cold shower. The icy countenance suddenly assaults you. What was once a dream is now real, but will the actuality match the aspiration that drove you to it?

Soar couldn't answer this question yet, but he undoubtedly felt conflicted. Once the initial euphoria and stomach-churning excitement that he felt at the beginning of his great quest had dwindled, it was replaced with a yawning chasm of doubt. Soar had felt himself to be locked in a dismal, uninspiring comfort zone in Aquilana, and his resentment of this had suppurated inside him, growing larger by the day, until it became a throbbing boil that he could no longer ignore.

However, Soar now recognized the scale of his challenge. Uncertainty stretched out in front of him, like an immense satin sheet. Soar began to realize that he had been delusional about one critical aspect of his character; his self-assurance had not been entirely derived from confidence in his own ability. This was not to downplay his actual level of skill and resourcefulness; this was, unquestionably, of rare proficiency.

But it had become clear, in the days since he'd abandoned Aquilana, that he had underestimated the role that the community and his family played in his identity. We can come to resent the familiar, but, equally, it brings comfort. And family and community can feel like a prohibitive ball and chain, curbing our movement, restricting our freedom, scattering rules, regulations and repugnant rationality across our path with such seeming abandon that we inevitably become resentful. But as much as family and community had been a constant annoying presence back home, repeatedly chivvying Soar like a woodpecker chipping away at a sycamore trunk, it was no more conspicuous than when it was no longer there! Soar now missed what had once goaded him. He was homesick. He was fighting against this realization internally but was also too honest to deny it. He had never felt more alone. He had never *been* more alone.

There was also a predictable yet reassuring structure to Aquilana. Everyday life was painstakingly planned around the needs of the community, with every aspect carefully planned out by the Elders. You largely knew what you would be doing each and every day. Conversely, Soar now had everything ahead of him—but also nothing ahead of him. Soar reflected on how fascinating it is that we become emotionally dependent on the things that hold us in bondage. The schoolmaster spends his whole life dreading the cacophonous interruption of the bell, then as soon as he's retired, he finds that he anticipates, and even misses, the school bell's jarring interventions!

Nonetheless, Soar's determination to explore and learn more about the world remained intact. And one critical motivation drove him forward: the fear of failure. Although he knew there would always be a home for him, and in that sense, Aquilana represented something of a safety net, Soar had absolutely no intention of returning with his tail between his legs. He did not wish to meekly concede that the glorious experience he'd envisioned had failed to materialize. Soar was far too proud for that, and he still believed in the principle underpinning this expedition. He would push forward.

Soar took a moment to imbibe the ambience of his surroundings. It was evening, shortly before sunset, and the tangerine-colored sky seemed somehow broader, more immense than usual. It was as if the sky was steadily swallowing the earth, while the fading sun dropped leisurely beneath the horizon. Daylight was vanishing into Cimmerian gloom. But there was still enough luminosity in the sun that Soar was able to perceive the immense serrated extremities of the snow-covered mountains, as they reached illimitably into the vermilion backdrop, resembling a row of needles attempting to puncture the dusky heavens.

For a moment, Soar's state of anxiety dissolved, his psyche focused solely on savoring the sumptuous scenery. This was precisely the sort of transcendent moment that he'd set out to experience. But life in the wild afforded little time to dwell on such aesthetics. There was always another consideration just around the corner, and the immediate concern for Soar was identifying a comfortable and secluded place to nest for the night. He began to adjust his altitude, his spirit galvanized by what he'd witnessed. Tomorrow would be a better day, Soar vowed, as his eager eyes spotted a smallholding in the distance.

Soar felt his state of consciousness and awareness lifting, as his usual state of alertness returned. He had soon drifted off to sleep amid the comfy confines of the cattle shed, with only a smattering of harmless four-legged creatures to keep him company. As an eagle, Soar couldn't help feeling slightly sorry for the cows—they weren't very bright, they couldn't fly, and they spent their lives being entirely domesticated. If only they could break out somehow, forge an alliance, Soar reflected. They sat there dimly surveying their surroundings, doing little to convey any impression of vigilance or vigor.

Still, there was no time for lying around and pondering such matters. Soar meandered his way out of the tin building, preparing to spread his wings. He noticed that they were a little stiffer than usual, perhaps not surprising considering the extra mileage that he'd been cramming in on a regular basis. Soar had never previously ventured outside of the confines of Eagles Land, and while he was a Grandmaster within that world, he was a rookie in the real world. Every day he was learning new life lessons, whether it was developing more efficient ways to forage for food, identifying different methods of sheltering from inclement weather, or encountering new sights, smells and sounds that he'd never previously been confronted with, and indeed the dangers and opportunities associated with them. It was a challenge, but one that he was beginning to relish. He was growing wiser by the day.

Soar began the morning ascent that he'd made so many times previously, comforted by the familiar sight of the sun, the regal giver of life. Its powerful beams were glinting off angular greenhouse panels below Soar, refracting the light; its reflective properties creating a fascinating fusion between natural and human-made.

There was a dichotomy churning within Soar at that very moment. This was the biggest day he'd faced since he left Aquilana. His plotted path would see him enter uncharted territory, crossing the ocean for the first time in his spiritual journey. In some respects, this was nothing new to Soar; he flew over bodies of water on a regular basis and had done so for many years. But although challenges both real and perceived had already crossed his path, there is perhaps no greater challenge than the unknown. Tales of seething seas resounded in local folklore. There was a rich seam of aquatic fables stitched into the fabric of Aquilana that rivaled anything from *Moby Dick*.

Soar instinctively treated this scaremongering with scorn but there was also a part of him that wondered if there was no smoke without fire. Why would there be this apparent fear of the planet's mighty oceans, if there was actually nothing to fear at all? This thought was enough to create a little apprehension in Soar as he contemplated the day ahead, though he attempted to temper this by telling himself this was nothing that he hadn't encountered previously. It was an unknown, but it was a known unknown! And regardless of any reservation, nothing could thwart his desire to know more.

After a short sail towards the coast, Soar finally laid eyes on the huge expanse of water that he'd been anticipating since the previous evening. As he'd neared the ocean, Soar had noticed the temperature dip precipitously, while the skies ahead had dulled to a shade of gunmetal gray that was far from welcoming. Nonetheless, flying conditions couldn't be considered a particular impediment; there was a stiff breeze wafting across the ocean, causing persistent undulations in the tide, but no more than that. Soar's potent eyes watched the foaming spray being whipped up by the wind, creating a frothy milkshake-like topping to the fluctuating waves.

The initial flight began without incident. Soar chose to adopt a much lower altitude than usual, keen to absorb the unfamiliar surroundings. He was acutely aware that there was an ecosystem of such magnitude beneath the shimmering surface of the ocean that it must be considered its own sequestered world. Soar had respect for this kingdom of marine life, populated by a fascinating collection of immensely diverse creatures. He recognized that they were capable of modes of existence that would always evade him. Yet despite its vibrancy, it was always concealed, invisible, mysterious by its very nature. This tantalized the inquisitive nature of Soar, and he couldn't resist peering futilely into the murky depths, hoping to catch a glimpse of some sleek, slippery creature sliding silently beneath the surface. But there was no marine life to be seen; merely the unalterable rise and fall of the waves.

By early afternoon, Soar's trans-oceanic journey had progressed enough distance for him to find himself in the uniquely uniform surroundings that only flying over the ocean can create. There was nothing as far as the eye could see, other than the continuing swell and retraction of the inky water, and overhanging frame of the heavens. It was an incredible feeling of freedom, soaring above this immense expanse of water, without a care in the world. Soar turned the reasoning for his adventure over in his mind once more; it had revolved around his brain more times than a tumble dryer spin cycle. He knew that he was doing the right thing. It was all worthwhile for feelings like this, frozen moments in time that would be engraved in his consciousness forever, creating these indelible impressions that would otherwise remain distant and imaginary. Soar was transfixed, reaffirming his rationale in his mind continuously, while memories from his past flooded back to him, competing for attention. It was valuable simply to have these periods of reflection, almost meditative in nature, that always seemed impossible amid the endless planning, meetings, and organization of Aquilana.

But while Soar's mind wandered, the atmosphere was tending towards the mildly foreboding. The sky had morphed from grayish to gray to decidedly dark, as if the ether was systematically cycling through an ominous color chart. In the distance, Soar heard the unmistakable warning that rumbles of thunder provide; something menacing was brewing in the clouds ahead. Instinctively, Soar began to climb, urgently flapping his wings with all of his strength. It is incredible how quickly a storm can close in when traveling over the sea, he reflected. The optical illusion of the unending horizon had disguised the impending arrival of the weather front, and it had only been the booming sound of thunder that had suddenly alerted him. Still, there was no cause for alarm, as he could easily climb above the howling winds, and view this spectacle of nature from a pleasing vantage point. If anything, this was an opportunity, rather than a cause for alarm!

However, this particular storm was a whirling dervish, and Soar had seriously underestimated its proximity. There was no time to mentally chastise himself for his neglectful attitude; all of his energy was invested in a desperate attempt to rise above the gale-force winds. But his body was weakening. Unaccustomed to flying long distances, Soar's wings were tiring as he tried to elevate himself, and it began to dawn on him that he wasn't strong enough to overcome or overpower it. Instead of gliding with his usual majesty, he suddenly realized that the storm was carrying him; the sheer irresistible momentum propelling him through the sky against his will.

Soar panicked, investing the remaining strength in his body in beating his fully extended wingspan as quickly and powerfully as possible. But it was no good; his enfeebled body had become as ineffectual as cotton candy against a hairdryer. Soar felt his heart pounding in his chest as he registered the sheer terror of the situation. Rain was beating down with such ferocity that he couldn't see where he was going; there was no visual indication now of where the storm began and ended. All Soar could do was feel it all around him, feel it overwhelming him physically. There was neither fight nor flight left in his body; his fate was in the lap of the infinite divine intelligence.

This uncontrolled flight continued for what seemed like an eternity. Soar was at least able, via the most frenzied flapping, to keep his head above water. But he had never experienced tiredness like this before. The intense spirit that typically pulsed through Soar's veins, that was symbiotic with his very being, was fading. He felt defeated. Helpless. No more in control of his destiny than a beachball bobbing aimlessly around on the ocean.

Bang! Out of nowhere, Soar felt a juddering smash to his cranium. Although it was a sickening thud, it wasn't sufficient to knock Soar out cold, but he went into a state of shock, laying completely still with almost no awareness of anything. Eventually, after little more than a minute, but what seemed like an eternity, Soar's body allowed him to think with clarity once more. It soon became apparent that he hadn't drowned. He was lying prostrate on an island, with the choppy seas washing over his body, coldly indifferent to this fate. The tide was beginning to slowly but surely sweep him out to sea.

Soar was groggy, barely conscious, dazed from colliding with what must have been a tree. He tried to rouse himself, but his vision was seriously blurred, and he could barely move. Even his nervous system wasn't blinking red, as expected in such a dangerous situation. The clattering thump into the rigid tree trunk had reduced his body and mind to a gelatinous state. All Soar could hear was his father's words ringing around his throbbing head.

Soar, why do you have to be so headstrong?!
Soar, listen to your mother and me!
Soar, there are rules for a reason!
Soar, this will be the death of you!

For so many years in Aquilana, Soar had considered those around him to be comatose. But now it was he who was literally struggling for consciousness. His left wing was badly damaged. His body was still in a state of shock. He had no strength left. His eyelids felt heavier than anvils. He just couldn't keep them open. They were drooping, closing, the last remnants of life were steadily seeping out of him. The sea took hold of his limp, lifeless body, and began to ease it away from the shore.

Soar didn't fight it. He was powerless, resigned to his fate. He allowed his eyes to close. Everything went pitch black. He was dying.

4. The Island

As the aquamarine tide lapped the yielding, golden beach of the island, the midday sun beamed down pleasingly on its inhabitants. The distinctive chirping of crickets filled the air, with not a single breath of wind to disturb the sound. It was the ideal setting, the ideal climate, to do anything, but particularly to do nothing.

The island was unquestionably one of aesthetic beauty. Over half of its surface consisted of labyrinthine forests, bottle-green, beautiful, but baffling to the uninitiated. It was possible to become lost for days amid the palm and mango trees, but this verdant presence also helped provide the islanders with all manner of delectable produce. The island was a mini-ecosystem all of its own, with plentiful opportunities for fishing and foraging, ensuring that those who chose these shores as their home received a bountiful and varied diet throughout their relaxed existence.

Aside from the acres of forest, the island also boasted many miles of the softest sandy beaches, and an incredible array of mountain ranges that reached into the ether, beyond the vision of even the keenest eye. It provided endless opportunity to explore, with caves and coves littered across the bay area. Its balmy summers stretched beyond the reasonable length of any season and its winters were mild and tolerable. Life is never perfect, but this setting provided a quality of life that made anything surpassing it seem inconceivable.

On this particular day, a colony of seals were making their way back towards the coast of the island in seemingly leisurely fashion. Their flippers slithered through the cleansing water with an unhurried ease that can only be derived from true mastery. They had made this journey a million times before, but they never allowed its majesty to become commonplace. As the sun's rays collided with the gentle waves, it created a phosphorescent glow, so brilliant in nature that even the experienced eyes of the seals needed to squint slightly. Their powerful noses smelled swordfish up ahead, swiveling succulently on a barbecue, and the anticipation prompted these expert swimmers to increase their pace.

The seals typically coasted at a fraction of their potential maximum swimming speed, yet even their gentlest efforts touched a velocity faster than any human has ever been able to swim! At their fiercest, they could bomb through the water with extreme ferocity. They were swimming slowly this morning, lapping through the tides smoothly, but with no apparent haste. But then there was a good reason for their indifference.

Eight seals formed a military-like pincer, scything through the water with the ease that a combine harvester beheads corn plantations. From a distance, there was no particular reason for this arrangement; it appeared an instinctive composition, much as migratory birds orchestrate a v-formation when flying south for the winter. But as one surveyed the scene more closely, it became evident that the herd was determinedly dragging an object of not inconsiderable size.

Not an object—a body. The body of an eagle.

"Is he alive?" Samuel asked insistently.

Carmel paused thoughtfully before answering. "We think so. His vital signs were all functioning adequately when we picked him up. He was out cold, but his heart was still beating. He didn't even need any CPR or medical intervention." She looked around her immediate surroundings, searching for something in particular. "Give him something potent to smell, and I bet he'll come round immediately."

After a short spell of scavenging, a fresh herring was presented to the island's medical practitioner. "If this doesn't wake him, nothing will!", Carmel proclaimed, placing it straight under the eagle's nose. Sure enough, in a matter of seconds, the wounded animal began spluttering, and his eyes opened slightly feebly, as if the creature had endured an extremely powerful bout of sedation.

"Nearly as good as smelling salts!", Carmel noted.

Soar's eyes struggled to acclimatize to the sudden influx of light. He attempted to recalibrate, so that he could perceive his immediate surroundings. But for some moments, all he could do was blink protectively against the dazzling glare of sunbeams, as his eyes came to terms with the sunlight, and his body with the battering it had received. Soar was stiff and sore. He didn't feel like an eagle; he felt weak and ineffectual. Still, his eyesight steadily restored itself, and he was able to peer upwards at four apparently friendly faces gazing down at him.

"Who are you? Where am I?", Soar began by asking.

"Just take it easy." A third seal named Shakina eyed Soar sensitively. "You've been through quite a distressing experience. You're safe now and we're here to help."

It had taken Soar a few moments to clock these creatures as seals, and now his usually nimble mind was attempting to piece together his immediate past. But his thinking was sluggish, not helped by a thumping headache that felt like the repeated pounding of a bass drum. After a little while, Soar admitted to himself that he simply couldn't remember anything that had happened. The last 24 hours weren't even a blur; they had been erased entirely from his memory. He vaguely recalled nestling down in a barn, and after that... nothing whatsoever. But even in this dazed state, Soar was still aware enough to recognize that these creatures were his only hope of survival.

He began again, slowly and patiently. "Please could you tell me what happened. I have no memory of anything. I don't know where I am, and I can't remember anything that occurred before arriving here. All I know is that my head hurts!"

The seals all turned to their physician, awaiting her verdict. "We don't know either! We can't be certain. However, you've obviously smashed into a hard object at a rate of knots, and this has caused bleeding and some concussion." Carmel smiled at Soar warmly. "However, I do have some good news. There is absolutely no sign of *internal* bleeding. Your injuries are all superficial, and you will have to tolerate some rest and recuperation, but your body will heal if you exercise some patience and acceptance."

"How did you find me?" Soar inquired.

"Well, we have patrols that circle the islands every day." A fourth seal, known as Zander, began to explain. "Honestly, it's pure good fortune that we spotted you and were able to scoop you up. We could easily have missed you. It was just something that was destined to happen. You must have been sent here for a reason."

Soar groaned a little. He wasn't responding negatively to Zander's assertion, even though currently it did seem a little fanciful! His body simply ached profusely. It felt as if his every bone had been used as notes by a particularly vigorous xylophone player. There didn't seem to be a positive reason for this horrifying situation, but Soar was always aware of his vulnerability, and was genuinely grateful towards his saviors.

"And why did you save me?"

On receiving this query, the seals glanced around at one another quizzically, failing to comprehend the underlying implication of the question.

"What do you mean?", Samuel asked.

"You had no reason to save me. There is nothing in it for you. Where I come from, an outsider in this state would have been viewed as a liability, or even a threat."

"This is our culture and mindset," Samuel explained. "We view it as our obligation to help those less fortunate, or anyone in a challenging predicament, not to mention the unwell and the vulnerable." Samuel shrugged as he continued. "It's just what we do. Sharing is at the heart of Eudaimonia. Once we found you, we never considered anything else other than saving you."

Soar pondered what he'd heard, contrasting it with the suspicious perspective that reigned supreme in Aquilana. "Well, I'm very thankful. I owe you everything. As soon as I'm in a fit state to repay you, I will do anything. I feel an enormous debt of gratitude towards you for your compassion and bravery." Soar may not have been at his sharpest but he was still alert enough to offer these words with true sincerity. He had not the slightest idea of what to expect from the islands of Eudaimonia, but he vowed that he would never leave them without fully recompensing these gallant creatures for their life-saving act of heroism.

* * *

As the days unfolded, Soar steadily acclimated himself to life in Eudaimonia, and to the mode of living that the seals had adopted. It was a remarkable experience for Soar; after all, he'd exited Aquilana barely a week previously and had never known anything else. He hadn't been sure what to expect from his pilgrimage, but to be completely accepted so quickly by an entirely unfamiliar community was astonishing.

But the mentality of the seals was fundamentally different from anything that he had encountered previously. They resonated a calmness and reassurance that was completely foreign to Soar. It seemed that their openness to strangers and non-judgmental mindset directly emanated from this. The seals fundamentally believed that the world would provide for them, and therefore tending to a stricken stranger was natural and logical. This was diametrically opposed to the prevailing mindset in Aquilana, which was self-serving and miserly; as if the community was a pensioner clutching a cloak around his body to protect himself against the winter chill.

Indeed, Soar had wanted for nothing from the moment that he inadvertently landed in Eudaimonia. It seemed to be a land of plenty that offered an assemblage of foods that were beyond Soar's wildest imagination. Never before had he encountered such a kaleidoscopic array of colorful fruits and vegetables, with the salmon-pink and speckled innards of the pitaya being a particular favorite. Soar was positively bombarded with fish of every conceivable variety. Although there was a little less meat than was customary, Soar had quickly appreciated having his palate acquainted with all manner of new flavors, and he vowed to be more open-minded about his food choices going forward.

But despite landing on his feet, despite his paradisial surroundings, and despite the steady healing that he was undergoing, Soar was still hurting. His body was in pain, but it was really his mind that was enduring a period of suffering that he needed to heal and reconcile. He was hugely conflicted about his whole journey, even though he appreciated the settlement in which he'd found himself. It was informative and educational to witness a superior mode of existence, but it wasn't reason enough to abandon his native land and people.

Was there any point in this physically exhausting and dangerous journey? Was he going to get anywhere and experience anything profound or meaningful? Should he stay with the seals, return home to Aquilana, or venture further off into the unknown? No matter how much Soar contemplated these questions, no obvious answers were forthcoming. For the first time in his young adult life, possibly his entire life, Soar's self-belief had suffered a tremendous blow, and his spirit had yet to return. He knew objectively that every moment spent in Eudaimonia should be joyful, but there was no joy in his heart. He hadn't drowned in the ocean, but he was drowning in thoughts, memories, emotions and an overwhelming process of introspective questioning. Before he had been so certain, so certain of himself, and now he felt a pale shadow of that boundlessly self-assured being.

But maybe this very process is just part of the journey, Soar reasoned. Perhaps nothing of real value comes without struggle. This could be my most valuable life lesson!

Gradually, Soar felt his customary physical powers returning. His wing was healed from the accident, and he was able to swoop and swirl with his usual lightning velocity. As the restoration of his skills continued, his mind began to heal in unison. The level of irritation and diminution of identity that an eagle experiences when unable to fly can barely be overstated; it is the equivalent of an aardvark being deprived of eating ants. It was no wonder that Soar hadn't felt like himself; he literally hadn't *been* himself.

As his recovery continued, Soar was even able to venture out on a couple of successful hunting excursions and was proud to present his rodent prey to the seals. Nonetheless, his attitude towards hunting had already softened. It had previously dominated his existence and defined his being, but now he recognized that there is more to life than simply pursuing other animals. However, he could feel his character morphing into something new and altogether more rounded.

The seals certainly appreciated having Soar as part of Eudaimonia. He could warn of changes in the climate, sudden storms brewing in the distance; to some degree, Soar fulfilled the position of an eagle weather forecaster! This was particularly useful, as the islands also benefited from excellent drainage, and this made it possible for the animals to grow a range of indigenous crops. Fields of leafy bamboo shoots, striking magenta eggplants, and tasty sweet potato competed with fish and meat whenever the animals supped, and Soar could feel his attitude toward food gradually but perceptibly shifting. He had certainly been an advocate of a meat-based existence, and while he was no vegetarian, he also recognized and relished the fact that his new balanced diet was having tangible physical benefits. He hadn't just healed from his accident; he felt leaner, stronger, fitter, even younger. It contradicted Soar's previous beliefs and tendencies, yet he had no problem with acknowledging this new reality.

Soar turned all these revelations and revisions over in his mind, as he feasted on fish and vegetables. It was a temperate evening, but they had lit a sizable bonfire, as much for the ambience as the warmth. He watched the mighty orange sun dominating the horizon, as it steadily began to vanish behind the acuminated peaks that watched over the island, as imperious and impervious as a squadron of soldiers. Such was the isolation of Eudaimonia, there was a silence in the evenings that bordered on the surreal. It was hard to imagine such a profound degree of soundlessness, as if someone had muted the cosmos with a galactic controller. Soar's heightened eagle senses always had the paranoid feeling that it was too quiet. But it was also undeniably magical.

An eagle's life, Soar reflected, is indivisible from the four basic elements; intrinsically entwined with earth, water, wind, and fire. The sun, after all, is just a colossal fire! It is for this reason that we develop such an acute appreciation of the elements; a respect that is engraved on our souls. We're not merely intertwined with the elements, we identify with the elements, we *are* the elements. We are the sun rising in the morning, the river rushing through the mountains, the wind that carries us out to sea, and the magisterial enormity of the lands that we've conquered.

Soar sat peacefully content with his current circumstances, but with an increasing realization burning inside. His journey must continue.

5. The Dolphin

From Soar's elevated standpoint, or, to be more accurate, flying-point, the flourishing forests of the island offered an appealing counterpoint to the ocean, their blooming, billowing mass creating a seemingly impenetrable emerald wall.

With his superlative eyesight, Soar was able to peer beyond this viridescent sheet and distinguish the individual properties of the trees. Some of the trunks were bold in their burnt sienna magnificence, while others were tarnished, sporting fragmented silvery patches. Even these immense organisms could display signs of vulnerability, of pain, their twisted and knotted trunks indicative of their grasping, striving quest for life, in what could be an unforgiving world. Soar contemplated the dichotomy at the heart of the forest; each individual tree was a mighty structure, yet also immersed in a far greater and more immediately obvious whole, just as individual snowflakes are ornate and beautiful, but vanish unnoticed and unappreciated into snowdrifts.

His period of physical convalescence had passed, but Soar was still healing inside. It was a glorious morning, with the resplendent rays of daybreak searing through the intermittent gaps in the maples and pines like laser beams. Soar was in a pensive mood, as his wings fluttered gracefully.

Eventually, the acres of woodland parted, revealing the seductive bay area. Soar began to glide downwards, readying himself to land. Ahead of him, the azure waters stretched out for many a mile, interrupted only by patches of turquoise discoloration. Soar landed softly on the silky sands, as the pleasant warmth beneath his talons seeped through his body. When the midday sun was at its most intense, perching on the golden beaches of the island could cause discomfort, as the sun baked the surface of the beach like pottery in a kiln. But the weather was more temperate at this early hour, meaning that Soar could contemplate a leisurely breakfast amid the sands.

Soar was particularly hungry, so as he attacked his breakfast, lychee juice running gloriously down his chin, he didn't notice the dolphin approaching him. This wasn't altogether surprising; the creature's slippery body slid silently through the ocean, parting the water with casual dexterity. But as the animal approached the surface, the sun's rays penetrated the translucent waters, bouncing off the dolphin's smooth exterior. This immediately caught Soar's attention—his highly-strung senses were wired to detect such temporary disturbances—and within a fraction of a second he had perceived the dolphin's presence.

This was a lean, muscular, and impressive creature, but one with a reassuring demeanor. There was nothing threatening about the dolphin; his expression was one of contentment and openness, friendliness even. Soar immediately felt comfortable, and approached the dolphin less gingerly than would usually be the case with an unfamiliar outsider. Perhaps the island was beginning to influence his outlook...

As he surveyed the dolphin, Soar immediately noticed its lighter underbelly, intended to conceal the prodigious swimmer from predators, which contrasted starkly with its oil-black abdomen. The two of them began to exchange pleasantries, reflecting on the splendor of their surroundings, the tranquility of life in the region, and the agreeableness of its climate. Soar was affecting a chirpy countenance, partly due to the weight of social expectation, but also as a form of learned protection; better to appear chipper and confident than disheartened and susceptible to weakness. But this astute Delphinidae saw rapidly through Soar's facade.

"I hope you don't mind me asking," the as-of-yet nameless dolphin began, "but why aren't you happy?"

Soar straightened his vertebrae and raised himself to his full height. "What do you mean? Why do you say that?" he replied defensively.

The dolphin retained a content and friendly expression. "I can sense your discontent. If you should be content anywhere, it should be here, so what's wrong?" He paused before explaining. "I don't mean to be rude; I only intend to help."

This last comment was well-meaning but misguided; it was not the ideal way to induce the proud eagle to open up! Soar had grimly resisted all forms of assistance throughout his life, and any offer of help was likely to result in his clamming up. Snapping down the shutters of resistance, like a convenience store closing for the evening.

"You wouldn't understand! How can you understand an eagle? You never rise above the level of the surface, while we soar on the breeze, thousands of feet above you! You're not qualified to offer an opinion!"

Far from becoming agitated or defensive, the dolphin retained his steadfast composure. He retained his serene air, his response delivered with a mellow calmness.

"Well, young one, although I can leap out of the ocean, I concede that I can't fly as high as you! So you're quite right. I'm also closer to shuffling off this mortal coil than you are; I envy your energy and passion. But I have seen a few things in my time, perhaps experienced a few things that you are yet to encounter, and for my sins I have learned a little about life."

This was no idle boast. Dolphins are arguably the most perceptive aquatic creature, but also the most cooperative, often coordinating their behaviors, and displaying exceptional empathy and kindness towards outsiders. This creature had clearly imbibed many of the planet's richest experiences.

The dolphin continued patiently. "I wish that I had listened more when I was younger, but I suppose that the energy of youth also brings its pitfalls! I would just hate to see an extraordinary creature such as yourself allow the sands of his youth to slide through his talons. Time is the most precious commodity that you have; you will never get it back. Don't waste it being dissatisfied or despondent."

There was a momentary pause, as the two of them felt an unspoken bond. Soar felt emotion coursing through his body, yet the magnitude was so great that he couldn't even recognize what he was feeling. All he knew was that the dolphin's words had resonated profoundly.

"I'm sorry, I didn't mean to be dismissive or rude. I've been through a lot recently, and I don't quite know which direction I'm headed. I only know what I don't want to be, I haven't yet decided what I do want to be. My future is uncertain, and I guess that makes me a little apprehensive."

"Well, there is no future. And there is no past. There is only this moment. You are allowing some imagined future to consume you, but when you arrive there it won't be some nirvana. You will just find yourself imagining another future, and then reaching for that. Or you may keep analyzing the past for what happened or didn't happen. You have to be *present*. You have to learn to deeply relish what you're experiencing *right now*." The dolphin paused for effect. "I know that is inside you, I know you must encounter incredible things when you're thousands of feet in the air. The immediate sensory experience should consume you, not just some goal lurking on the horizon. If you allow that goal to consume you, you may possibly never reach it."

These wise words opened the floodgates. Soar allowed everything that had occurred at Aquilana to pour out of him. The dolphin listened patiently with barely an interjection. Soar divulged everything that had happened to him from a young age, explaining that he'd always felt like an outsider. He filled the dolphin in on the storm, his family, his feelings, his dreams, things that he had never shared with the island's residents, or indeed with anyone. He wasn't specifically seeking advice; the words cascaded as naturally and inevitably as a cliffside river forms a waterfall. However, when he'd finished he paused with anticipation. He was surprised that he was actively seeking the counsel of this creature, but this didn't grate with him; he was instead gratified with his newly discovered sense of openness.

"It seems to me, young man, that you're carrying a lot of baggage with you, and that you've been carrying it for a long time. So there's one important thing that I want you to know and remember."

Soar leant forward in expectation.

"You can put that heavy bag down now."

And with that, without warning, the dolphin flipped over elegantly, and swam off, disappearing as rapidly as he had appeared. Within a fraction of a second, there was not the merest fragment of evidence that he'd ever existed. It was a moment frozen in time, that only the two of them had shared and no one else would ever know. Fleeting, yet hugely important.

* * *

As dawn broke, the island gradually awakened. From the very moment that natural light began to penetrate the all-consuming blackness, its sounds, smells and sights revived from their dormant state. There was an intimacy with the natural world that impacted one profoundly. At some point, there was no natural world and divisible self any longer—the two melted into oneness.

It was the sounds that struck first before the other senses had awoken. The piercing calls of avian life would be initially perceptible, echoing across the ecosystem defiantly, whether it was the shrieking caw of the gorgeously colorful Eclectus parrot, or the contralto mating squawks of the roseate spoonbill, whose incessant grunting resembled the distorted droning of a down-tuned guitar. Then the subtler slithering and scampering of the reptiles and rodents became audible, scurrying and slinking through the plentiful tall grasses. Confined in the aphotic regions of the island, among the dingy and unilluminated crevices of obsidian rock, insects buzzed, ants scuttled, and those that sought to feast on them listened intently.

Soon the ravishing odour of breakfast drifted enticingly across the island. The seals would sometimes sleep in the water, bobbing as effortlessly as corks. Occasionally they'd replenish themselves on the beach itself, sleeping in a position in such proximity to their natural habitat that the water would wash sensuously over their prostrate bodies. It always amazed Soar that this seemingly didn't disturb them. But their sleeping location meant they often smoked fish in the bay area, even before the morning light had fully bloomed, and this aroma floated through the air until it could no longer be resisted.

Since he'd arrived in Eudaimonia, Soar had experienced an increasing proclivity to nest. This had been trained out of him in Aquilana; Long-Tail Lodge had seemed such a reassuring haven, somehow the family had developed an attitude of indifference towards their natural instincts. But in this environment, Soar had steadily returned to his indigenous ways. It felt good. There were no buildings, furniture, clocks, and schedules—the paraphernalia of the work and responsibility-driven society was conspicuous by its absence. Instead, Soar found himself settling into a more emancipated mode of existence. He snoozed when the light failed, and he stirred when it returned, his circadian rhythm fully restored. There was no fastidious measuring of time, no induction into an organized industrial complex, and no limits to one's inclination and imagination. It was intoxicating.

Of course, nesting amongst the treetops meant that he was separated from the group of seals; this was not an option that was open to them! The variety of collective nouns associated with seals was fascinating to Soar— they could legitimately be described as a colony, a rookery, a bob, a herd, and even a harem!

But however he chose to describe them, he had formed a meaningful bond with these enchanting creatures. There was a serenity about them that was thoroughly disarming. It was impossible not to juxtapose and contrast their outlook, not only with the one he'd been inculcated into, but also his own organic perspective. Soar had considered himself a libertine, but the more that he reflected on his attitudes, the more he realized that it wasn't as profoundly disconnected from the mentality of Aquilana as he had believed. Though he had considered himself to be superior to those around him, his mind hadn't been as permeable to new ideas as he would wish, and his consciousness hadn't been as harmonized with nature as he would desire. This had made Soar question many of his assumptions, about others and about himself. At the same time, he missed his family. Being separated from them could be agonizing at times, even though he still deeply believed that the path he had chosen was essential, even involuntary.

Soar was turning this over in his head as he swooped down to the bay area to join the seals for breakfast. They were always generous with their reception, and this morning the portion of mackerel, herring and lobster that they'd provided was just as lavish. Soar didn't forget his manners, thanking the seals graciously, and there was a dearth of conversation for some moments as the collected creatures chomped through their food with glee.

Once they'd all finished, Soar decided to spill his figurative guts; he had a burning desire to tell the seals about everything he'd experienced in their company, and how it had made him feel about himself and indeed life itself. The seals listened patiently, apparently in common with all animals that Soar encountered in Eudaimonia, before offering any verdict.

"Well, Soar," Samuel began, "it's hard for me, for any of us, to have an opinion on Aquilana because we haven't heard their side of the story! But it seems to me that you've been trying too hard to change what's on the outside, when it's what's inside that you should be concentrating on." Samuel took a sizeable quaff of mango juice, before continuing. "You're combing the mirror. And combing the mirror will never change your reflection."

Soar ruminated on this assertion before responding. He was learning to be more measured and philosophical in his thinking, and less driven by passion and dogmatism.

"That's an interesting notion," he observed. "But I don't know where to begin. I have so much that I want to achieve, and I have no idea how to get there."

Shakina smiled at him. "Every great journey begins with a single step. If you think of what you want to achieve as a huge, unconquerable mountain, of course it will be intimidating. But if you think only of the task in hand, the immediate thing you are experiencing or trying to achieve, suddenly it becomes more manageable."

Carmel interjected, "And the other thing, Soar, is that you're still thinking outside of yourself. I am a physician, I deal with the body, and even physical health all begins with what you put into yourself. Garbage in, garbage out!" Carmel eyed Soar earnestly. "Have you noticed an improvement in the time that you've stayed here, since your diet has become more diverse and balanced?"

"Oh, unquestionably," Soar agreed without hesitation. "I feel that I could fight the world and win!"

Carmel chuckled. "Okay, well now you need to take some of that passion and channel it in the right direction, instead of all in the wrong directions!"

The unyielding Soar that started out on this journey would have instantly balked at any such comment, such was his headstrong and defensive manner. But he was evolving. Instead of responding angrily, dismissing such suggestions derisively, he paused and considered the implications of the statement.

"Okay, Carmel," he began, before juddering to a halt as he realized that he had no concept of what to say next. "I think I understand what you mean, but I have absolutely no idea what you mean!"

Everyone laughed, and Soar appreciated spreading some merriment. "Maybe being self-deprecating has more value than I realized," he thought. He resolved to be more willing to laugh at himself in future.

"Have you been introduced to the walrus?" Samuel asked.

"No. Never heard of him," Soar replied.

"I didn't realize that," Samuel said with surprise. "He's one of the wisest and most experienced creatures that you're ever likely to encounter. He has taught me a huge amount about life. Why don't you take a trip to see him, we'll show you the way."

Soar was immediately skeptical. "I've already lived in one place where I was dictated to by Elders. I don't want someone else telling me what to do and what to think."

"Well, there are a couple of things that you need to consider here, Soar." Samuel spoke slowly and calmly, breaking eye contact with Soar for a second, attempting to ensure that what he was about to say didn't come across as too intense or accusatory. "Firstly, the walrus really isn't like the Elders, or how you perceive the Elders to be. He will be guiding you, not dictating to you. Secondly, if you want to be open to new ideas and experiences, you do actually have to be *open* to them! It's easy to talk the talk, but you have to walk the walk. Only you can choose this."

Soar didn't respond immediately, so Carmel quickly interjected for the second time. "Put it this way, Soar. What do you have to lose?"

6. The Walrus

From his immense height, the vast mountain range seemed no larger than pimples that had acned the earth. Soar hovered calmly, fixing his bearings, while trying to recall the precise information that the seals had divulged. As they explained the directions, it had felt as if he was being ushered into some clandestine cult, such was the mysterious, and curiously specific, directions he'd been given. Not least that he had to travel and arrive in the late evening. Not early evening. Not late afternoon. Just before sunset.

"Speaking of directions, I'd better reduce my height," Soar thought abruptly, realizing that he was in the approximate vicinity of the apparent opening to what the seals had described as Simplicitas Glacialis. As Soar swooped to a height that was roughly adjacent to the apex of the summits, he located the identifying feature that the seals had mentioned. "Follow the winding footpath until it disappears," they had informed him cryptically. Soar, slightly bewildered, wondered how he could follow something that disappears!

But there was indeed a hazy pathway twisting and meandering its way through the peaks. Suddenly, Soar experienced the strange sensation of the air stiffening. His feathers and wings were so acclimated to the wind rushing through them that he could detect the merest alterations in climatic conditions almost immediately. Yet this wasn't some mere meteorological movement. It felt as if the temperature had dropped dramatically in a matter of seconds, and, sure enough, Soar soon realized that he was shivering. It was difficult to estimate precisely how cold the weather had become; after all, Soar had become accustomed to the tropical climes of Eudaimonia. But it certainly felt perishingly cold, and the sun seemed less powerful, appearing washed out and lighter, lemon in color, as if it was being systematically softened, like broccoli in boiling water.

Soar had no time to react to this unexpected occurrence, as he noticed that the pathway had disappeared. Before he could wonder what to do next, the mountains narrowed before him, ushering him toward the one negotiable aperture between them. As he soared through this crevice, darkness enveloped him, and Soar's vision was seriously reduced—traumatic for a creature so utterly reliant on sight.

The darkness endured for a few moments, and then Soar was catapulted into the most dazzling light that he had ever experienced. It was as if he had passed through a portal into another world; a void in which neither time nor space was perceptible. Soar automatically shielded his eyes as his pupils instantly retracted, before realizing that such evasive action was unnecessary. He could see everything, but also nothing. There were no physical features perceptible, no landmarks; he was simply surrounded by a milky-white brilliance. It was a totally surreal experience, but also a surprisingly calm one. For some seconds, Soar was split asunder from any awareness of his own body. He drifted as weightless as a cloud, separated from all earthly concerns. He felt nothing but pure joy.

It was impossible to estimate time in this translucent atmosphere, and barely possible to use mundane language to describe it. But after a period of some indistinguishable length, the tiniest black dot appeared on the horizon, no larger than the period at the end of a sentence. As Soar was drawn towards it, instinctively heading in that direction, the dot expanded like an inkblot spreading outwards in a Rorschach test. Soar felt himself being transported back into a normal state of consciousness, returning to his customary physical state. Meanwhile, in his line of vision, the dot gradually broadened, until he was surrounded by an utterly unfamiliar universe.

While this new world didn't share the unique lighting of the apparent vortex through which he had just passed, it was immediately obvious to Soar that it was the polar opposite of Eudaimonia. In fact, 'polar' was precisely the right word to describe this setting. Soar had passed through an area of scintillating whiteness into another realm that was dominated by this color.

There was snow and ice as far as the eye could see. The mountains that he'd traversed had completely disappeared from view. Instead, Soar experienced the undeniable, if confusing, sensation of feeling as if he was underground, in a vast enclave. As the sedimentary walls around him began to narrow, and he first spied the flickering, flaming torches lining the walls, it became clear that this impression was correct.

The icicle-clad ceiling rapidly became low and restrictive, and Soar took the opportunity to land, continuing the final furlongs of his journey on foot. Beneath his talons, he felt the glassy bite and squishy softness that only snow can bring, yet he felt oddly warm. The few wall-mounted torches were the only source of heat, yet Soar was entirely comfortable. It was as if his vital signs had been temporarily becalmed and were invulnerable to the usual sensations of coldness.

Soar sincerely hoped this was Simplicitas Glacialis, if only because he had no idea where he was, nor how to get back to where he was before, wherever that was! He had more than a faint sense of disorientation, and yet no sense of concern manifested within him. Rather than unsettling, the muted lighting of the torches seemed seductive and sensuous; he was being genially cajoled and was a willing participant in this process.

The corridor weaved and wavered its way, until eventually Soar spotted an extremely comforting sight—a distinct opening, with light pouring through it. There was a rectangular crimson carpet with gold fringing, paving the way to what appeared to be a doorway. Soar remembered Samuel describing this and felt reassured that he hadn't become irretrievably lost in an unidentifiable parallel universe! The light emanating from the opening began to inundate the corridor as he drew ever closer to it. As he approached this interruption in the limestone, it opened out into the abdomen of the cave—a gigantic subterranean complex. It was akin to an open-plan living quarter; cozily heated, classically furnished, with endless rows of leather-bound books housed by chestnut and glass-fronted bookcases, all pleasingly draped in mood lighting. Yet the unadulterated rawness of nature was also present. Stalactites formed surreal and spiny decorative features on the ceiling, as if the cave was stretching, straining, reaching downwards in defiance of gravitational force. A spring of natural water ran undisturbed towards the left-hand wall of the cavern, filling an area of rock that appeared to have been hollowed out deliberately to form a bathing pool. And the air was redolent with the balsamic scent of amber, which swirled around and mingled with the far muskier aroma of incense. It was like two dancers encircling one another.

Sat in the middle of this improvised room was an implacable male figure, reclining in an armchair, draped in an ornate robe, almost regal in demeanor. There was time to perceive him, and even time enough to notice the unkempt yet distinguished gray hairs that sprouted from either side of his razor-sharp tusks. But there was no opportunity to consider him properly, before his gravelly voice declared authoritatively, in a manner that conveyed the impression that he never had, nor never would, experience even the most fleeting moment of uncertainty...

"Ahhhh. You must be Soar. I've been expecting you."

* * *

Soar sipped on a replenishing mug of ginseng tea, partly wanting to continue surveying his surroundings, and equally recognizing that this would be impolite. It hadn't been easy to find the walrus, and he had developed enough awareness during his journey to understand that he must make the most of this opportunity.

If the walrus had cut something of an imposing figure initially, his rasping pronunciation and commanding presence soon graciously recoiled to reveal an inner warmth. He had made Soar feel at home immediately, plying him with steaming hot drinks and thickly buttered crumpets. Touched by this hospitality, the once impudent hunter had felt humbled, recognizing a newfound sense of respect that ran through his being like a promising seam of coal. There were so many questions that Soar wanted to ask, but whereas once he would have lunged in gauchely with all guns blazing, this more refined and considered Soar was able to restrain his innate curiosity. Rather than immediately satisfy his sense of wonder, he was able to simply enjoy being in a new place with a new acquaintance. He was learning to live in the moment.

Nonetheless, the conversation soon turned to everything that had happened to Soar, and his multitude of questions about life and the universe. Soar felt slightly reluctant to discuss Aquilana, and particularly the Elders, partly because it was personal, but also because he didn't wish to appear biased against the elderly. But he knew he had to open up, so he explained to the walrus that he'd found them so limiting, and that life at home had been unbearable because he was constrained, squeezed to bursting point, until he felt like a failing dam.

The walrus listened, occasionally interrupting with charm, patiently clarifying some detail or another with Soar. And after Soar had finished, the walrus reclined in his luxurious seating, and delivered his verdict politely but unsparingly.

"I understand how you felt, Soar. But there are some important things that you need to appreciate. Firstly, there are two sides to every story. You have only considered this from your side, you haven't really attempted to empathize with the Elders. That doesn't mean that they were right and you were wrong; perhaps even the complete opposite is the case. But you will never be truly enlightened unless you can appreciate the perspective of someone that you profoundly disagree with."

Soar had barely begun to consider this assertion before the walrus continued.

"And, secondly, you can't fight fire with fire. You just end up emulating what you condemn. You become the very thing that you despise. All you do by pushing against the people you grew up with is make them more entrenched in their position. You can't change their mind for them; you have to demonstrate to them that they will benefit and allow them to make this transformation of their own accord." The walrus paused briefly before delivering his final checkmating observation. "Remember, Soar, if someone confrontationally told you that you were completely wrong about everything, how likely would you be to accept this? I can see that you've grown, but even the eagle that I see before me today simply wouldn't accept it! You can't tell people that they're wrong, you can only show them what is right."

Instinctively, almost before the words had left the mouth of the walrus, Soar realized that he was correct. This was an important aspect of his evolution: the development of acceptance. He might never have quite the relationship with his family that he desired, he might never convince the dwellers of Aquilana to branch out beyond their narrow confines. But he could be at peace with it. And yet, before he had even processed this epiphany, it was as if the walrus had reached inside his brain and excavated his very thoughts.

"And I want you to know something else, Soar. Acceptance doesn't mean living with something indefinitely. Acceptance doesn't mean that you don't try to change something. It means that you actively practice the conscious awareness of knowing that you can only truly control your own experience." The walrus chuckled. "And even that is currently a little beyond you!"

The air was silent for a second, but Soar was pleased to note that the atmosphere was contemplative rather than hostile. There was wisdom in the walrus' words, even though he would have rebuffed them violently, like a rutting stag, at the time that he'd begun his journey. Before he could consider this any further, Soar surprised himself by blurting out a particularly unintelligible sentence.

"I want to feel the white thing!"

The walrus was far from unfriendly, but he also rarely smiled. He was simply too wise and experienced to be taken by surprise, as is required by humour. But on hearing Soar's rash comment, the walrus couldn't help grinning, perhaps even secretly pleased that Soar had been so affected by his sojourn in Simplicitas.

"I think you'll need to expand on that concept slightly, Soar!"

Soar returned the smile and composed himself. "Okay! Okay… When I was traveling here, I went through what I can only describe as a portal, and it was surreal and amazing, but I felt something inside myself that I'd never felt before. It was as if I had no body. I felt an unadulterated joy that was unimpeded by any of the usual bodily functions. It was a side of myself that I'd never experienced before. I want to feel that again! Very much!"

The walrus fixed his eyes unstintingly on Soar. As he inhaled and began to speak, the looser, malleable flesh beneath his giant tusks, that formed something of a double chin, quivered like the vibrating string of a plucked harp. "That was just a taste of something that is inside you. That is inside all of us. You were connecting with the universe, with the infinite, with everything that there is. You are intrinsically connected with this, but if you want to experience this regularly then you first need to remember what you already know."

This was a little too much of a riddle for Soar to truly understand, and he spent a few seconds staring into space, observing how an array of tightly packed stalactites formed a jellyfish-like structure, albeit with more solidity. "What is it that I need to know?", he asked with his most sincere curiosity.

"There isn't a single answer to that question, and there isn't an easy solution. You need to do a lot of inner work. You need to look inside yourself for the answers. You need to actively practice inner awareness, and you need to fully commit to this on a daily basis. If you do this, if you take my guidance on board, and if you cultivate discipline, serenity and openness then there is no limit to what you can achieve. And suddenly the world will be your oyster, you'll never want for anything. You will connect with something far greater than the most breathtaking vista or sunset. And yet you will be free to explore the world with joy, with equanimity, with purpose, and with certainty at the core of your being that will guide you and sustain you no matter what you encounter."

And so the two of them discussed Soar's development at length, everything that he was doing wrong, and what could be done to remedy this. It was a sign of burgeoning maturity in him that, although the walrus wasn't reluctant to praise him, Soar no longer required this. He didn't need to be patted on the back, he had no desire for his qualities and lethal hunting ability to be recognized and acknowledged. He just wanted to become better.

Soon it was time for Soar to leave, although he was glad that the walrus pointed him in the right direction! He thanked him with true gratitude and turned to exit. But before he reached the corridor, the walrus stopped him, and offered him one last piece of advice.

"I want you to hear this, Soar, and hear it well. You should live your life like a sculptor. You should be constantly chiseling away at the world around you, and yourself, to reveal form, not grasping for some halcyon monument that doesn't exist yet. It requires patience, it cannot be rushed. But eventually, if you do the work on yourself, you will find that you've reduced that apparently immovable slab of stone into something remarkable. And that comes from following the same process, day in, day out, with fortitude, determination, and acceptance."

Soar savored every word, nodded appreciatively, and crept back out into the sparse and tapered surroundings of the cavern.

Ambient music filled the air with a soothing resonance. Soar's eyes were closed, but in a relaxed rather than resolute fashion. He allowed the tranquil melodies to guide him, the notes lingering and alternating unhurriedly. As he recognized this, allowing himself to slide into the meditative state that the warming sounds encouraged, he let his mind consider everything for which he was grateful. His health. The air. Fresh water. The sun. His ability to fly. His friends. His family. The beauty of the planet. The bountiful abundance that it offers. Soar turned these things over in his head repeatedly, allowing himself to drift further into this reflective state, feeling the energy of the universe steadily pulsing through his body. Most importantly, he was beginning to genuinely vibrate at the frequency of gratitude, feeling appreciative in his heart and soul for everything that he had and would experience.

The session finished, Soar allowed himself to enjoy the slightly sedated sensation for a little longer, keeping his eyes closed, as he allowed the soothing qualities of the forest to wash over him. Then he opened them, ready to seize the day with renewed fortitude.

Soar had revisited the walrus twice since that initial foray, and this had helped accelerate a process that was already developing. There was a new Soar growing inside him; this was perceptible, undeniable. It wasn't as dramatic as a phoenix rising from the ashes, nor was there any silver bullet that precipitated this growth. It was, instead, small processes that were collectively cumulative. Daily meditation, tailored exercise, improved sleep, better diet, practicing mindfulness, positive self-talk, cultivating acceptance. When all these things coalesced, there was a vision, a vitality, a vivacity at the core of Soar's being that seemed to become more strongly reinforced by the day.

And yet, this increased energy and amplified state of being was tempered with calmness. Soar no longer felt frantic, like a drowning cat thrashing around in the water randomly. He was stronger mentally and emotionally, systematically learning to view the world with compassion. As an eagle, a hunter, a feared and formidable specimen, Soar had relied on his instinctive behaviors. Now, conversely, he was strengthening his conscious awareness slowly but deliberately, and learning to depend on that as well. He was steadily evolving, fashioning a new version of himself, becoming the sculptor that the walrus had spoken of.

As Soar began his daily flight to the beach, he considered the most important transformation of all. There was an inner joy that was germinating inside him, sprouting like a juvenile sapling. This spirit was emanating in his heart, but being disseminated throughout his body, mind, and soul, spreading, flowing, just as tributaries gush into the mighty ocean.

Soar no longer merely observed the splendour of the island; it was now indelibly engraved on his soul. He felt ineradicably connected to it. The way that nightfall descended on the island like a gargantuan satin sheet. The tide that sometimes meekly, almost apologetically, barely brushed the shore, and on other occasions swirling waves and currents crashed against the beach with an indignant ferocity. The surreal way that the early morning silence seemed to permeate the air as much as the most reverberating sound.

Even the resentment that Soar felt towards Aquilana was steadily dissipating. It hadn't dissolved completely, but the familiar yet restrictive feelings of denial that had limited his thinking were steadily clearing, like a chink in the clouds after a thunderstorm. He recognized now that blaming others was futile, and that he had been too engrossed in himself to see beyond his selfish desires. He had been an unwilling but decisive participant in his own constraint. Not anymore. The congestion that had clouded his thinking was lifting. He could see himself and the world with a new clarity. Instead, something else was consuming his conscious mind.

This conversational gambit with the walrus had begun so innocuously, and his sage companion had so casually tossed in what turned out to be a considerable revelation. There was another Aquilana! Far away to the east. In a dim and distant land. He had never once heard this mentioned back home; as far as he knew there was no one in the community who was acquainted with it, even intellectually. But the seals were aware of it; in fact, its reputation was seemingly famous in this part of the world. There was talk of this being an incredible kingdom that beguiled all who witnessed it.

It might not be his ultimate destination, but Soar knew that he must seek out this mystical paradise. And he knew in his heart that he was ready.

7. The Unknown

Everyone agreed that it had been the happiest and most memorable Christmas that they could remember. Snow had tumbled down liberally, covering the entire neighborhood with the crunchiest, most aesthetically pleasing coating imaginable. It had been one of those incomparable winter days, where the temperature barely lifts above freezing, and yet the sun still anomalously cuts through the chill, shining brightly, almost bravely, undeterred by the temperature.

There had been no shortage of turkey on offer this time. Roast turkey can be a notoriously tricky dish to prepare; no matter how much basting, seasoning and stuffing, the results can still be disappointingly dry. But this year, Jemima had upstaged even her usual standards of excellence, cramming pounds of bacon into the bird before using the creamiest butter as an ideal basting agent. The result was tender, succulent, and irresistible.

Steaming Christmas pudding with lashings of cream and brandy sauce followed. By the time that this had been savaged with glee, the whole family felt slightly food drunk! A bracing flight through the mountains, a Christmas tradition, soon awakened the senses. The undulations of the snow-covered peaks always seemed more distinct, as if the temporary veneer of snowfall somehow acted to accentuate their positive qualities. The sun mingled with the powdery covering to create a fluffy haze, as the family surveyed the natural beauty of their surroundings. You never felt more alive than swooping between the towering mountains with a hearty meal in your belly. You *couldn't* feel more alive than this.

When nightfall arrived the family toasted a successful day, a prosperous year, and their deep connection and bonds with one another. Inevitably, the day ended with Carrie tinkling the ivories, bolting through some time-honored favorites, while the rest of the family joined in merrily. Solomon's voice was rather powerful, somewhere in the range of baritone, and he belted out his vocals with quite evident relish, as invigorating sea spray suddenly whipped up into Soar's face. He immediately awakened from his daydream, no longer allowing the wistful memory to distract him from the task at hand. He could glide so effortlessly that it was perfectly possible for him to drift off every bit as deeply as the snowdrifts that formed on this idyllic Christmas Day.

Soar missed his family. This was an undeniable fact, much though he had attempted to bury this inconvenient reality deep within his subconscious. He knew that he would reunite with them in some form, at some point. But he didn't know when this would be, or what sort of reception he could expect when he did. He wished deeply in his heart that they'd wanted to join him, or that they could see the world and life in a similar way to his own perception. Every important aspect of his being had been ruptured by the decision to leave; it had torn him right down the middle. Yet despite the pain and heartbreak, despite the trials and tribulations, despite the occasionally overwhelming feelings of loneliness, Soar could still reconcile his emotional state with the reality that he had no choice. If he had allowed his resentment to percolate any longer in his gut, it could have grown into something monstrous and immovable. The feelings of affection and belonging would have almost inevitably crumbled when confronted with this greater force. And the damage to those important family relationships would have been potentially far greater, possibly irreparable. It was paradoxical, but the only way that he could preserve his love for his family was to embark on this journey.

Those halcyon islands on which he had spent quite some months had already disappeared into the distance. Eudaimonia may be in his future, but for now it was in his immediate past. The seals had been hugely supportive when he'd sat them down to reveal all. It was one of those moments that

Soar wished to defer, or even cancel completely. But he knew that he must disclose to them that his time on Eudaimonia was over.

There was no fierce response, or even any sign that this announcement was unexpected. The seals graciously accepted that it was time for Soar to depart. A lingering part of Soar ached to stay a little longer on this bountiful island. He felt that he hadn't yet truly repaid the seals for their kindness. But they were entirely philosophical about this, opining that Soar had been an asset to them while he had resided in their vicinity, and that he would always have a place in their hearts. He thanked them warmly and was grateful not only for their hospitality and guidance, but also that they intrinsically understood the need to spread his wings. An inner calling was more powerful and profound than the competing need that Soar felt for comfort and security. Which meant it was his unfortunate duty to bid farewell to the seals.

He would miss the walrus as well. Their relationship had never exactly been an equal one; Soar had unashamedly assumed the role of a protégé, the walrus frequently dispensing his instruction. One of the most memorable aspects of his advice concerned the concept of making mistakes. He explained to Soar that the reason he chastised himself for his perceived errors was that he had been taught this from an early age. Education inculcates us into the fraudulent understanding that mistakes are undesirable, the walrus divulged, and we indeed are often punished in this environment precisely for making mistakes. Yet how can you learn without them? Did you fly perfectly the first time that you took off? Or the second time? Of course not! You learn by failing. If you never fail, you never learn anything of substance.

Soar had railed against school in all its grisly forms, but he had latently absorbed the notion that doing things badly is wrong. He had rebelled against this—boy, had he rebelled against it! And yet, the idea had still penetrated his consciousness, wedging itself stubbornly in his cranium; such is the power of social conditioning. The strain of perfectionism that had been an Achilles heel could undoubtedly be attributed to this. Bringing this into his conscious awareness was helping to heal this self-inflicted wound.

Such self-awareness was becoming an invaluable tool in Soar's arsenal. He reflected that it was natural for these feelings to surface at this fork in the road. The next chapter of his journey was about to begin; it was therefore logical to reflect on his past. Overall, his time in Eudaimonia had been overwhelmingly positive; a valuable sabbatical of inquisition and expansion. He left this paradise stronger, more experienced, and healthier, with a burgeoning awareness flourishing in the crux of his being. Furthermore, Soar was armed with new and instructive knowledge that would inform him as he negotiated the undefined path that lay ahead.

Breathing at high altitude never posed any difficulty for Soar. But today he had adopted a much lower flying height than usual, not for any particular reason, simply for the benefit of variety. On this mild morning, the waters seemed almost turquoise in colour, swelling and retracting with an aloof delicacy that gave no indication of the ocean's destructive power.

Soar remained conflicted. The wheels had been set in motion for a deep awakening, and there was part of him that was inspired by the challenges ahead. But there was another part of him that wondered if the whole process was a mythical dream; a phantom that would never materialize. And there was still a third part of him that wondered if he should return to Aquilana, that longed to see his parents and his sister, and generally felt very alone on this nebulous and uncertain journey.

But his mood that day matched the placid seas. Soar was learning to heed his inner voice and trust his intuition. And this compelling counselor was pushing him east, toward the other Aquilana that he'd heard the seals speak of with such regard. His internal compass was set in this direction, and this direction only.

* * *

It was not entirely unusual for Soar to encounter ships, but they were still something of a curiosity. This particular multi-tiered vessel was filled to the brim with passengers, who were evidently enjoying a cruise. It must be frustrating being so constricted in where and how you can move, Soar reflected. Imagine never having felt thermal power propelling you through the air. Imagine witnessing a smoldering apricot sunset and being unable to get close to it. Imagine moving with such painful sluggishness through the water. And imagine this process being divorced from any form of anatomical mastery, or even effort. Poor creatures!

Soar's attention to the lavish indulgence of the cruise ship then moved back to his journey. This was now completely uncharted territory. His internal compass was bereft; it was a region that was completely new to him. Once the ship had disappeared into the distance, there was a surreal calmness to the panoramic dominance of the heavens and the ocean. How long had he been traveling? Was it days? Was it weeks? Soar had no idea. Time had ceased to be a meaningful variable within the equation of this universe, aside from the elliptical journey that the sun made across the sky each day. It rose, it meandered towards its inevitable destination, it sank, another day ended. That was all he knew.

There were only three considerations that consumed Soar: finding a place to rest once the gloom had descended; scrabbling together enough food to convert into sufficient energy to survive; and making progress towards the Aquilana of his dreams. This second task was proving difficult enough in itself; there had been the occasional sight of land, but foraging in these locations had proved rather fruitless when it came to sustenance, largely limited to fishing excursions. Soar kept his eyes studiously trained on the azure depths throughout his journey.

The elements were usually a source of wonder and fascination for Soar. But the nature of his expedition had effectively twisted his perception of them. The respect was still present, but its emphasis had morphed into something decidedly darker than usual. Rather than a giver of life, the sun appeared relentless; like a triathlete that simply never stops running. It appeared immediately in the sky at dawn, and soon reached an intoxicating intensity, beating down mercilessly, seeming to infuse the entire skyline. Dominant, imposing, unflagging. Soar was thankful for the cooling properties of the sea but was finding it difficult to cherish its beauty. It appeared cobalt blue in colour on this day, but didn't transmit its usual allure, seeming implacable, indifferent, and infinite, almost taunting him.

Nonetheless, Soar felt no inclination to surrender to his fatigue. Challenging thoughts were pulsating through his brain. His central nervous system was indeed begging him to surrender, or at least allow his mood to descend into one of depression and despair. But he was able to recognize this bubbling cauldron of internalized feelings and resolve it. The self-work he had started, the meditation that he continued to practice, the questioning and self-questioning that he repeatedly engaged in, and the numerous fireside chats that he'd enjoyed with the seals and the walrus—these had all collectively raised Soar's emotional intelligence. He was able to take a figurative step back and observe his emotions; he was now consciously aware of this process. Soar was becoming a judicious curator of a carefully balanced emotional state. He looked back now at the suspicious Soar who had left Aquilana, recognizing him to be a bundle of unfocused energy and emotion.

Soar continued on his planned eastward path, occasionally ticking off a landmark on the way that had been mentioned by the seals. This was only indeed an occasional process, though, as nothing appeared within Soar's line of vision for what seemed like hours at a time. But being alone with just the primordial aspects of the universe for company wasn't disheartening. He had learned to cope with the challenges that he faced, along with the sheer determination and stamina required. Eventually, after he'd been flying for many hours, he even encountered a storm, but this posed no particular problem. He sidestepped it by climbing in a fashion that seemed precipitous but was actually surgically controlled. It soon passed. Nothing would deter Soar from continuing with this quest.

Eventually, night began to fall. It was another day where he had felt himself steadily drifting away from the familiar. At this point, he didn't have the slightest clue where he was, and even his usually impeccable sense of direction was failing him. Thus, he wasn't quite sure where he was in relation to anything else either! As light rapidly began to turn to dusk, Soar was tired and hungry. Admittedly, he had managed to consume some pelagic fish earlier in the day, but there was a more pressing concern than even hunger; there was not the merest indication that there was any land within reasonable distance. He was astray amid the vast ocean, as helpless as a newborn fawn. He could do nothing to address the situation—literally nothing. All he could do was struggle onwards, point himself in what he believed to be the correct direction, and fly faithfully through the night. Soar instinctively adjusted his altitude, hoping to encounter a thermal at some point. The light was fading fast; he had mere minutes of daylight remaining. Then he would become a solitary figure in the wilderness, with only his lesser functioning senses for company.

Fortunately, there was a full moon that evening. Sparkling stars were abundant, visible across the entire extent of the blackened skyline. They were not quite lighting the way, but providing enough illumination that the immediate environment wasn't plunged into all-encompassing darkness. Soar's pupils had dilated sufficiently for him to absorb this new source of light, and he became hopeful that the night would be more manageable than he had first feared. There was a beauty to the stark duskiness; each star seeming like an individual pinprick bursting through the celestial expanse.

Still no immediate respite was forthcoming. The night was so still as to be motionless; there was no prospect of any thermal assistance. Many more hours of purposeful flying lay ahead for Soar, as he hoped—probably in vain—to be drifting in the general direction of his appointed outcome. This must be a secondary consideration; his primary focus must be on preserving his energy, maintaining level flight, and living to fight another day.

The moon cast a shimmering field of conical light across the rippling, raven seas, and Soar steeled himself for an almighty challenge to his stamina.

8. The Master

The lively rays of morning sun seared across the atmosphere, spearing the cerulean carpet of the sea, refracting, before being reflected back into the planet's lower atmosphere. After the bleakness of nightfall, suddenly the world seemed to exist ontologically again. Having been camouflaged from vision in the dead of night, the ocean appeared even more gargantuan than usual, almost elasticated, stretching beyond the extent of even eagle perception.

This sight was more than a glimmer of hope for Soar; it was a blessed relief after ten torrid hours. Ten torrid hours during which he had absolutely no perception of time! He had squeezed nearly every ounce of fight and energy from his body during that period; disorientated, exhausted, yet never allowing his determination to diminish. The seals had warned him that there may be a considerable period during which his senses would be pervaded by nothing but ocean, but he had somehow imagined that they were exaggerating.

How wrong he had been! Days had passed since he had last encountered anything other than the boundless, unconquerable brine. Witnessing nothing but the same horizon, the same linear progression of the sun, and the same heaving sea, with nothing to disrupt it other than the seemingly impossible task of traversing it. But the unforgiving bleakness of nightfall had sharpened his senses, making him re-engage with reality. No matter how tired he might feel, he was ready to meet any challenges head-on.

It was a hazy morning, and the sun was so low it appeared that it would collide with the ocean. With no buildings, mountains, trees, or indeed anything else to deflect the burning orb, its potent rays danced playfully upon the ocean without interruption. It was a dazzling sight, a spectacular one, and Soar was forced to avert his gaze, instead staring into an unoccupied area of the blue yonder. His latest fishing expedition would have to wait.

Instead, he focused his eyes intently to the east of the sun, zooming in with laser focus, testing himself to ensure that his eyesight was still intense. But there was nothing to see except the infinite. The unceasing, blazing sun. The eternal atmosphere. Nothing to see whatsoever….. except for that land that was looming into view! Soar's heart skipped a beat. At last, there was something tangible! Could this be his destination?

Soar's recent travails and sense of exhaustion dissolved as quickly as sugar in coffee, as an intense bout of adrenaline propelled him in the general direction of the land. He had never been so relieved or grateful. Even if it wasn't the Aquilana that he sought, he could hopefully rest up here for a few days, feed himself up, and continue with renewed vigor. Indeed, although Soar was passionate about locating this esteemed paradise, the identity of the island wasn't of any immediate concern. He was simply desperate to land, and crushingly in need of rest. He was praying to whatever force compelled the universe that the island would provide ample food and water.

As Soar approached the sands that constituted the coast of the island, he scorched through the air like an atomic bomb. There was no time for niceties; he didn't care for an elegant landing, nor even to rudimentarily survey his surroundings. He landed with an unsightly thump, but barely felt a thing. Instead, Soar lay motionless, allowing the revitalizing water to lap passively over him, as if it was an embrocation for his entire body. The seals were right; this did feel good! Soar lay there, contented, resting his limbs, with no desire other than to recuperate.

* * *

The first word that came to Soar's mind when describing this region was pristine. It was almost unnaturally clean, as if it was a newborn land that had yet to be sullied by the inconvenience of being occupied. In the immediate rejuvenating moments after alighting from the beach, Soar surveyed his surroundings, noting their metaphysical beauty. This was an ideal home for any eagle; this land was characterized by dense woodland. There was a variety of trees to gorge on, but barely a breath of wind to whistle through them. As soon as Soar realized how copious the forests were on the island, he immediately took flight, rising himself high above the tallest redwoods, so that he could survey the magnificence of his surroundings.

He was instantly elated. This land was far greater in scope than the Aquilana with which he was familiar. In fact, it was probably bigger than his birthplace and Eudaimonia combined. It was an immense region of luxuriant forest, with few signs of clearings, akin to a rainforest in density, but featuring a less equatorial climate. The only thing he could spy, other than impenetrable throngs of trees, was the shimmering, silvery coast on which he had originally touched down. The temperature was a little cooler than his previous residence, but this didn't concern Soar; it would help make flying expeditions more comfortable.

On one level, this world seemed to be the antithesis of Eudaimonia; absent of any signs of life. On the seal-infested islands, it was almost impossible to avoid other creatures. The whole region was teeming with biology; this was one of the captivating aspects of Eudaimonia. This new land, whether it was the Aquilana he sought or not, provided a calmer backdrop, a silent enclave that seemed almost designed to aid concentration. Nonetheless, Soar had been alone for quite some time, and he craved contact or a smattering of conversation.

No matter, Soar concluded. He would find a suitable sapling and settle down for a protracted snooze. Weaving in and out of the sturdy trunks was a wonderful experience, and Soar was proud to note that his reaction time was as honed as ever. Suddenly he spied the perfect nesting region. This time Soar landed with more decorum, gently bringing himself to a halt and bedding in for some well-earned rest. Despite the tiredness that he felt, Soar was also proud of the newfound strength of his wings. He could have carried on flying such was the increased stamina in his arsenal nowadays. Nonetheless, he was still glad to have settled in peaceful surroundings.

It was strange that this place was so eerily bereft of animal life, but investigation could wait a few hours. There were more pressing matters to be dealt with first, such as getting forty winks! But before Soar could even contemplate closing his eyes, the nest he had identified was plunged into darkness. As Soar turned to investigate how and why this had occurred, an imposing figure loomed over him. It was startling, as he hadn't perceived the merest suggestion of life in the region. He began to chastise himself for his careless survey of the area, but quickly realized that it was a fellow eagle that stood over him.

"Good morning, stranger," the figure said in measured tones. "Welcome to Magna Aquilana."

Not for the first time during his journey, Soar was taken aback by the rapidity of hospitality offered. He was soon tucked up in a cozy blanket and his new hosts immediately provided a mug of warming mushroom soup. His early impression of the climate in this part of the world was that it was more capricious than that of Eudaimonia. After he'd landed, dark clouds had snaked their way across the skyline with apparent haste, parking themselves inconsiderately in front of the sun, casting a moody shadow across the land. Soar was fine, it wasn't excessively cold, but he was also willing to concede that it was pleasant to receive these small tokens of comfort.

His initial inspection of what he had now been inducted into as Magna Aquilana was misleading. The land was indeed jam-packed with trees, many of which were particularly impressive specimens, extending with such avidity into the heavens that it was impossible to see their peaks from the ground. But Soar had effectively approached the land from an errant angle and had thus failed to encounter the settlement that monopolized the other side of the island. Such was the density of greenery that it had simply been concealed from view. In fact, Soar wasn't entirely sure how he'd been located so quickly, but when he'd inquired about this, his inquisition was brushed away brusquely.

Conversely, it wasn't altogether surprising that Soar had overlooked any signs of life, as the buildings on the island were only conspicuous by one quality—their absence. This was the major contrast between his birthplace and Magna Aquilana; there were seemingly no dwellings whatsoever. When he asked about this, explaining that the eagles in his Aquilana tended to reside in housing, he was immediately posed the rhetorical question: "What could be a greater place of residence than living in the natural world?" And this resonated with Soar. The best things in this world are free; the simplest life is the most fulfilling life.

The initial impression Soar had was that the land represented a veritable haven for eagles. Once he'd been escorted to the primary area of residence, it became obvious that this region was populated by hundreds, if not thousands, of eagles and eaglets. He watched them nesting in the jagged eclogite rocks, swirling in and out of the totemic mountain ashes and statuesque spruces, surveying the pellucid waters. He saw them gathering together socially in what appeared to be a regular meeting place on the shore, preening and grooming themselves as they did so. Almost immediately, Soar's soul was suffused with a deep sense of belonging.

Another facet of the island that was instantly attuned with Soar's consciousness was the irresistible, unmistakable aroma of meat! Soar was glad, proud even, that he had broadened his nutritional palate, but it remained an undeniable fact that meat was seductive. Eating meat was conjoined with his soul. It would thus be gratifying to feast on grilled flesh once more and relish the sumptuous juices and inimitable taste and texture; it was already a tantalizing prospect! But maybe he could also introduce the residents to more varied foodstuffs.

In those early hours in this new location, Soar steadily acclimatized to his surroundings. It was strange to be among the familiar, and yet for it to be unfamiliar. Soar had yet to be inculcated into life in Magna Aquilana—or Magna as the locals referred to it—but he could already see that it contrasted with that of the Aquilana in which he'd been raised. Back home, the emphasis was on hunting, family and the tribe. Conversely, it was clear that in this part of the world personal growth was heavily accentuated. Magna was almost like a boot camp for eagles, where they were, on the one hand, drilled and trained, but also given the apparatus required to evolve into the best versions of themselves. Education here didn't mean memorizing answers, it meant developing the tools needed to think critically. Physical training wasn't about filling some predetermined role, it was about developing yourself precisely for the very purpose of development.

It also occurred to Soar that the region was isolated from any other signs of civilization. There was nothing on the horizon; the view far into the distance was characterized by having nothing of character to discern. But when he asked about this seclusion from other species and lands, it was explained that this certainly wasn't intended to induce an inward-looking tendency in the inhabitants of Magna. Everyone residing at the settlement was deeply prepared for the outside world, for fulfilling any and every role that they could ever assume, and they were entirely free to leave whenever their soul demanded it. Magna was intended not to imprison, but to impress and imprint strength, independence, and character.

Soar had begun to mix with the other eagles to some extent, but it was the wizened, elderly figure that had initially located him that interested him the most. From the moment that Soar was around him, he immediately realized that this was an unusual figure, with similar qualities to the walrus, but also with an ethereal calmness at the core of his being. The walrus was a bibliophile, and an insightful fellow, but he never struck Soar as the biggest meditator. Instead, his focus was always on deriving wisdom and meaning from the life lessons that inevitably accumulate on this mortal coil. But this particular eagle conveyed a tangible and distinct aura of spirituality; a masterful presence. It was evident that he was serene and focused, with a strength for his age and a warmth of expression that conveyed a life lived according to the most noble principles.

It didn't even surprise Soar when he was informed that this esteemed figure was referred to simply as Master. He had played a central role in building Magna, structuring the way that eaglets were raised, and ensuring that this systematic approach was passed down from one generation to the next. This didn't, superficially, appear that different to Aquilana, but there was one crucial difference—Magna was based on the key principle of empowering the individual. In this society, you were free to become whoever and whatever you wanted, rather than the emphasis being on the potentially self-limiting perpetuation of the tribe.

"However, Soar, if you want this freedom then you first have to earn it," the Master explained to him. "We respect you; we can already tell what you're capable of doing. But you're not permitted to sail in here, with your prodigious hunting abilities and physical capabilities, and take over! You will learn much here but first you will learn discipline."

This wasn't exactly music to Soar's ears, yet he accepted it. The concept felt like the first step towards something greater; akin to a samurai warrior studying Kendo diligently before they finally receive a blade. He was expecting to be immediately summoned into an inner sanctum; an illuminati of eagle knowledge. Yet the reality jarred somewhat with this assumption. It was relayed to Soar that he would effectively begin his time in Magna at the bottom of the food chain. It would not be a "cakewalk," as the Master put it.

"Remember, Soar, we are building character. This stage of the process is every bit as important as any other facet of personal growth that you will ever experience."

And so, Soar reluctantly found himself being inducted into a seemingly unending litany of menial tasks. He spent hours removing shells from crustaceans. He prepared and broiled meat dishes for an array of, admittedly gracious, eagles. He cleaned a myriad of cooking pots and utensils. He even waited on tables a few times, although there was always a delicious meal awaiting him once he'd completed his mandatory tasks. Soar fetched, carried, scrubbed, disinfected, and polished, working with unending industriousness. It was tiring and unedifying, but Soar figured that this spell of humdrum labour would pass swiftly, and he would soon graduate on to something more stimulating.

But this didn't occur as quickly as he'd hoped. Several weeks passed, but there was still no sign that Soar would be invited to do anything other than scurry around attending to multitudinous chores. It was tiring, monotonous, even degrading. He could almost perceive his senses and skills steadily dulling through neglect, while he watched the other eagles enjoy engaging activities—debate, discussion, learning, hunting, along with all of the organizational tasks that ensured Magna ran like clockwork. He observed the other eagles and reflected that something was working. There was an extremely mature and intelligent level of interaction that predominated, and there was a palpable sense of joy that pervaded the entire atmosphere of Magna. The eagles present there had, without exception, undeniably strong characters, yet there was never any hint of conflict. Problems and disagreements were resolved through rational discussion, with no preconceived or dogmatic insistence that things must be done a certain way. Magna was constantly evolving. As new information and insight became available, the land remolded itself to harmonize with this greater understanding.

Nonetheless, Soar was far from accustomed to being, as he saw it, barred from participation in intellectual life. He could easily see the good in Magna, but he also felt excluded like an outsider. He was becoming bored and irritable—he considered his role to be thoroughly beneath him! It felt as if he wasn't needed, as if his skill set was nothing of particular note in this world, and that he would never be afforded the opportunity to progress and develop. This was hugely frustrating for Soar, and there were several moments when he considered abandoning the land completely. He fantasized about fleeing in the dead of night, leaving not the slightest residue to indicate that he'd even been present.

But he didn't know where to go, except returning from where he came. And Soar had set out on this journey to move forwards, not backwards.

* * *

The candle flickered and wavered in the gentle evening breeze. Shards of liquefied wax slowly submitted to the pull of gravity, snaking their way sinuously down the sides of the main body of the candle. Soar ruminated in the subdued lighting. His mood was somber, but not defeated. He would not be vanquished by the drudgery that had been put in front of him; he would prove his worth to the entire community. He had been promised that he would gain enlightenment from his sojourn in Magna, and he was determined to drink in this experience, whatever it took.

As it turned out, the residents of Magna already had a balanced diet. They were more aware of the importance of this than the eagles back in Aquilana. They were impressive specimens; smart, open-minded, lean, and powerful. Soar soon realized that he had more to learn from them than he himself could impart. And if that meant earning his reputation through grit first, so be it.

Once dusk had cascaded down on Magna, the land was muted to the point of being mildly surreal. It was as if Soar had traveled to an Atlantis, an otherworldly location that had been systematically removed from maps, charts, and all known consciousness. There were no external noises within audible distance; the silence would only be occasionally punctured by the shrill whistling of mating calls. Soar would be tempted by the single, soft, soprano note of the female, indicating that she was prepared for copulation. But he recognized that he had yet to rise to a satisfactory enough position in the society to heed such calls. "My time will come," he vowed.

Soar's contemplation was suddenly interrupted, as the Master landed next to him without warning. He had a habit of surprising Soar, and this was another occasion on which the younger of the two eagles had been completely unprepared for his presence.

"Sorry to disturb you, Soar," the Master began. "I'm sure you're ready to turn in for the evening, but there is something pressing that I need to discuss with you that can't wait until the morning."

"Of course, what is it?" As much as he respected the Master, the notion of addressing him as Master still stuck in Soar's stomach!

"I've been watching you closely since you came to Magna. I'm particularly impressed with how hard you've worked." Soar's expression turned marginally from neutral to mildly favorable. "You have a lot of maturity. You've accepted your role as a newbie with real determination. It was never our intention for you to remain in this role; you're here to learn, you're here to grow, and to become the best version of yourself. And tomorrow that process begins."

Soar could barely contain his excitement but managed to retain a dignified appearance.

"You have the grit and determination. You're willing to sacrifice yourself for the well-being of others. You're hungry to learn. You're ready."

Soar couldn't prevent himself from inquiring. "Ready for what?"

The Master raised his eyebrows slightly, turned his body in a 180-degree angle, and began his preparations for take-off. He offered but a few words of explanation, spoken ambiguously over his shoulder. "You'll find out tomorrow." But just as he stretched his wings out, the Master turned to Soar meaningfully, and offered one final statement of importance.

"And, Soar, there's one last thing that I want you to understand."

Soar nodded solemnly.

"The real work begins now."

9. The Awakening

The usual gradual awakening that Soar experienced was replaced by a different sensation that morning. In its place was a sudden jolt of recognition just as soon as the day that lay ahead of him seeped into his groggy consciousness. It felt like the first day of the rest of his life; the enticing point at which his existence on Magna was to truly begin.

Despite his heightened sense of anticipation, Soar wasn't quite ready to leap out of the nest with abandon! A few moments of introspection would aid the process of arousal. He lay silently, amid a carefully assembled concave structure of intertwined twigs, warm, comfortable, brimming with relish for the learning experience that he'd been promised. Although there was significantly less wildlife around Magna than in Eudaimonia, it wasn't entirely bereft of other species. From his vantage point, Soar spotted the wriggling movements of a python in the undergrowth. Its reticulated physique almost oozed across the ground in liquid fashion.

After just a couple of minutes, Soar stretched his weary bones and headed out. As he swooped between the towering trees, it became evident that he was the first eagle to leave the nest. A morning mist hung stubbornly in the air, refusing to be summarily dismissed by the arrival of the sun. This always cast a slightly surreal shadow over the atmosphere, Soar thought, as if daybreak was refusing to reveal itself. He headed toward the northern extremities of Magna, an appreciable flight of several kilometers, zigzagging between a palisade of three ancient firs, not allowing the immovable presence of several tons of sturdy trunk to impede his momentum. The greens of summer were beginning to capitulate to the impending browns, reds and oranges of autumn, and though the temperatures were becoming more bracing, this was compensated by the aesthetics of what Soar considered to be the most striking season.

Soar had been informed that he must make for one particular enclave, located approximately 300 yards away from the northern coast of Magna. Soar had never ventured in that direction and was geographically unfamiliar with the region. However, he had been assured that there was a clearing within the trees that was sizable enough to be unmistakable; if Soar ascended to a decent altitude, he would easily spot the destination. He was initially skeptical, yet as he reached what seemed to be the approximate location, there was a sudden annular parting in the evergreen fortification, as if the forest was experiencing an early onset of alopecia.

Soar slowed and braced himself for landing. As he steadily descended, an intricate stone circle in the center of the clearing became evident. A bonfire had been lit within it, and the dancing flames helped illuminate his path as he brought himself delicately to the ground. The clearing was actually huge, so large that it was more appropriate to measure it in square acres than square meters, and there was already an assemblage of eagles waiting for him. Among them, inevitably, was the Master.

None of the other handful of eagles present were recognizable to Soar. For some moments they all sat among the carefully arranged slate-gray rocks, studiously ignoring one another in the slightly awkward way that is common for coltish strangers. Soar could feel the churning presence of nervousness in his stomach but knew that this guttural cocktail also contained excitement and anticipation. And then the Master raised himself perceptibly above them, and indicated that he was about to speak.

"Beloved eagles, we are gathered here for the noblest of purposes—to begin the great work that will harness the innate potential that you all have within you. As you begin this program, you float through the world naively, uncoupled from your true selves. By the time that it ends, if you demonstrate dedication, attentiveness and patience, you will have reformed that primal connection, in the process ascending to a new level of existence."

Soar was captivated, unable to even glance fleetingly at the other eagles, such was his burning passion for the sentiment.

"That doesn't mean that this will be an easy process. You will all have to challenge yourselves and be willing to leave behind some of your existing habits, beliefs and even identities. In a sense, if you follow the assistance that we will provide over the days and weeks to come, you will cease to exist. The old version of yourself will expire, as redundant as a discarded banana peel. In its place will be a new and better version of yourself. More aware, more focused, stronger, wiser, with greatly extended boundaries of purpose."

The Master paused, pointedly, seemingly awaiting any verbal response. But there was none—each of the smattering of eagles present remained silent, patiently awaiting further instruction, as the bonfire crackled unnoticed in the background.

"Does anyone have any questions?" Silence. "Then let's begin."

*　*　*

Soar had been through other challenging and unfamiliar experiences before, and his mind drifted nostalgically back to some of these during his early days in the clearing. He remembered venturing out on the first hunts with his father and some of the other neighborhood eaglets, greedily eyeing voles and mice and rats and, frankly, anything and everything that was scampering in the tall grasses. He recalled his first day at school; the sensation that he was leaving behind the sheltered familiarity of his infancy. And the tribulations of the episodes that he'd endured and enjoyed on his journey to this point were inescapable; they drifted irresistibly into his cognizant mind, inciting memories that triggered explosions of endorphins.

But this was different. So much of Soar's life had been focused on survival. Now the focus was not on developing some skill for the practical purpose of more efficient hunting. Nor was it about acquiring knowledge for the benefit of Aquilana. This wasn't about survival; it was about personal growth. It was indeed about growing for no other reason than the principle that growth and improvement should always be the ultimate outcome and endeavor of existence.

From day one, they began a program of deep work, comprising numerous modules. There were several friendly tutors involved in this process, and the ambience, despite the seriousness of the material, was always congenial. Soar soon began to relax and started to feel an enveloping oneness at the core of his being.

The program had begun with some simple awareness exercises. And yet, despite their uncomplicated nature, Soar had never tried them before.

He was instructed to focus on gratitude, to identify and give thanks for everything that was life-affirming. This began as a tricky exercise but Soar soon realized the immense abundance of objects and experiences for which he could be grateful; it was a granular extension of the process that he'd begun in Eudaimonia. He attempted to compile an exhaustive list, and although this proved beyond the confines of his memory, it all contributed to the process of learning and growing. The air. His wings. Clean water. The powerful sun. This diverse planet. Being here in this moment. That last insight reverberated sensuously throughout his mind and body, slowly but surely supplanting the notion that he should be ravenously pursuing some future goal. "There is only this moment. Be grateful for this moment," Soar repeated internally.

Gratitude meditation became a twice-daily practice, and even in the earliest days of his spiritual evolution, Soar could feel the incessant mental chatter skulking off to the background of his cranium, replaced in the foreground of his consciousness by a new, focused mindset.

But this was just the beginning. An entirely new Soar was being forged, like molten metal being shaped in a steelworks. In the days that followed, the tutors challenged Soar to identify his core values, and then compose a personal manifesto in line with those beliefs. He discovered that attaining excellence, intelligence, curiosity, and freedom were at the epicenter of his identity. His mental manifesto, therefore, reflected these qualities, as he crafted several maxims to guide his future endeavors. This was all part of the process of creating intentional thoughts; the Master explained to him during a personal session that this would raise his level of awareness.

"Most creatures live in a prison of their own making," he divulged. "They restrict themselves due to the maelstrom of impulses that subconsciously shape their existence and limit their potential. That's why we teach everyone here to live consciously, intentionally, to cultivate positive patterns of thought and language. This is what defines your perspective on life, and, more importantly, yourself."

Each day in the clearing, Soar was cultivating attention to what really mattered; centered around the core values of his true identity and unquestionable gratitude for all that surrounded him. He was circumventing his ego and waking up to his true self. The frequent guided and freeform meditations that all participants engaged in simultaneously, contributed to this process. An unfamiliar yet indisputable sensation of sheer joy began to lap over Soar. It was every bit as perceptible as the waves washing over his body on the shore when he first landed. The external began to melt away. There was only the clearing, the learning, the moment that he was experiencing right now. Anything beyond the immediate became unimportant, then irrelevant, then non-existent.

There was quite an atmosphere of camaraderie in the camp. Soar became familiar with the other recruits who were new to Magna and found that the same origin story cropped up repeatedly. Most of them had abandoned other settlements of eagles, seeking more fulfilling and enlightened lives. Somehow, they had sensed, felt intrinsically, that there was something more gratifying out there. Soar strongly identified with their sentiments, and they bonded in the evening, regaling one another with tales of bravery and youthful alienation. Soar found that he was willing and able to open up far more spontaneously than before. He no longer restrained his personality and character when with strangers; the spiritual work and his incipient awakening had instilled a newfound confidence and openness in his heart.

Another intriguing development was that Soar found that he needed far less food than usual. Everything he required was provided; the participants consumed a pseudo-paleo diet comprising meat, fish, fruit, vegetables, and nuts. And they all gathered around the invigorating fire of an evening, slurping soup as a second source of warmth. Yet Soar was eating quite lightly; it seemed that the energetic work provided ample sustenance.

The next part of the training involved cognitive restructuring. Soar was challenged to explore his mental and intellectual distortions, in the process creating new and productive thought patterns. During this exercise, Soar reflected that many of his underlying assumptions were based on emotions, rather than facts. That didn't mean that they were all unfounded, but as he negotiated the process of Socratic questioning, it became increasingly clear to Soar that he had clasped on to so much baggage from his childhood. It had felt restrictive and cumbersome, and yet he also experienced a growing realization that it was a form of safety blanket. The more that Soar grasped these memories, the more he could convince himself of his innate superiority. Holding on to these recollections wasn't merely indicative of childhood trauma, it was also an ego-driven process.

His thoughts flashed back involuntarily to the dolphin, and the proclamation that Soar should put down the bag that he was carrying. Perhaps he was finally ready to do it.

As the exploration continued, one area where Soar had established positive cognitive processes was self-talk. He had never burdened his soul with negative internal monologues about himself. He had never suffered the emotional torment of feeling that he wasn't good enough—that he was some kind of impostor. If anything, he was too confident in his abilities; too impudent and self-regarding! Soar vowed to temper that slightly, while retaining his core self-belief.

Patterns of restrictive thoughts, impulses and behaviors were being systematically stripped away like unwanted wallpaper. In their place, as inevitably as the river melds into the ocean, flowed freedom and joy. Soar could intermittently feel a nirvanic bliss pulsing through his body that he had only previously encountered in the vortex that led to Simplicitas. It wasn't yet quite as potent, but it was nonetheless unmistakable. One evening, as they sipped on their nightly soup, he recounted his experience to the Master, disclosing the internal transformation that he was currently undergoing.

"In that case, young eagle, you are becoming truly aware of yourself. You have laid the first stone in the path of living intentionally. Now is the time for you to take the next step."

Soar was captivated by this prospect, and intrigued by what was to follow. But he had learned to hold himself back slightly. There was a composure to his behavior now; he recognized the value of patiently waiting for things to manifest, rather than charging forward with all guns blazing. He would find out soon enough, when the time was right.

When the next day arrived, Soar found himself spreadeagled on the floor, covered practically from head to toe in autumnal leaves. They were crisper, drier and more friable than their summer counterparts, but had remained intact as a makeshift blanket throughout the darker hours. The clearing was some distance away from the main settlements of Magna, and thus the atmosphere was bathed in a quietness that could have seemed eerie, particularly before the morning had cast light on their increasingly sienna-infused surroundings. But such was the serenity of Soar's disposition, the forest symbiotically absorbed this quality from him. Whereas once he was wired to detect even the slightest disturbance, he had now become more centered and accepting, and in the process less prone to fear the worst. Soar's alertness was undimmed, but the way that he dealt with sensory inputs had evolved.

Before he could rouse himself, a familiar figure alighted next to him. "Soar," the Master began, "you have no requirement for breakfast this morning. You will receive all of your nourishment from what we are about to discuss." Soar instantly and instinctively understood precisely what was meant by this. He shook off his improvised bedclothes, and made his way over to the area of the clearing that had been designated for learning.

The Master viewed Soar with open eyes, and the younger eagle thought he could perceive a tincture of pride in his expression. But there was no time to reflect on that, as he began to address Soar with purpose.

"Young Soar, you have made extraordinary progress during this process, which demonstrates to me that you were fully prepared for this transition in your life. You have experienced some deep healing and transformation through your inner work. Perhaps if you had arrived on Magna a little earlier, you would have been less developed, and therefore less ready to take on board what we've asked of you." Soar nodded subconsciously in agreement. "But I believe that you're now ready to rid yourself of all worldly influences on your life. From here on in, you will be *in* the world, but not *of* the world. You will be living in accordance with your own values, and in the absence of any other influences, whether nefarious or otherwise. It is only by achieving this that you will be able to ascend to the highest level of existence. Everything that you have encountered up until now, all the personal growth and experiences are part of this process; now you are entering the final furlongs."

It was this very issue that was at the heart of Soar's disconnection from Aquilana. He had not truly understood it at the time, but it was crystal clear now that he had never been afforded the opportunity to live intentionally, and to feel fulfilled. But it was doubtful that this would have been possible, as Soar hadn't even established his core values. He hadn't quite known what he wanted, only what he didn't want. This journey had never been about seeking something external, as Soar had initially believed. Its kernel was always an internal quest. This was now as plain as the beak on his face.

As Soar's evolution into the best version of himself continued, he vowed to permanently, yet gently, sever all ties with his previous self, particularly his belligerent, rumbustious, indignant tendencies. He was instead encouraged to cultivate intentional habits, and this began most critically with the nurturing of a positive mindset. Soar would no longer allow himself to wallow in negativity, for his thoughts and soul to be consumed with dissatisfaction and vengeance. "No matter how much we hold on to the past, no matter how much we rationalize things, we still just go on living anyway," the Master explained during one philosophical discussion; an assertion that immediately made perfect sense to Soar.

Increasingly, where there was once a bubbling cauldron of emotion within Soar, there was now no more than a gentle simmering. And when these emotions did surface, there was no longer a detonation. Soar found that the awareness of his state of mind had become acutely heightened.

Whereas once he would have exploded, he was now able to take a step back and observe his emotions. Above all else, Soar realized that his emotions were *not* his identity. They were a part of him, and not to be denied, but they didn't and shouldn't define him. His whole was far greater than these mere electrochemical impulses.

Each day in the clearing was filled with exercises and consultations, and the intensity was steadily ratcheted up as the days and weeks passed. Time became hazy, nebulous, and then ceased to be a property of the universe. Nothing mattered, except for the rising and setting of the sun, perfectly in tune with the innate rhythms of the body. Encouraged by the tutors, Soar began mentally journaling at the end of every day. He started navigating his feelings and thoughts systematically, allowing them to discharge naturally, but peacefully, rather than restraining them. In the past, he had allowed his mental state to oscillate wildly between repression and explosion. Now there were no longer such dramatic fluctuations; he had reached a tranquil emotional equilibrium. But it was not neutral; instead, his soul was resounding with positive energy, flowing within him as powerfully and perceptibly as the crisp north wind whistling through his feathers on a winter morning.

Soar found that as his spirit awakened, his habits automatically evolved. The language he used became solely positive. His outlook was entirely constructive. Any negative feelings were dealt with, and then rapidly dispersed. And he was listening more actively to others. Soar was happy to contribute, but no longer experienced the burning sensation of needing to passionately catapult his views and feelings into the ether. When the time was right to speak, he would speak. That time would come, as surely as the stars twinkled in the satin sky.

New realizations and insights were surging into Soar uncontrollably every day, as he became more conscious in his thinking, and more intentional in his outlook. He could sense the profundity of the universe. Nothing of terrestrial significance was *really* significant; he was a dot in the greater scheme of things, a speck in the monumental spectrum of infinite universal energy. And yet, equally, he was indelibly connected to it. The universe was within him, and he was within the universe, and at some point the two became inseparable and indistinguishable; akin to the simultaneous presence and absence of a Heisenberg electron.

Soar had already begun the practice of gratitude meditation in Eudaimonia but he was now doubling down on this exercise. After all, there was so much for which he was grateful. It was one day, while he was giving thanks for the abundance in the universe, that he suddenly experienced a sensation of immense energy, pulsing through his solar plexus and throat chakra. It was a curious experience, but Soar felt strangely calm, as if he had been expecting it. He then perceived it cooling; what started as burning morphed into a tingling feeling that began vibrating rapidly at the base of his spine. As Soar observed this process, the energy felt like a coiled spring, and then began to unfurl, spreading out through his lower limbs, then reverberating throughout his body.

It was a sensation of such potency that Soar had rarely experienced anything remotely comparable. It was as if a cosmic fountain was spraying universal energy all over his body. Nonetheless, he remained entirely self-possessed and serene, intrinsically understanding that his chakras were awakening. He could feel a powerful whirring sensation in seven explicit areas of his body, although his crown, heart and sacral chakras were revolving with particular intensity.

Soar's eyes remained closed throughout, and yet it felt as if he could perceive more than when they were open. His soul was enlivened with a feeling of ecstasy; he became increasingly euphoric as the pulsating energy surged through him. Soar was experiencing a process of karmic rejuvenation; he could feel all that was negative leaving him. He was being purged of the undesirable perceptions of his past, the troublesome emotions and reflections; everything that he had jealously guarded and grasped to himself as if they were critical fragments of his being. They were all disappearing, incinerated by the irresistible force of universal energy, as his body and soul became a boundless ocean of love. He felt an intense connection with the cosmos; this was true freedom. Soar's ego was dissolving, replaced by an emotional understanding that resonated peace and love.

As his chakras continued turning, Soar's visual perception was suddenly overwhelmed by an explosion of colour. It seemed that he had been submerged in the entire electromagnetic spectrum, as vivid red, orange, yellow, green, blue, indigo and violet illuminations dominated his field of vision. They were distinct, emanating harmoniously from separate chakras, yet they merged transcendentally into one. At this point, there was no time; Soar had entered a semi-permanent state of fermata. He could consciously observe the process, and yet miss nothing of significance, almost occupying two distinct places at once. It felt as if he could perceive every iota, each individual molecule of the universe, while also being intrinsically aware of its interconnected and infinite essence. At some point, warming, tingling sensations spread throughout his body, almost like the metastasis of a cancer, but in this instance entirely positive.

In that moment, Soar felt empathy, love and compassion for all and everything. He recognized himself as an intrinsic part of the whole; indeed, the two could not be separated. He felt a wisdom that was completely unrelated to conscious thought and intellect, experiencing profound insight and physical sensation, the magnitude of which far exceeded anything from the mundane realm. An immense strength and clarity flowed through him, as powerful and irresistible as the force of a mighty river. Soar felt dynamically powerful, yet utterly relaxed, overflowing with percipience, yet completely free from conscious thought. There was an illimitable understanding, consciousness and exultation vibrating through his heart chakra. Everything was possible.

It was in the clearing that Soar began to live joyously for the first time.

10. The Passing

Hordes of smoky nimbus clouds thronged threateningly on the horizon as Soar sailed peacefully on his way. Precipitation had been falling steadily on this bleak morning, and such was the temperature that the descending droplets alternated between rain, snow and hail; the persistent drizzle unable to decide what form it should take.

It was all the same to Soar. He enjoyed the sensuous feeling of the rain drumming on his wings. As the wetness accumulated, Soar would expertly shake off the excess water, ensuring that his body remained as close to his flighting weight as possible. Nonetheless, despite the dreadful weather, Soar had no intention of sheltering. There were things to do, and, anyway, he embraced the universe and all its variance. There would be no more cowering in cowsheds, nor secreting himself in shrubbery. Soar was radiant with energy and purpose, his mind teeming with ideas. Nothing could distract him from his purpose; the luminous flash of lightning and booming crash of thunder in his vicinity prompted only wonder in his heart.

A month had passed since that memorable experience in the clearing, and Soar had steadily readjusted to everyday life. He had rapidly integrated himself into the community, and immediately felt at home with the other eagles. It was everything that he'd hoped for, and precisely hadn't experienced back home. There had always been the gnawing sensation, pecking away at his brain, that he was an outsider. He'd tried to fit in with the regimen of

Aquilana, he'd attempted to acquiesce with the customs and conventions of the region, but it was to no avail.

Equally, and completely contradicting this notion, was the realization that he would return. Aquilana was still his home, his family was still his family, and this would always be a part of him. No matter how much he grew, Soar could never completely outgrow his past.

Although there were still challenges ahead, Soar felt extremely well-equipped to deal with them. He was attuned to the elements, aligned with his own senses to such a degree that it felt as if every aspect of his being was optimized. The inner and outer strength and confidence that he felt were stunning, and yet these qualities were perfectly balanced with an outlook of serenity. He had never been more powerful, yet his power had never been more purposefully restrained.

Soar was journeying to meet with the Master, and this wasn't just a social visit. Despite his generally calm mood, there was still a persistent murmuring at the back of his mind. It wasn't quite enough to prompt restlessness but he intrinsically sensed that he still hadn't reached the end of his pathway. He had experienced and evolved so much, but he wasn't the finished article; still further exploration and growth lay ahead of him. Although Magna had germinated his awareness more than he could have possibly hoped, the land was also but a mere globule in the infinite universe.

They had arranged to meet back at the clearing. A new group of initiates were being put through their paces, and Soar had agreed to arrive ahead of their induction. In accordance with this, the sun had barely even peeked over the horizon by the time that Soar reached his destination. Only the smallest fragment was visible; the scintilla of light provided just enough to create minimal visibility.

As Soar carefully descended, all of the familiar apparatus from his memorable awakening was undisturbed. The stone circle remained untouched and he inevitably found himself thinking back to the challenging and glorious times that he'd spent in this magical setting. Electricity charged down his spine, and the feathers on the back of his neck suddenly stood up. There was an emotional bond with this location that would never dissipate.

Amid the stones, arranged like a rudimentary rockery, the remnants of a fire were burning. As Soar drew closer, he realized that, rather than being leftovers, this fire had just been lit, and was in its embryonic phase. It was steadily growing, as it spluttered and spat on its fuel of coal and ash. In the short amount of time that Soar had studied the flames, the Master had appeared as if from nowhere. He raised his wing in greeting towards his protégé, and Soar was glad to see that he appeared to be in good form. Rumours had been circulating that the Master's health was deteriorating. This had troubled Soar, but also acted as a reminder that our days on this mortal coil are small in number.

The two of them embraced, and Soar was offered some hot chocolate, which he gratefully accepted. It was barely dawn, and there was an autumnal sting in the morning air that served as a chilly warning of harsher winter weather ahead. Soar sipped the warming drink, using the palate of his mouth to cool the liquid before swallowing. The two exchanged pleasantries, ostensibly as equals, but Soar couldn't help admitting to himself that he would always look up to the Master. This was something that he would have been fundamentally opposed to at one time. But this improved version of Soar was prepared to fully acknowledge the contributions that others had made to his evolution.

"Soar, do you know why all eagles succeed?", the Master enigmatically asked him.

"I don't mind admitting that I don't know," Soar replied curiously.

"When you're an eaglet, before you can really do anything else of consequence, do you remember what your parents did?"

Soar shook his head quizzically.

"They picked you up, dropped you, and you learned to fly in the most challenging circumstances. You were taken way outside of your comfort zone. You learned to flap your wings on your own—no one taught you."

Soar agreed with the Master. "Yes, that's true, although I barely remember it."

"That's why all eagles succeed. Even if we don't reach our full potential, we stand on our own two feet from the youngest age. We learn because we have to learn. Humans don't have that privilege. They often have the privilege of safety. They often have the privilege of security. But many of them never have the privilege of independence and freedom. That is something that I want you to cherish, because it's something that is embedded deep in your DNA. More so than even most eagles."

Soar retained an external appearance that was unmoved but inside he was glowing from the compliment.

"We all have a different path through life. Our life goals should always be attuned to our internal characteristics. What is right for you is not necessarily right for someone else. That's why we maintain Magna, for those who are homely, who belong in one place, or whose journey is at an end. But your journey..."

"...is only just beginning," Soar finished the sentence in unison with the Master.

"Exactly! There is a sense of adventure and wonder within you that will probably never be pacified. Well," the Master chuckled before continuing, "perhaps it will when you're as old and disheveled as me! But your internal and external journey must continue. It would be unfortunate for you to confine yourself, limit yourself, at this juncture."

"I know," Soar agreed. "You're right. I feel this in my heart."

The Master nodded in agreement. "There is something important that I want to share with you."

Soar felt his stomach churning with anticipation. "Please do, Master." As soon as the word left his mouth, Soar realized that he'd used the word Master for the first time. His self-respect was becoming indivisible from the respect that he had for others. He had come to realize that even the most innocuous creature has something to teach him. All entities know something that you do not. Everything in the universe, whether visible or otherwise, should be respected.

"I'm not going to be here much longer. I don't mean in Magna, I mean in this realm. I'm old, I'm weak; my vital signs are failing me. I know this is sad, young eagle, but I've lived a rich and full life. I have no regrets." The Master paused before continuing, regathering himself and summoning up some final remnants of physical energy. "There are a few reasons that I'm telling you this. Firstly, I want you to proceed precisely in that manner—without regrets. Never looking back, never squinting too far into the distance. You are well on the way to living consciously, in full awareness of yourself, but achieving this is a marathon, not a sprint."

Soar was captivated. Emotionally moved, as silent as the most timid mouse.

"Secondly, I wanted to speak with you, as you won't see me again. I won't be here when you return... if you return. Your time on Magna is drawing to a close, even faster than my fading existence. And that leads me to the third point."

"There is a Lost Kingdom, many miles from here, that you must seek. I am unaware of its exact location. I can't describe it; I have only heard rumours. I can't tell you what you will experience there; I can only inform you of its existence. I cannot accompany you. I would love to try," he turned to Soar and smiled, "but this is a journey for a younger eagle than myself!"

"I believe you've been heading east?" Soar confirmed this impression. "Head further east. It may be north of here; it may be south of here. You may have to seek further guidance. You will need to strive with a fortitude that you have never invested in anything previously. All I know, and you need to know, is the legend that the Lost Kingdom is so far east that it's almost at the edge of the known universe."

The Master cleared his throat. It became evident to Soar that speaking was something of an effort for him; even the saliva glands that would usually lubricate his throat were slowing, dwindling, as his essence and life force steadily ebbed away.

"Sorry, Soar. This life is nearly over for me! But I wanted to say that there is so much for you still to discover—about the universe, and about yourself. I have learned a lot in my time in this world, and there is a vast amount of collective knowledge here in Magna—but we don't know everything. Wisdom is knowing how little you know. Equally, you have everything before you. There is no such thing as the unknowable, only that which we don't yet know. I want you to take the hero's journey and seek out lands and experiences of which many only dream."

Soar was choked. He moved his head upwards and downwards, in what he approximated to be a nodding action. Tears were welling in his eyes.

"I acknowledge your sentiment, Soar. But this is merely part of the inevitable passing from this realm to the next. It is no more significant than dust being deposited elsewhere by a swirling breeze. It's time for you to leave, young eagle."

There was a tincture of trauma to this moment, yet Soar could already feel himself shifting into a state of acceptance. The Master had clearly accepted the situation, and this would not be the end of his soul's journey in this universe of infinite possibility. Soar wiped away a tear and began to contemplate the journey ahead. He would move forward without fear, allowing the universal intelligence to guide him in his quest for joy, fulfillment and meaning. His relentless desire to search, to grow, to seek out the exact unknowable experiences of which the Master spoke was undimmed. He would succeed, no matter what.

"And, Soar, I want you to remember this," the Master's voice called out for one final time.

Soar turned in expectation.

"There are no limits to what you can do if you truly commit to being the best version of yourself."

Soar spread his wings, and balletically ascended from the stone circle, leaving this esteemed figure in his heart, and those of many other eagles, to pass gently away. The still falling rain teemed down, mixing with his tears, until the two were indistinguishable.

11. The Encounter

There was something particularly satisfying about viewing a cornfield from above. Or maybe it was several things combined. The plant itself is aesthetic, with its unusual, bunched construction, and striking yellow grains. There is a pleasing symmetry to the countless rows of virtually perfectly aligned plantations. And the crop is visible from many thousands of feet in the air, immediately signaling one thing and one thing only — lunchtime!

Soar delicately lowered himself towards the cornfield, his mouth lubricating itself involuntarily, beginning to salivate, as he contemplated the starchy sweetness. As he approached the field, the musty smell of the vascular crop filled his senses, heightening anticipation of the imminent gorging. Maize was the ideal find at this time; exactly the sort of carb-heavy, energy-dense food that Soar needed. He spotted a particularly juicy looking cob and began gnawing his way through it, with all the subtlety and etiquette of a buzzsaw.

Several days had passed since he set out on this most nebulous of journeys, with not the slightest notion of when or where it would end. Thankfully, the route that he'd chosen had thus far frequently been punctuated by signs of civilization, and he spent the first night curled up amid the bells of an octagonal-shaped belfry. Its slanted, slate-gray medieval design incorporated a pyramidal roof; it was certainly an architecturally rich way to spend an evening.

Water had also been relatively plentiful. Soar had flown directly over a crystal lake and had instinctively stopped off to replenish his reserves. Soar was intrinsically proud of being an eagle, but he had to concede that camels had an advantage in this department! Although eagles derive water from food, on a long journey such as this, food could be in short supply. Even humans, with their ability to store water in those hideous manufactured bottles, could last longer without an obvious source of water than flighted birds. Soar had frequently witnessed areas of natural beauty being defaced by plastic, and thus loathed this artificial substance and its consequences.

Food had been more intermittent in recent days, hence Soar's unplanned sojourn at the lake. He was glad that he'd developed a more judicious palate since he left Aquilana, as it meant that he could feast on anything edible that he encountered. Juniper berries disappeared rapidly and corn struck a chord with his taste buds. He had also brought a premature end to one unfortunate field mouse. After he'd successfully hunted down the rodent, he offered his mental gratitude to the abundance of the universe and wished the creature a smooth transition to the next realm of existence.

The crops had ripened, as Soar sailed over a horde of meadows and farmland, virtually all of which were flourishing. Poppies radiated with vermilion ambience; boundless rows of wheat matched the golden glow of the sun. Teams of diligent workers attended to rice plantations, splashing through the inundated fields as they toiled. Soar was always on the lookout for the latest opportunity, and he devoured every detail. The way that occasional ears of wheat grew irregularly, stretching up above the great mass of this year's yield, as if they were yearning to escape. Four labourers gathered in a circle, sending wispy plumes of smoke into the air from the cigarettes that they were smoking, as they took a well-earned break. And poppies swayed tenderly in the light breeze, in different states of development. Some had opened up, proudly displaying their wares to the bees, while others were more bashful, remaining constrained and compacted.

Conditions were warm enough to be pleasant, cool enough not to provoke perspiration; perfect flying weather. It was always delightful to be airborne when visibility was perfect. This was a particularly flat portion of Soar's journey, with the greener regions resembling immense billiard tables. From a technical perspective, this made flying much easier, but it was also marginally less joyful than careering through mountain ranges. It was always a privilege to be an eagle, but pancake-like areas possessed neither the physical allure nor thrilling scale of mountainous landscapes.

Nonetheless, this less arduous period was relaxing, enabling Soar to replenish his energy ahead of whatever it was that would extend before him. He had also managed to locate some of the most powerful and unimpeded thermals that he'd encountered for quite some time, and the gliding phases that this enabled eased the efficacy of his progression. Soar floated effortlessly above an irradiant array of kaleidoscopic tulips. The vividity and variety of the hues was breathtaking; earthy lilacs mixed with gentle lemons and scintillating ruby reds to create a wonderful iridescent display. Fluffy lambs gamboled playfully in the field next door, blissfully unaware beneath their cotton candy coats that they were about to be guillotined into steak.

The whole day passed in this casual fashion. It seemed that the universe had provided Soar with a picture book of beautiful sights, ensuring that this undemanding juncture of his journey wasn't too laborious. Soar was even able to meditate in the air on occasion, floating as silently as a cloud, closing his eyes to the external world, enjoying the sensation as the limitless energy and wisdom of the universe flowed through him.

By sunset, Soar happened upon a suspension bridge, a gigantic wrought iron construction, with a black tarmacked runway disappearing way into the horizon, beyond the two pillars that guarded the structure like sentries. From his elevated height of hundreds of feet, Soar could see rows of vehicles teeming back and forth, no bigger nor more significant than ants. As he wondered what to do next, he also couldn't help noticing that much of the concrete composition was covered in a malodorous white substance. "I'm a big supporter of the pigeons," thought Soar, "but they really have no class or decency!"

The existence of this bridge meant that the road must lead towards a populated area. "Yikes, civilization!", Soar recoiled. It was therefore logical to head in the opposite direction, veering southward, hoping to encounter something uncharted, as he migrated away from the human-scarred regions. Soar's intuition was shifting him away from the path that he had followed for much of the day, but that had still been largely eastward — he was merely making a minor correction towards a more south-easterly direction. Regardless of whether this was correct, Soar could always rely on the internal compass that would return him to this point as reliably as any form of technology.

It had been a day of steady progression, but now it was coming to an end. As Soar sought a place offering sleep and perhaps a little sustenance, the sun was sagging wearily in the evening sky. The palette notably differed from the burnished sunset of summer; it was softer, subtler, akin to a washed-out watercolor, the heavens visibly tinged with apricot.

He had only traversed perhaps a mile or so when he encountered a whitewashed building with a distinctive thatched roof. Outside the extremities of its garden, a suspended sign swung back and forth squeakily, proclaiming the establishment to be a public house. Soar recognized this as a drinking den and realized that this would be an ideal venue for seeking food. Indeed, as he swooped towards the intricately assembled heather that comprised the roof, a seductive assortment of scents wafted airily towards him. Soar followed his nose, climbing above the sloping roof, seeking out the source of the odour of roasted chicken in particular.

And then, suddenly, without warning, she was there before him. Soar would never forget the moment that he first laid eyes on her, nor the way that his sacral chakra immediately began spiraling like a pinwheel. She was a white-tailed eagle; one of the largest and most formidable breeds, with an elongated wingspan that was probably even slightly wider than his. Her combination of sooty, coffee-coloured, and chalky feathers created an almost speckled impression. For some moments, Soar admired her distinctive plumage, his eyes immediately drawn to her snowy tail feathers. And then she became aware of his presence, craning her neck towards him. She revealed a striking yellow beak, with its distinctive, razor-sharp eagle-defining point that hung beyond the main structure, almost as a warning of her hunting prowess. Their pupils met, and Soar reflected that her eyes were slightly beadier than his, perhaps a little softer, but still piercing and alert.

No word was uttered for a moment. And then Soar began instinctively, primevally calling her, shrieking in a high-pitched tone. Not as loudly as some breeding sounds, for he was merely a few yards away from her, but forceful enough to create a shrill noise that sharply scythed through the air. The female watched him, and then returned the call, beginning to echo the sounds precisely. The two of them continued joyously in unison for what seemed like forever to Soar, but that was actually no more than a minute.

And then, without warning, Soar took off. There was no indication given to the female of what he had in mind; somehow, they were already innately connected. He began climbing with all his might, flapping his wings ferociously, and before he had risen even feet above the thatched roof, he saw his female acquaintance following him. Soar climbed and circled and weaved and twisted, showcasing all his flying skills in an adept aerial display. But his companion was just as powerful and proficient, matching his maneuvers, as the pair of them sailed across the skyline with a dichotomous combination of grace and force that was quite breathtaking.

Soon they had risen several hundred feet. The building that was once their place of rest now appeared the size of a cardboard box. Soar ceased the process of gaining altitude, hovering in one spot. Almost simultaneously, this enticing female joined him, gently wafting her wings back and forth, like an ancient aristocrat being fanned. The two of them surveyed one another, making not the slightest sound, but with already an unspoken bond between them. Soar stared straight into his companion's probing gaze, finding it to be penetrative and discerning. She oozed perceptiveness and character. Soar moved towards her, finding that his movements were mirrored, and as they reached proximity they locked talons, remaining in this intimate pose for a few seconds.

Then the descent began. The two of them were locked together as a pincer, and they began corkscrewing through the air, swirling and gyrating prodigiously. They were barreling through the air at an incredible rate of knots, twisting with the impetus of a cyclone. Their entwined bodies headed straight downwards towards the earth, at a pace that would be terrifying for any less courageous creature. It was an incredible and alarming display, and yet their conjoined bodies continued helter-skeltering the whole time, revolving rapidly with complete abandon. It seemed certain that they would plummet with tremendous momentum straight into the very roof on which they'd met, as they closed in rapidly, merely yards away from catastrophe.

And then, at what appeared to be a nanosecond before disaster struck, the two of them separated, easing themselves apart. They brought their bodies to a perfectly safe and almost delicate landing on the thatched surface. They were both breathing slightly heavily but were invigorated rather than frightened. The female bowed slightly before Soar, and this encouraged him to approach her, sitting close to her, gently touching her luxuriant feathers, beginning to groom her slightly as they continued to lock eyes.

"I'm Soar," he explained.

"I'm Sama," she replied, without blinking once or remotely averting her gaze.

They lay together for a while, Soar slightly shielding Sama under his wing. He could feel Sama's chest rising and falling with her breath, moving in the manner of a gentle sea, and immediately felt protective of her. They watched the sky gradually darkening in colour as the late afternoon unfolded like an inkblot steadily seeping into loose-leaf paper. Nothing was said, nor needed to be said. Time slowed and melted away; nothing mattered except their proximity.

Eventually, after what could have been minutes and could have been hours, Soar stirred, recognizing a pressing reality that needed to be addressed.

"I would love for this moment to last forever," Soar began, "but I must insist we seek out that chicken before nightfall!"

There was a smile of agreement from Sama, and the two of them had located some discarded drumsticks within a matter of seconds. Soar swept into the kitchen of the pub through a marginally opened bay window, rescuing two particularly juicy specimens, clutching them firmly in his beak. He was starving, and so the two of them immediately returned to the peak of the thatched covering of this quaint building, munching and ingesting the chicken speedily. They surveyed one another as they ate, exchanging occasional furtive and flirtatious glances.

The level of connection that they achieved through communication that was entirely divorced from language surprised Soar. He relished it. There was an immediate bond of trust between them, which even exceeded the usual level of openness that Soar experienced as an evolved being. It was as if they both intrinsically realized that there would be time ahead to express all their thoughts. In this moment, the emphasis should be on connecting spiritually.

Soar found Sama captivating; she was robust but demure, powerful but tender. He knew that she would be a formidable companion, yet this didn't remotely detract from her sensuous femininity. It seemed that Sama was able to live entirely in the moment, and Soar realized that he too had morphed into a creature much more able to be present. In the past, he would have been racing ahead, wanting things to move quickly, perhaps trying to impress Sama with some rambunctious behavior. Today, he could savour everything, never allowing experiences to pass without proper acknowledgement, nor for the sands of time to slide through his talons unappreciated.

After finishing their impromptu meal, the two of them briefly discussed where they should spend the evening. Sama noticed a couple of apple trees in the front garden of the establishment, and this immediately appealed to them both. By the time they'd weaved their way over there, it became apparent that some previous residents had abandoned an entirely serviceable nest. Maybe they'd migrated, or perhaps just fled, but the artfully arranged basin of twigs was more than accommodating, even for two large eagles.

Soar and Sama arranged themselves within the structure, warmth emanating from one another's sinewy physiques. They were soon cozily conjoined, safe and snug. Their eyes rather rapidly surrendered to the twin forces of gravity and exhaustion, until everything was black and peaceful.

That apple tree and conveniently assembled den would act as their base for some time to come. They spent these days meandering around the village, enjoying the leafy and unthreatening environment, while foraging for anything delicious, or, failing that, edible. It was a magical time of courtship. The couple barrel-rolled between the church spire and adjacent sycamore trees, patiently fished for trout and sculpin, and watched the dusky horizon protractedly swallowing the blood-red sun each and every evening, content within the confines of one another's wings.

It was also a time for talking, for opening up and familiarizing themselves with the journey that had brought them together. Sama radiated calmness and joy. Her lived experience had always been one of freedom; it was this that instantly united them. Perhaps the most tangible difference between the pair of them was that Sama had felt a comfort with her early life that had somehow escaped Soar. She had roamed around from the tenderest age, absorbing diverse experiences along the way. Soar recognized that this underpinned the powerful sense of contentment that poured like wine from Sama; this was as immediately evident as any of her physical qualities.

As they chatted away about memories and formative experiences, Sama told Soar that she had originally been named Samantha, but later it had been shortened to this Sanskrit term. When she informed him that the word relates to the quality of calmness and tranquility of the mind, Soar could immediately see that the name was indelibly connected with her identity. She conveyed an innate serenity that was enchanting, yet this in no way undermined the vigor of her convictions. There was a charm that exuded through every word she spoke and every movement that she made; as if she possessed some profound secret. Despite his own spiritual progress, Soar admired and envied the perpetual state of undisturbed equilibrium that he observed in Sama.

The two love birds talked at length as these soothing days unfolded, Soar reflecting that they actually spoke fewer words than was usual. This was not because their conversation was stilted or awkward, quite the opposite. There just wasn't the same requirement for language, as their connection exceeded the confines of mere vocabulary. When they did speak, they would finish one another's sentences, or be nodding in agreement before the full idea had been vocalized. They instantly understood one another; it was as if they had been forged from the same block of universal matter. It was increasingly evident that they were soulmates, but even this didn't need to be said. It was as undeniable as the earth beneath them; it developed as naturally from their meeting as thunder following lightning.

There was an essential kindness and compassion to Sama that afforded her an evident emotional depth that few creatures could rival. She was able to express herself so fluently and candidly, yet she listened intently to the words of Soar as well. As they alighted on an elliptical wooden bridge one day, broiling sunshine glinting from the water flowing under it, Soar ruminated on the reality that no man nor woman could be an island. The journey of existence was intrinsically associated with the self, but it couldn't be completed alone. Forging meaningful relationships is a critical constituent of development. No voyage of self-discovery could be concluded otherwise.

Buoyed by this conclusion, Soar merrily tossed twigs into the stream with Sama. This tributary that gushed straight into a neighboring lake was particularly insistent, babbling by with such velocity that it seethed and frothed, in the manner of a rabid dog. Sometimes the sticks would hurtle unhindered along the length of the river, and the casual race would end in a photo finish. And other times, one branch would be ushered away on an unfortunate route, floundering on one of the moss-covered rocks indefinitely, perhaps never to be released. Soar reflected that this was so much like life itself; we all begin on an equal footing, with seemingly limitless potential, and then some of us are spirited away in an unforeseen direction, never to return to the path of progress and fulfillment.

There was a danger that such a loving connection could diminish Soar's competitiveness, dampening down his senses, and softening his resolve. But instead of making him sloppy and complacent, it acted like rocket fuel. It was the wind beneath his wings, driving him forth more passionately and energetically than he had believed possible. And his heart chakra wasn't merely spinning; the floodgates had positively opened. Energy flooded into the central region of his spinal column almost unendingly, as if it had become a reservoir for truth, love and understanding. It was one of the many pleasing anomalies of the situation; Soar felt calmer than ever before, and yet there was a cauldron of emotion bubbling inside him!

One late afternoon, the two of them were sharing some herring that they'd managed to purloin from a local fishmonger. Soar wasn't generally receptive to pilfering from others, but it seemed that these fish were to be discarded, and eagles are far thriftier than any anthropoid. Waste was not to be tolerated for those that resided in the natural world; let alone the scandalous squandering of resources that humans appeared to deem inevitable, or even preferable. Nonetheless, Soar found the people in this sleepy community to be more tolerable than those in urban areas. There were fewer of them — that was a great start! But their way of living was altogether more attuned to sustainability. They walked and cycled, instead of pumping out those horrible fumes into the ether, they were somewhat observant of the world around them, and they were more appreciative and welcoming of animals generally.

As they guzzled the salty fish, Soar felt innately connected with Sama. Again, they'd never voiced their preference for concentrating on eating during mealtimes, rather than silly chatter, but it was something that they instinctively sensed in one another. Eat first, talk later! Thus, the only sound that emanated from them for some minutes was the grinding and crunching of these craniate vertebrates. They made for an ideal entrée; all that was needed now was something sweet to cleanse the palate. But that would have to wait for another day.

Satiated and satisfied, they leant against a drystone wall. This irregular slate-gray barrier had been erected from thousands of slabs of granite that were arranged like rows of unruly teeth. As dusk approached, the sky had taken on the color of rosé wine, flushed in appearance. Soar closed his eyes, disconnecting briefly from the external world, becoming absorbed in a heartfelt state of gratitude, giving thanks for all the abundance of the universe and his existence. But this meditation was suddenly and unexpectedly interrupted by deliberation.

"Hey, listen for one second," Sama began, her jolly voice immediately bringing joy to Soar's heart. "We've talked a lot about where you've come from, but where are you going? What are you looking for?"

"When I started this journey, Sama, I wasn't looking for anything other than the journey itself," Soar replied earnestly. "But along the way, I encountered someone who suggested something to me. I hadn't forgotten about it, but meeting you changed things a bit; let's call it a pleasurable pitstop along the way!"

"Don't be so coy!", Sama teased Soar. "Are you going to tell me more about the suggestion, and what it entailed?"

"Well, it was another eagle, a Master I met a little while ago, who told me that there was a special place, a Lost Kingdom, that I had to experience to understand joy and fulfillment, as well as purpose and meaning."

Sama sat up immediately, sharply tapping Soar on the side of the head to rouse him. "Someone mentioned the exact same place to me just days ago!"

Soar turned to face her, intrigued. "Who was it?"

"It was when I was off the coast of Eudaimonia. It was a dolphin; quite a striking and thoughtful creature."

Soar was shocked and excited, and answered in a less coherent fashion than usual. "Hold on, hold on, hold on! Rewind a second! You've been to Eudaimonia?!"

"Yes, quite recently. I didn't stay there for long; it was just a passing visit."

Soar explained everything that had happened to him, recounting the walrus, and his own encounter with the dolphin. They couldn't be sure that it was the same creature, but it appeared too much of a coincidence to be otherwise, particularly after they'd both described his appearance and countenance.

"But how did you get here so quickly?", Soar wondered.

Sama shrugged her shoulders. "I'm not sure. I just drifted here. I had not intended to make searching for the Lost Kingdom an immediate priority, as there is so much else for the senses to drink in. I just allow the breeze to guide me and take me where it chooses."

"This is kismet," Soar concluded, and Sama nodded in agreement. "But one thing is puzzling me. Why didn't the dolphin tell me about the Lost Kingdom when I encountered him?", Soar pondered.

Sama paused before replying, ensuring to choose her words with love and diplomacy. "Perhaps he could see that you had internal issues to resolve and heal before you completed your journey. You had to become the eagle that you are today, so that you're no longer constrained by your past."

"Yes, you're right," Soar agreed immediately, gathering his thoughts before continuing, "But nothing is stopping me now."

"Correction! Nothing is stopping *us* now."

12. The Humans

Amid the moments of sheer bliss, Sama could be extremely playful, provoking merriment in both eagles. She was forever teasing Soar, friskily needling him for some perceived slight or other. Generally, Soar would tease right back, while on occasion he would engage in a feigned defense of his more turbulent tendencies. When she became too persistent in her pestering, Soar would begin tickling her soft underbelly, and that soon put an end to her schemes! The two of them would end up giggling and embracing, their affection further cemented by this amorous activity.

They had decided collectively to embark on a great journey in the foreseeable future. It felt like the ideal time; in fact, their whole meeting felt destined. Soar wondered if the universe was entirely random, or whether there was an intergalactic itinerary that unified creatures by design. Regardless, it was inspiring and invigorating to have encountered this first love experience. The two of them were inseparable, meditating peacefully, hunting as a pair, gyrating through the clouds, sharing all of life's rich tapestry in a perpetual state of togetherness.

Soar understood the profound resonance of love for the first time. It served a greater purpose than merely the compelling feelings that it engendered. Although he felt content when he had been alone, since meeting Sama every fiber of Soar's being was galvanized. And he could also feel the infinite love of the universe commingling with this more personal form of love, in the process creating something of immense force. These two distinct manifestations of passion and joy entwined and blended, becoming condensed until the sensations that this new concoction created were overpowering. There were moments when it felt genuinely intoxicating, and Soar even experienced some of the light-headed inebriation that one associates with the consumption of liquor.

As such, those indolent but rewarding days in the village passed in something of a daze. It was as if their blossoming courtship was already a honeymoon, and it seemed entirely appropriate that there was a vernal mood to everything that surrounded them. Daffodils sprouted like golden trumpets, livestock arranged themselves in pleasing configurations as the pair swooped over them, and each sun-tinctured day seemed longer than the last. It was a testament to Einstein's theory of relativity!

It was one such morning that Soar and Sama found themselves stretching their wings, enjoying what was a clear and clement dawn. In the distance, immense expanses of oilseed rape and buttercups varnished the land bright yellow. Throughout this delightful enclave, charming buildings were predominant. There were no unsightly red-brick monstrosities; everything had been constructed from traditional materials, creating a pleasingly rustic impression. Soar particularly favored the raw yet charming beauty of the village's sandstone cottages.

They passed over the local green, where a gaggle of humans were engaging in one of their curious ball-related pastimes. Two groups had apparently split into teams, based on their matching attire, and they appeared to be pursuing some form of globular object. It had all created quite a commotion, and some of the local spectators had even surrounded the whitewashed markings that seemed to indicate the extent of the playing area. Humans aren't so bad, Soar told himself, even if they do engage in some incomprehensibly pointless activities!

The field gave way to a slightly hilly region. It wasn't a mountainous area by any means, but this wooded section of farmland was somewhat sloped. More humans, decked in bottle-green jackets and rubber boots were grouped together and preparing something or other. Probably planning a picnic, Soar concluded. He suddenly accelerated, sneaking up behind Sama, bumping into her unexpectedly, and then darting off in the opposite direction. She joined in exuberantly with his capering, chasing after Soar, and the two of them circled repeatedly, happily, playfully, without a care in the world.

BANG! BANG! BANG! The sickening cacophony of harsh booming instinctively jolted Soar into immediate evasive action. Terror spread rapidly from his amygdala, through his central nervous system, as electrical currents surged along the length of his vertebrae. There was no time to be scared, no time to recall his father's sage advice about woodsmen and guns and hunting dogs, barely even time to worry about Sama. Yet such was the heightened emotion and trauma of the situation that time virtually stood still. He had time to contemplate all of these things, even watching the waxed-jacketed predators reloading their weapons almost in slow-motion, as he circled away from them. Soar weaved deliberately, climbing, descending, at maximum velocity, attempting to make himself the slipperiest target possible.

BANG! BANG! More shots rang out, as Soar twisted like a pretzel, his heart beating faster than his wings could carry him, the air suddenly feeling weightier, more restrictive and friction-inducing than ever before. He desperately attempted to put some distance between the gleaming metallic weapons and his body, straining every tendon, every atomic particle of his body, in search of an additional knot of flying speed.

And then, suddenly, relative quiet. The shooting seemed to have ceased. Soar realized that he'd put enough distance between himself and the hunters. He was safe again. He breathed a sigh of relief, but this air was barely exhaled before he began panicking again.

Where is Sama?! Where is she?! He scanned the horizon frantically. There was no sign of her. His eyes scrutinized the surrounding area once more. Nothing. He called for her, as forcibly and piercingly as possible. He paused for several seconds waiting for a response. None was forthcoming. He called again, becoming distraught now. Still nothing.

Soar bowled back into the fray, straight into the line of fire once more. He would never leave without her. He descended as he neared the field, hoping that this would serve the dual purpose of making his body trickier to spot, while enabling him to detect Sama. He called again, wafting his wings delicately in virtual silence, attempting to ensure that the hunters weren't alerted and so that he could perceive any noises of response. But none were forthcoming. Soar zig-zagged around, his eyes welling with salt tears of sheer despair, calling repeatedly, observing the hunters in the distance, noticing that they had their backs to him now, and were apparently leaving the area.

He called out again, this time more loudly and in a shriller tone, emboldened by the retreat of the humans. This time he heard a muffled reaction. Soar triangulated its position immediately and plunged towards the noise fearlessly. As he approached the source of the sound, he called again. This time the response was both quicker and more recognizable. Thank Goodness! It was Sama. He descended, spotting her prostrate body amid the boggy field. She looked up at him with a dazed expression, wounded and startled.

"It hurts, Soar, they winged me! I can't fly!"

Soar peered at her bloodied left wing, which had been serrated by scorching lead.

"It's not that bad, girl," Soar told her. "It could have been a lot worse. There is no terminal damage, it just needs a little time to heal." Soar surveyed the area once more before continuing. "Anyway, there's no time to talk, hop on my back, and let's get the hell out of here!"

Sama did as instructed and Soar took off, finding extra reserves of strength that emanated from his unadulterated adoration of Sama. As they flew across the fields, keeping to a much lower trajectory than usual, Sama was even able to flap both of her wings somewhat tentatively, offering additional force to Soar's restricted flying effort. But despite the rather awkward contour of their melded physiques, they made steady progress. Within a minute or so, Soar knew that they had escaped from danger, and brought them to rest back on the bridge where they'd cavorted with such innocence and joy just moments before.

Neither spoke for some seconds. They just held one another, enveloped in the comforting warmth of life itself, never more appreciative of how fleeting and fragile this precious gift can be. Soar felt the familiar sensation of Sama's abdomen retracting and expanding as it gulped in oxygen, and offered mental thanks to the universe that she was indeed still breathing.

Eventually, it was Soar who spoke first, still guarding his love, their wings wrapped around one another gingerly.

"You scared me. I don't want to lose you."

"I don't want to lose you either," Sama replied earnestly.

Soar chose his words carefully. "We have to be more alert from now on. Because of everything that we were feeling, we allowed our guard to drop."

"I agree. We can't do that again." Sama paused, considering her response, still feeling bruised and tenderized from their tremulous encounter. "I want to experience everything in life with you, but we can't forget that there will always be challenges along the way. We have to support each other, but not get so wrapped up in one another that we lose sight of the whole."

Soar nodded solemnly, returning to holding Sama, feeling incalculably relieved that he could still wrap his wings around her. They remained silent for some time, Sama appreciating the assistance and Soar relieved that disaster had been averted. But his thoughts were already turning to the future, feeling that their bond was stronger than ever, contemplating the journey ahead of them that they would share in union.

"I'm glad that we had this talk. As soon as you're healed, it's time for us to move on. This changes nothing. We still have our great adventure ahead of us. And it wouldn't mean as much to me now if you weren't accompanying me at all times."

Sama smiled warmly. Soar could already perceive her strength returning, the fight seeping back into her indomitable veins.

"I wouldn't miss it for the world," Sama agreed, summoning every ounce of sincerity in her heart.

Soar searched assiduously for the right words, but only three short ones came to mind.

"I love you."

"I love you too."

13. The Voyage

Thankfully, the external appearance of Sama's injuries was much worse than the prognosis. A bullet had caught her, but it had merely brushed her pneumatized skeletal structure. Soar couldn't tell if it had chipped any of her bones, but it certainly hadn't broken any. Some superficial ligament damage, yes, but nothing that wouldn't mend itself naturally and relatively quickly. Her body had automatically entered into a state of shock after the incident, but the damage was no more serious than some grazing and mild concussion.

The incident was sobering but ultimately a lucky escape; Sama's injuries could have been much worse with a miniscule adjustment to the firing angle of the rifle. If she had been penetrated a few centimeters to the left of where the bullet struck, her bloody death would have been inevitable and virtually instantaneous. Leaving this aside, it was even fortunate that she'd been able to cover enough distance that the slavering Labradors hadn't caught her scent. That could have resulted in a far grislier demise.

Soar had grown immeasurably fond of Sama but he would be the first to opine that she wasn't the world's best patient! She despised the feelings of dependency that her wounded state brewed within her, and equally hated someone fussing over her. Soar understood this, realizing that he would be the same, or possibly worse, and, in response, demonstrated a level of stoicism that was hitherto unknown to him. Perhaps it was his personal growth, maybe it was the deep feelings of love and their consequences, or quite possibly both, but something had caused him to become unusually composed. He soothed Sama's outbursts, responding calmly and sensitively at all times. And the more he exhibited his patience and understanding, the more she accepted her predicament.

It would take a few diligent days for Soar to nurse Sama back to full health. During this time, he took on the role of medic, counselor, and forager. He spent many hours talking with her, massaging her, attending to her injury, ensuring that her spirits weren't allowed to dwindle. And Soar also located and acquired food for both of them, encouraging her to eat heartily. This would not only buttress her recovery; it would also help build resilience for the long road ahead. They drank goat's milk in the evenings, warmed by a discarded camp stove that Soar had rescued, sharing anecdotes, hopes, and dreams, while petting one another affectionately. Sama seemed more determined than ever to seek out the Lost Kingdom; this incident had merely hardened her resolve, rather than compromising it.

After ten days of recuperation, Sama tested her wing for the first time. She took off cautiously, slightly raw in her movements after a period of inaction. But she was soon moving through the air with some degree of freedom; an encouraging sign. Soar warned her to stick to relatively level flight and was somewhat surprised when she agreed. There was a level of respect and understanding between them that permeated their relationship, both feeling deeply in the core of their souls that they cared about one another's well-being more than could ever be expressed with words. It hadn't gone unnoticed that Soar had surged back into the jaws of death simply to save her. That would never be forgotten. "Some day I shall repay this bravery," Sama vowed internally.

As they awaited the healing of Sama's wing, the two of them frequently discussed their plans with almost delirious enthusiasm. It was exciting enough for Soar to be simply setting off on the final leg of this epic journey, but the opportunity to share this adventure with Sama ramped up the anticipation by several notches. Although contented in one another's company, those final days ahead of their departure seemed to drag interminably. As they awaited twilight, and another day ticked off, it seemed on occasion that the sun had stopped in one place indefinitely, as if paused by a universal remote.

But, eventually, the day of departure arrived; Sama pronounced her wing to be as good as new. They had tested her strength and recovery systematically throughout this period of convalescence, steadily increasing her workload. After four weeks of studied patience, Sama was able to twirl and swoop and sear through the sky with all her previous verve. She triumphantly circled the church spire, bursting out in fits of joyous laughter as she did so. "It begins!", she announced humorously, but jubilantly. As soon as the flight was completed, they wolfed down a hearty brunch of cuttlefish and peaches, barely bothering to chew, such was their excitement.

Making time for one final stroll, the frolicking pair absorbed the sights, sounds and scents of the village, purposely imprinting them on their long-term memories. It seemed appropriate to pause on the bridge; the location had become symbolically associated with their time here. They lobbed broken branches and twigs into the river once more, uncertain of the path that they would assume, and whether they would flounder or flourish. Much like the journey that lay ahead of them.

* * *

After some deliberation, they agreed to proceed in the southeasterly direction that Soar had adopted during the earlier stages of his journey. Soar was quite insistent on this matter and Sama was happy to go along with him. Both eagles had mentally prepared themselves for a punishing psychological and physical process. However, they had no concrete notion of what they would encounter. It was possible that their final destination was in their vicinity; equally it could elude them for eternity.

What was abundantly clear was that their immediate future would require them to traverse a generous portion of ocean. It was a fraction warmer than back in the village, as they soared over the crystal waters, with nothing more than the egg-yolk sun and globular lumps of altocumulus clouds decorating the vista. The clouds were fragmented, alternating between snowfall white and smoky gray, the hue and patchiness giving them the appearance of an elderly gentleman's thinning hair, with azure patches of skyline peeking through.

Soar was immensely proud of Sama's toughness, but inevitably at times he felt protective of her. They had taken every reasonable precaution to ensure that she had returned to full strength, yet Soar couldn't help wondering if she was ready for this undertaking. When he had attempted to delicately voice this concern to his mate and companion, it was brusquely dismissed. He empathically recognized her personal pride, acknowledging internally that he himself would have reacted similarly. Nonetheless, he still hoped that her wing was properly healed, and that her skills were fully replenished.

The first hours of their quest passed without incident. Soar was well aware that ocean flying is all about passing time as mindfully as possible. It isn't for no reason that lengthy excursions at sea have become associated with an irrevocable descent into madness. The environment is shorn of the usual markers of navigation, time whittled down to an infinitesimal process of progression. Eventually, it seems as if you have entered a permanent void, in which nothing will ever occur, and no tangible object will ever be encountered again. And all the time, the sea bulges and retracts with an irritating inevitability, coldly indifferent to both your state and your fate.

What made this particular oceanic passage less anesthetizing was the presence of Sama. If there were incipient signs that their spirits were dwindling, they picked one another up again with encouragement, or even the simple stimulation of chit-chat. The early hours of their flight were illuminated by persistent sunshine, but Soar was grateful that the weather was temperate, warming rather than baking.

By early evening, the light was fading reluctantly, the palette of the cosmos shifting. The sun had assumed a peach-like tone before the pinkish-red havens. As the marmalade-colored sun sunk wearily in the sky, it cast a column of shimmering crimson light that shimmered and oscillated with the marginal undulations of the placid seas. "Red sky at night, shepherd's delight," Soar thought, before reflecting on what unmitigated nonsense such observations frequently turn out to be!

However, there was already some excellent news on the horizon. An imposing, yet welcome, range of mountains had emerged, and it seemed likely that they could reach them before nightfall. Hopefully, this discovery would obviate the need to fly through the night; in an ideal scenario, the range could even provide plentiful sources of food. Both Soar and Sama felt somewhat relieved to encounter this potential haven.

As they closed in on their target, it became obvious that the peaks would be too steep for many animals, but such considerations are immaterial to eagles. The mountains stretched arrestingly into the distance, with an unshakeable permanence. Their very physicality conveyed the notion that they would outlast any mere organism, retaining their incisive presence long after those who observe them have perished.

Still, they were overcome with an awesome feeling of power in viewing something remote in the distance, and observing it steadily materialize, simply through the sheer magnitude of their own exertion. And then, finally, its full form was revealed, it was possible to reach out and touch it; what was once immense eventually rendered as routinely conquerable as an anthill. It was, unquestionably, the ultimate terrestrial experience. Nothing could ever equal it. Soar had grown immeasurably in empathy and was hugely grateful for the various creatures and species that he'd encountered and learned from. But he still retained his eagle soul, and profoundly identified with the eagle experience, even if he had broadened the parameters of his perception.

Once they had closed in on the mountains, it was evident that they were constructed from granite; the most immovable and sturdiest of materials. Craggy spikes and jagged edges sprouted from each and every coarse surface of the ashen cliff faces, which were displeasingly barren when it came to anything resembling lifeforms. Nonetheless, Soar and Sama remained hopeful that there would be something at least palatable in their vicinity. In the meantime, the couple landed smartly, and began surveying their immediate surroundings. Sama had spotted a hollowed-out cavity in the rock, and as the two of them judiciously investigated, it became immediately obvious that it was, indeed, a cave-like structure.

By this time, dusk had reduced the available light to a nominal level. But there was still enough light to enable the two wary eagles to peek inside. Ten, possibly twelve, feet were observable, before the visibility yielded to the black of night. It wasn't hugely reassuring.

"What do you think, Soar? Is it safe?"

Soar considered Sama's question for some seconds, continuing to peer deep into the cave, as if his eyes would somehow act as flaming torches if he stared at the darkness for long enough.

"I don't know. I really don't know. I do know this—we need some rest and some food." He paused for effect. "And we don't have any immediate prospect of the latter, it's getting too dark to have even the remotest chance of finding something," Soar turned to Sama with compassion in his eyes, "so we might as well try to get some of the former."

Sama nodded. "Okay, well I've got an idea. Why don't we take it in turns to keep watch? One of us could sleep for a few hours, and then we could swap."

Soar concurred. "Sounds like a plan. We can wake with the dawn, and properly investigate this area. There must be something to eat somewhere!

You can't have a mountain without any sources of food whatsoever, surely!"

Sama put her wing around Soar in consoling fashion. "Of course we'll find something! We always do! Let's get a bit of rest, and we'll be feasting on something delicious before the sun has even fully appeared."

They entered the orifice of the cave, snuggling up against one another in a cozy corner. "Hey," Soar suddenly exclaimed, "your wing is holding up pretty well."

Sama rolled her eyes for a second in mock disbelief, before reminding Soar that she had informed him it would be perfectly fine. Soar conceded this point and suggested that if she was so smart and perceptive, perhaps she might like to keep watch first while he rested his eyes.

"How could I refuse such an irresistible offer?" Sama quipped.

Soar smiled, closed his eyes, and soon his consciousness subsided.

* * *

The two of them were awoken, rather rudely, by the most blood-curdling growl. They both roused themselves immediately.

A colossal, barrel-chested female black bear darkened the path to their escape. Although her voluminous physique blocked out significant portions of the morning brightness, there was still enough light shining through the cracks to reveal something chilling that hadn't been evident in the bleakness of nightfall. Soar and Sama had huddled together just feet away from an array of desecrated skeletons. Some were still fully formed, others had been shredded and summarily dismantled; torn asunder and deposited dismissively.

It was an alarming situation, and yet Soar felt quite calm. "Come on," he encouraged Sama, "let's show him what we can do."

And without warning they both began circling the bear with incredible rapidity, spiraling briskly, just as Sama had twisted around the church spire. The powerful creature attempted to swat them like pesky insects, but her movements were too cumbersome. Soar and Sama swooped niftily, almost teasingly, under her armpits, congratulating themselves on their athleticism, before being assaulted with a whiff of malodorous body scent.

"That's what you get for showing off," Soar reflected.

Nonetheless, it passed quickly, and they were soon outside of the confines of the cave, climbing significantly out of the reach of any carnivore. The bear turned to look up at them, and Soar couldn't help calling out slightly derisively. "You don't get to catch us that easily! Hope the rest of your day goes better!"

The bear let out a gravelly grumble of frustration, but there was a marginal smile on her face, recognizing the expertise of fellow hunters.

"In retrospect, Soar, maybe having that lie-in was a mistake!", Sama observed.

"Oh, do shut up!", Soar responded in mock annoyance, pretending to clip her ear with his wing as a rebuke.

Sama giggled. "Come on, let's find breakfast."

The two eagles were already located within reasonable proximity to the pinnacle of the mountain, which meant that they could squint down its surface, while rotating around its circumference. After a certain period of doing precisely this, the optical illusion made the ridge begin to resemble a spinning top, albeit a rather drearily colored example. But within ten minutes this low-level exploration had paid off; Sama spied a clump of bushes sporting edible berries some distance down the mountain, and they quickly descended to investigate.

As it turned out, the waxy shrubbery offered a plentiful assortment of huckleberries; not the most lavish provisions but still nutritious and appreciated. Soar and Sama took the time required to collect as many of these violet fruits as possible. They were approximately the size of blueberries, smooth and spherical, forming a solid structure, rather than the drupelet formation of the blackberry. Sweet with a little tartness, the huckleberries were guzzled with relish. In fact, Soar perhaps indulged slightly too much, developing some minor flatulence that amused them both.

Shortly after they had completed breakfast and meditation, they took wing. It was a little more chilly and blustery than the previous day, as the westerly wind whipped up off the frothing tides. Soar was incredibly glad of Sama's companionship; he could feel his root chakra vibrating gently—an indication of safety and comfort.

One day became two and then three, and yet there was still no sign of anything resembling a kingdom of any nature. As their journey opened out before them, like intricate origami being unfolded, they took an increasingly pragmatic approach to recuperation. With any chance to stop and refuel, they took it. The first day was thankfully punctuated by an overnight stay on a bijou island, where the two of them appropriately feasted on the passion fruit, maracuya, known to be an initiator of passion. This bright yellow lemon-resembling fruit could be prised open easily, revealing its innards to be arranged in a triangular pattern. Thankfully, despite its appearance, it was by no means as bitter as lemon, possessing a subtle sweetness that was akin to the still citrus, but more agreeable, flavor of mango.

Although not a huge amount to see or do on this tiny island, nor seemingly any sentient life with which to interact, the two of them were still inclined to investigate. Their inquisitive natures were rewarded, because the island did house one of the more extraordinary specimens of flora that one could ever encounter. A rainbow eucalyptus stood proudly as the centerpiece of this largely nondescript land. Its incredible and incongruous multi-colored bark would have been conspicuous in any setting, but here its twisted kaleidoscope of beauty seemed particularly magical; as if they had been drawn to this place by design.

They also drank some much-needed milk before departing, after Soar sent a coconut tumbling to the ground from within the fronds of a palm tree by repeatedly bashing into it forcefully with his talons. The sugary energy that flowed from this slightly honeyed liquid was hugely welcome.

A sultry tincture to their surroundings remained; temperatures were comfortable, inclining towards balmy, and trees tended towards the tropical. But as they ventured further on their quest, the weather became gloomier. The skies blackened, light diminished, and the inky waters stretched out immeasurably, resembling an immense oilfield.

Neither of the intrepid eagles knew what lay ahead. There were no signposts pointing the way, no convenient barometer nor yardstick of progress available to them. All they could do was venture forth with optimism, attempting to derive insight from the signatures of the universe, trusting their intuition to guide them. Nonetheless, as much as their mental states remained relatively buoyant, and their camaraderie eased any anxiety that might otherwise have developed, there was no denying that their journey was becoming increasingly taxing. Islands were intermittent and barren, and food was scarce. It was quite some time since they had encountered any life other than one another; it was plainly evident that little other than avian life could ever make it this far.

And the further that they strayed from the beaten track, the more tempestuous the conditions became. The skies glowered at them and persistent fine rain stung their eyes. Eventually, it seemed as if the entire atmosphere consisted of precipitation; the palette of their locality had become almost monochrome, dominated by insipid grayness. Soar and Sama continued to offer words of encouragement to one another and were genuinely fortified by this. But there was also a gnawing realization at the back of their minds that they were weakening due to lack of food and rest.

They implored the universe to send finer weather but if anything the resolve of the clouds hardened, and the rain became more vicious, lashing down in billowing sheets. By now, the reduced visibility was causing disorientation; even their internal compasses had let them down. Neither was inclined to take a backward step, but now there was no turning back, as the returning path to safety and sustenance had become murky and unclear. Both eagles trusted their prowess, but they had covered thousands of miles, they were effectively lost at sea, with climatic conditions worsening by the minute. They had no notion of where they were going, and they had been two days without food. A third day would be unsustainable.

Moments passed when they both felt that they couldn't continue much further. Their physical state was fading. It was only a combination of mutual encouragement, love, and determination that kept them going. Surely there would be some manifestation of land and life forthcoming. But still the rain came down, still the wind howled, and still there was no sign of anything more than an unending swathe of ocean. After a brief dialogue, they decided to veer around in search of a brighter path, but this failed to achieve anything of note. The ominous gloom was enveloping.

And yet their hope and conviction never deserted them. If they were handed the divine ability to turn back time, they would still make the same decision again. Soar and Sama were united in purpose and outlook. The covenant between them was that nothing would prevent them from reaching their goal, or else they would expire together in union.

"If you're terrified of death, you can never truly live," Sama told Soar.

On hearing these profound words his heart was infused with a cocktail of love, devotion, admiration, pride, and many other competing emotions.

No sooner had this decision been made than a flash of lightning illuminated the sky, shortly followed by a deafening boom of thunder. The threatening proximity to these two meteorological signifiers indicated that the storm must be extremely close. There was no avoiding it; they were soaring straight into the heart of these most turbulent conditions.

While they were both courageous to the point of audacity, they were also realists. Sama's wing had recently been seriously injured. They hadn't even seen food for days, never mind eaten any. They'd flown thousands of miles. They were both in an enfeebled state. The situation was alarming, yet they both felt an incongruous sense of certainty in the face of peril. They had developed their mastery precisely for this sort of challenge, stretching and straining to be the best versions of themselves. They were thoroughly prepared; in a strange way, they even welcomed it.

Still, the rain was utterly relentless, bucketing down in sheets, surrounding Soar and Sama. The thunder and lightning had become incessant, flashing, and roaring every few seconds. Neither spoke a word, instead concentrating on retaining level flight. It was an almighty struggle; they were both drenched, their wings weighed heavy, while gale-force winds assaulted them from all angles. Soar was panting like a thirsty hound, exhausted, praying that this ordeal would pass sooner rather than later.

Another burst of dazzling light came surging through the stratosphere, shocking both eagles, searing between their bodies at a blistering velocity, nearly striking them. It was close enough to interrupt their flight. Sama lost her equilibrium for some seconds and found herself flailing around, more disorientated than ever, trying to correct her trajectory, literally fighting for her life. She eventually managed to balance herself, turning to remark to Soar that it was a particularly close shave.

But before she could even begin to speak, she could already see that Soar was in serious trouble. He was floundering, flapping his wings desperately, with none of his usual elegance and authority. And he was falling fast, as if he was disappearing into quicksand. Sama immediately began to reduce her altitude to offer help. But before she could get close to Soar, another blinding flash was issued by the heavens, and she was forced to concentrate on her own flight, while shielding herself with her wing against the torrential rainfall, which stung her eyes like vinegar.

By the time she had recovered, she had lost sight of Soar. Even with her prodigious eyesight, it was barely possible to see beyond the end of her beak, let alone potentially hundreds of feet, through the dingy clouds, pelting rain, and shadowy skies. "Soar!", she cried out several times, but to no avail. She dived fearlessly downwards, ignoring the encircling monsoon. She had to find him. They weren't flying at a tremendous altitude, so within a relatively short period of time Sama was already close enough to the ocean to use its waters as a mirror, if indeed the visibility made this remotely plausible.

There was nothing. Sama knew that he could be anywhere. She flew parallel to the ocean, dangerously close to the surface, calling Soar's name continually. She bellowed at the top of her voice, while the formidable dusky waves raged and surged. She wasn't sure if Soar had been struck by lightning, and not even certain that he'd fallen into the sea. But it seemed likely, considering that he'd barely been moving with any forward momentum when she'd seen him last, and there was not the slightest sign of him in the air during her descent.

Sama was aware that these few minutes could be critical. Thankfully, the sea wasn't dangerously cold, but it was seething hazardously. Soar could easily be swept away. Hopefully, he would retain or regain consciousness, but there was no such certainty. She continued calling out despairingly, sweeping the general region where he'd begun to tumble so perilously. Her ears were primed for the slightest unanticipated sound, her eyes peeled for the most minuscule of movements.

As her manhunt continued, another forked detonation of electrical energy surged threateningly through the atmosphere. Each one was accompanied by another resonating, piercing crash of thunder. It was frightening. Sama became tearful, frantically screaming for Soar, terrified that she had lost him, and acutely aware of her solitude. Usually, she was as harmonized with the elements as a tuning fork. But at this moment she resented them, cursed them, feeling an anger percolating in her gut. At least anger is an energy, Sama reasoned, and she continued to call for Soar, peering into the leaden abyss of the currents, calling on the universe to guide her as calmly as was possible under the circumstances.

But all the universe sent was further convulsing bolts of lightning. Two followed in quick succession, pulsating on the surface of the sea, creating a flickering, fluctuating radiance upon the foreboding waters, like a failing fluorescent ceiling light. And then, for the merest fraction of a moment, there was a figure. It passed in a virtual nanosecond, as the lightning quickly concluded its latest strike, plunging the world into darkness once more.

But Sama had already hurtled in the direction of the figure, finding a strength she was unaware she possessed. She hurtled through the fierce winds, reaching the approximate area in a matter of seconds. But the evening was black as coal and Sama could barely see a thing, let alone identify a shadowy body. She called for Soar several times, but there was still no answer. She couldn't hear him. She couldn't see him. The situation was terminal. She could feel Soar slipping away from her.

She couldn't give up. "For the love of life!", she screamed with all her might. "Give me some more light! Please! I beg you!"

Sama kept her eagle eyes trained obsessively on the ocean at all times like a sniper searching for targets. She was fully aware that she would have virtually no time to spot Soar. Nothing occurred for a few seconds, but she retained her faith that more lightning would come. It had to come.

And then electrical energy prised open the heavens once more, casting a preternatural radiance over the threatening tract of oceanic gloom. It acted as a searchlight, albeit a highly intermittent one, and suddenly but unmistakably there was Soar! Sama bombed over and was soon right next to him. He was bobbing around in the ocean, as lifelessly as an inanimate cork. Once Sama was close to Soar, she could see him well enough for it to be clear that his eyes were closed. There was no time to check for vital signs or wonder what his condition might be; she massaged his heart, administering basic cardiopulmonary resuscitation. Sama closed her own eyes, making a silent prayer, having completely forgotten about any jeopardy that she might face. All that mattered was saving Soar.

After some moments, there was a splutter, and Soar resuscitated. He opened his eyes, and Sama stared straight into them, lovingly, unblinkingly. By now, they were both in the sea, vast, coiled waves towering over them.

"What happened, Sama?"

"There was a storm. There was lightning. I lost you. But I knew I would find you." She was cradling Soar as she spoke, ensuring that his head remained above water, until he regained his bearings. "How do you feel?"

Soar took a little time to gather himself. "I've been better, I've been worse!" He hadn't lost his sense of humor! "What are we going to do? How are we going to get out of this?"

Sama pondered the question, as lightning continued to cast sporadic radiance on their surroundings. During these dazzling bursts of luminosity, Sama caught sight of another creature. It was the unmistakable figure of a blue whale. Brilliant light danced upon its smooth, slick physique, as it sleekly slid through the choppy waters. And yet, even in this fleeting illumination, there was time enough for Sama to notice something decidedly unusual. This peerless swimmer was allowing itself to be carried by the current. There was no tangible effort to plot its own course, no squirming against the immense forces of nature.

It was a eureka moment for Sama. "Soar, look at that incredible creature, so powerful, but he's just allowing the tide to guide him. He is accepting the power of the ocean as inevitable. He's biding his time until the situation turns in his favor. That is exactly what we have to do. We just need to keep ourselves afloat, and let the tide carry us. We can do this!"

Sama knew that sometimes it was necessary to simply allow the manifest and unmanifest universe to guide you. Recognizing external forces that one can never control, it was senseless to thrash around attempting to exert some futile influence over them. Even in the bedlam of that moment, her composure suddenly returned, and she voiced her opinion to Soar. It resonated with him immediately, and they figuratively loosened their grip on the situation. It occurred to Soar that this was a critical life lesson, and an attitude that he should have embraced earlier in his life. Sometimes it is senseless trying to change other people and your immediate surroundings.

You must be willing to accept them for what they are, never losing faith in the potential for growth. He wouldn't make that same mistake again!

As Soar and Sama floated through the writhing seas, over time they became marginally, but perceptibly, calmer. It was as if their new attitude of acceptance began to pacify the ocean. As they drifted, time stood still. And all the while, the ocean became less ferocious and more manageable; its worst excesses placated. Eventually, it was even possible to exhibit a few butterfly-like swimming strokes to aid their progress. They circled their wings repeatedly, not with quite the grace and elegance of their flying but creating a somewhat awkward whirling motion, like a slightly unsightly windmill.

The further that they floated, the calmer they became. There was baby blue sky on the horizon, and they knew that the worst was behind them. The ocean had been tamed. Already their attention was turning to what came next.

"We're safe for now," Soar observed. "But we really need to find some food quickly. I feel weak, and I'm sure that you do too. I don't know how much longer I can last. I don't even know if I have the strength to fly."

Sama nodded in immediate agreement. "Let's float for a while. We can regain our strength, and then we can make one final push. We're going to hit land soon, I can feel it in my bones."

Soar felt a surge of optimism pulsing through his Maṇipūra—his solar plexus chakra. "I agree." And then something important came into his mind. "How is your wing doing, by the way?"

Sama was touched that he'd remembered her injury in these awful circumstances. "It's great! I feel fine. As good as can be expected." She paused for a second, choosing her words assiduously.

"Soar, there's something I want you to know."

"Go ahead."

"You saved my life, now I have had the opportunity to return the favor. There is a bond between us that is eternal."

Soar smiled warmly and reached over to sensitively stroke Sama's beautiful face.

"When we're together, nothing can ever defeat us."

14. The Arrival

It was exceedingly unusual, Soar reflected, for eagles to allow nature to wash over themselves with such yielding acquiescence. Yet he embraced it. He had long since made the decision to accept anything and everything that he encountered during this journey, while absorbing all accompanying life lessons. If that meant that he should float on this relatively placid ocean bed with all the passivity of a beach ball, then that was the path that the universe had intended for him.

In fact, Sama had been completely correct. It was replenishing to simply take a break and allow the tide to guide them. As they ventured along their way, their mindset correlated with the prevailing conditions; both were increasingly becalmed. The weather cycled through several gradations of ever-lightening hue and serenity, before settling on pastel blues and almost total tranquility. But still the eagles allowed themselves to drift, remaining confident that there was something of substance up ahead of them.

As the sun had reappeared, so the temperature had steadily risen, and it was now neither too hot nor too cold, like soup that had been meticulously warmed until it was perfectly palatable. And then an unusual cloud formation appeared on the horizon, fluffy and flocculent, while sweeping beyond the usual confines that one associates with cloud cover. They seemed to almost touch the sea, while stretching beyond the limitations of sight, far and high into the powder-blue heavens, as if they were deliberately concealing something.

By this time, Soar and Sama had developed an understanding and connection that was virtually telepathic in its intensity, and barely a raised eyebrow was required to convey their thoughts and intentions to one another. It was time to take to the skies again. They climbed out of the gently lapping waves, and immediately headed towards this pillar-like cloud formation. It felt incredible to move with freedom and grace once more, powering majestically through the atmosphere, splintering the breeze as they flew.

Such was their determination and velocity, the gap between themselves and the clouds was narrowed in almost no time. Before they knew it, they were submerged in a surreal mist, a silky atmosphere that surrounded them. Soar's mind involuntarily returned to the dreamlike state he'd encountered when he had journeyed to meet the walrus, the instructive time when he'd felt the energy of the infinite flowing through his unaccustomed frame. They experienced no panic, not the slightest feeling of apprehension at being subsumed by this vaporous haze. Instead, the two eagles began to climb, while still making forward momentum, feeling something, sensing something, instinctively being pulled in that direction.

Finally, there was a clearing in the clouds, a marginal but precise parting. The crevice created was perceptible only due to the incongruous brightness that seeped through it, puncturing the dark atmosphere, despite being no larger than the opening of a milk bottle. Unperturbed, the two eagles poured into the aperture without hesitation, throbbing with wonder and expectation. By the time they entered this portal-like fissure in the cocooning blanket of cloud, Soar and Sama had climbed thousands of feet above sea level. In a hushed moment of anticipation, they slid through this expanse. They shielded their eyes slightly, as their pupils acclimatized to an entirely new realm of light.

As they squinted through the now luminous brightness, a breathtaking vista was revealed to them. Immense mountain ranges dominated the skyline, beyond the scope of even their formidable ocular capabilities, verdant in appearance, covered in greenery. There was nothing bleak nor imposing about these structures; they were emerald in color, soft in texture, effusing the very source of existence, something to be celebrated rather than feared or negotiated. It seemed as if these towering pyramidal structures were floating in the air, as vast sheets of cloud formed an immeasurable flooring of gaseous carpet, segregating this world from the atmosphere below.

Several ridges sprung up ruggedly above the wider structure. Although tinged with green, these peaks were not entirely covered with shrubbery, the plant life being interrupted by jagged rock that burst from beneath its floral flesh like a defiant skeleton. Fleecy clouds billowed at their feet like smoke, and swirled around their apex, forming feathery coronets. Another structure appeared to be constructed from two gigantic cuboid building blocks, which were asymmetrically assembled in such a way that it appeared that the top one must tumble into the ether. Yet they remained conjoined and unmoved.

Elsewhere, an expanse of cuspated land stretched far into the distance, winding its way endlessly beyond the range of the eye. But before the couple had begun to gorge themselves on the feast of sights in this remarkable domain, something still more pressing was apparent. The Lost Kingdom was an incredible biological preserve, a rich ecosystem populated by all manner of different creatures. Gigantic elephants were wielding tree trunks like toothpicks, giraffes feasted with delight on treetops, gorillas held counsel, surrounded by captive audiences of enthralled creatures, while several buffalo were herding and grazing. Soar even noticed some smaller animals; there was a population of turtles that were spending some time on land.

For a second, Soar pondered how they could survive, then he spied a winding stone staircase, which twisted and meandered its way down to the ocean. It was an extraordinary sight to behold, and Soar wondered for some moments how these creatures had managed to culminate their personal journeys in this remote kingdom.

But his thought pattern was interrupted by a batch of familiar flocks swooping through the clouds, alighting on the spectacular scenery. It was already clear that the land was frequented by hundreds of birds, perhaps thousands, certainly many more than it was feasible to count. Soar was certain that it was the largest population that he'd ever encountered. He considered this for a second, connecting with his rational mind once more, and immediately realized something significant. If this many souls had already found the Lost Kingdom, there must be thousands, hundreds of thousands, perhaps millions more who would relish the chance to mix with them.

Truly a diaspora of avian life, Soar was soon engaging in a little ornithology, spotting the striking crimson-and-yellow beak of the bateleur, the double-jointed and remarkably monochrome harrier hawk, the unmistakable chocolate brown and snowy white plumage of a huge bald eagle, and the keen eyes and aesthetically impressive flying technique of the red-tailed hawk. There were so many potential friendships to form, so many like-minded creatures with whom to connect.

In those first moments in this new world, Soar was swathed in a mystical presence that seemed to perforate every cell of his being. He felt a calm beyond calmness; an entirely new state of knowing. It was partly from a sense of relief, partly due to recognizing that his journey had reached its culmination, partly from the unbridled joy that he felt at the recognition of this, and partly from something intangible that exceeded even these critical factors.

By the time they'd made their way down to ground level, they had already been spotted by several of the residents. It didn't strike Soar as the sort of place where everyone would know everyone; this seemed to be a logistical impossibility! But there must have been some form of organization inherent to the society, as they could see welcoming faces making eye contact with them well before they landed.

A Harris's hawk by the name of Jake greeted them first, welcoming them warmly to the Lost Kingdom. Jake had a mousey underbelly, but his wings bristled with a fierce orange that made his otherwise unremarkable plumage far more distinctive. They introduced themselves, explaining that they'd been flying for several days, but they'd been determined to locate this land. Jake nodded and told them that was the usual experience. Only those souls willing to strain for the extremities of their potential would make it here. "But few will leave," Jake added precipitously, and a little triumphantly.

Soon they were being ushered off for their first meal in their new abode. Neither Soar nor Sama had wanted to make abrupt enquiries about food, but both were relieved that Jake had been forthcoming. They thanked him warmly, but he airily dismissed their gratitude. "I know how hungry and weak I was when I arrived here, and if you're half as hungry then you desperately need to be fed!"

On this occasion, Soar could make no apology for feasting on the meat of some tender young mice. He had tried to curb his carnivorous tendencies but couldn't eliminate this aspect of himself completely. Having said that, both eagles were desperately in need of the influx of protein that perceptibly flowed into their muscles. They had been running on pure adrenaline for the last leg of the journey, but now their strength began to return. Soar could almost feel the viscous glucose internally restoring his body to its optimum state. He was ready to partake in life in the Lost Kingdom, whatever that entailed.

What soon became obvious, even without initiation, was that the society here was truly enlightened.

"There is so much solidarity here," Sama expressed.

"But I don't notice a rigid structure." Soar added. "I can't stop noticing how the freedom of an individual is accentuated. Yet there is a composite that is equally supported."

"I notice such an amazing organization here, with discipline, yet fluidity of leadership," Sama remarked. Each and every inhabitant was free to come and go as they pleased but there was always food, drink, companionship, and even entertainment available to all who were present, with no questions asked, without prejudice, and without checking up or monitoring. In fact, no authoritative or derogatory hierarchy whatsoever was present. The kingdom operated on trust, commitment, and collective spirit, and appeared to function like clockwork. There was cooperation and delegation, but no one was deemed inherently superior or inferior.

Soar considered how such a thing was possible. It seemed more appropriate to ruminate on this himself, rather than ask around; after all, the whole atmosphere of the society seemed to be rooted in personal responsibility. And that was really the crux of the matter. The Lost Kingdom was physically dazzling and mystical, but its true beauty was contained in the fierce sense of responsibility that its residents embodied. Simply by virtue of reaching this land, an inhabitant had already demonstrated an extraordinary level of determination and self-control, as well as an unblemished ethical core. There was no need for rules; personal pride and self-discipline dictated that the creatures here would always pull their weight, always accept their obligations, and deliver as a matter of course more than the society required. True self-mastery was contributing to a greater whole. Not because systemic regulations demanded this, but because it was ethical and just to *give* more than one expected to *receive*.

It transpired that many of the creatures present in the Lost Kingdom had traveled from the opposing easterly direction to that which Soar and Sama had taken. Rather than crossing oceans, many animals had undertaken mountainous expeditions to reach the kingdom. What became apparent to Soar was that any creature was capable of reaching this point, if they were truly invested in the process. The journey would never be the same for any two creatures, but if there was a determination to achieve, the way to do this would inevitably become apparent.

As the two eagles settled in, it was Sama who first pointed out one of the distinct features of their surroundings. There were colorful crystals spread across the land. Some were encrusted within the natural world, some had been embedded within certain objects as a design feature, and others were used ornamentally. Chalky white cliffs were embedded with glinting sapphire topaz and substantial chunks of serrated amethyst were encased within the magnificent oak banquet table. The sun would sporadically gleam through the orbiting cloud cover, catching the lavender stones, causing an enchanting purplish haze to mystically hang over the dinner table.

Banqueting was indeed a regular and memorable occurrence in this elevated kingdom. Hundreds of creatures gathered together on a regular basis to eat, drink, and be merry. There was *joie de vivre* at the heart of this settlement, and Soar found himself being propelled by this spirit. He was by nature more introverted than Sama, more comfortable with the company of a few trusted souls. But he found himself being swept up in the intoxicating spirit of camaraderie and companionship. They would sit next to different creatures every evening, often entering into deep conversations. Soar even encountered a bar-tailed godwit one evening; a petite bird that didn't seem capable of the undertaking required to reach the Lost Kingdom, but which was, in fact, capable of enormous feats of stamina. Although Soar and Sama were much bigger and stronger than this modest reddish bird, they spoke as equals, happy to concede that he could fly farther than them!

Being plunged into this daily social regimen was something of a test for Soar. He had always retreated to his own company, living life through his own eyes and perception. Even when he'd been resident in Magna and Eudaimonia, he had actively sought his own personal space. He instinctively erected an unseen barrier between himself and any society in which he operated; it insulated him against anyone getting too close. It was not that he was hostile to others, or even suspicious, more that outsider tendencies had developed in him from a young age, and this tendency had never been adequately healed. Soar had rarely felt far enough outside of things to be alienated, but nor had he been close enough to truly feel part of them. He had always maintained something of a distance between himself and his social environment. Perhaps meeting Sama had partly changed that, but he was also astute enough to recognize this new location as both an examination of his growth, and an opportunity to evolve.

It made it easier to have Sama alongside, as if he were already qualified in the eyes of others merely by her presence. But within days of landing in the Lost Kingdom, Soar had already resolved to turn over a new leaf, vowing to expose himself to all of life's experiences, rather than grasping his solitude around himself like a protective cloak.

And there was no shortage of social pursuits and occasions for the couple to partake in, nor any paucity of companions with which to share them. Aside from the vast banqueting evenings, there were a couple of special buildings for those that wished to partake in spiritual practices. One was an orthodox chapel, where those with religious convictions congregated to pray. But Soar was far more inclined to frequent the alternative; an example of contemporary architecture that combined modernity in design with tradition in material. It was constructed from red cedar and featured prominent ceiling-tall glass panels at the front, which acted as both windows and sliding doors. Natural light streamed into the main meeting room from dawn until dusk, and it had become a hugely popular meeting place for many of the kingdom's inhabitants.

In fact, there was a wealth of spiritual events that were held within the building's inspirational walls. Nothing was formally organized; everything that transpired there was arranged on a voluntary basis. But folk willingly gave their time, and a genuinely communal feeling was the principle and highly desirable consequence of these efforts.

Soar and Sama both loved to partake in as many of the activities as possible. Not everything resonated with them, but they still approached every new practice with open minds and hearts. The schedule for the week would be pinned on a noticeboard in what had become the equivalent of a village square, and then interested parties would flock to the venue in large numbers. Tantra sessions involved deep conversation, lengthy meditations, body talk, and massage. Another increasingly popular introduction had been holotropic breathwork, where participants used systematic breathing exercises to reach heightened and enlightened states of consciousness.

But that was just the start. Kundalini yoga sessions took place regularly in the evenings. Readings from many spiritual books and texts, including the legendary *I Ching*. Puja ceremonies were common, along with some straighter and guided meditations. And the centre wasn't limited to spirituality; music and dancing took place some evenings, also a debating society, and one creative eagle had even introduced the peculiar pursuit of skittles. Soar had never played games for the sake of games before, and found himself thinking back to some of the curious pastimes that he'd witnessed humans engage in. But after participating in a few games, he had to concede that skittles was more enjoyable than he'd imagined.

Spontaneous assemblies aplenty: dozens of animals gathered together in impromptu meditation symposia; Couples would sit together on the verge of vertiginous cliffs, talking, cuddling, sometimes sharing food or drink, staring into the vast ether, feeling as if they were perched on the very edge of the universe. Soar even became fascinated with a convoluted board game that was being played earnestly by two chimpanzees one evening, notable for its intricately chiseled marble pieces. This was his first introduction to the game of chess and Soar soon became intrigued by its sedate complexity. It offered a starkly different form of sensation to the primeval thrill of hunting, but it was intoxicating in its own way. The patterns that the pieces weaved were mesmerizing, and you could enter a deeply contemplative state when considering the myriad ways that the baffling knights could leap around the playing area.

One of the most notable aspects of the Lost Kingdom was the way that the different qualities and skill sets of animals meshed together into a coherent whole. Sometimes the might of the elephant would prove invaluable, other times the long-term flying capabilities of the hawks and eagles were irreplaceable. The wisdom of the great apes and speckle-feathered tawny owls were appreciated and respected and bison naturally worked together in collaborative groups. Dogs were fearless, with peerless energy, and the resident giraffes were able to reach extremities that were beyond the capabilities of any other mammal. Each and every creature strived to contribute uniquely to life in the Lost Kingdom, acutely aware of their own particular qualities and uniqueness.

In such an atmosphere, new ideas brewed and percolated with the rapidity of a coffee pot bubbling on a burning stove. When the sun peeked through the ubiquitous clouds that wrapped the land in a mysterious hazy atmosphere, small-scale equivalents of athletics meetings would be held. The mightiest and briskest citizens would compete against one another in a series of races and games, and at finals day at the end of each season, trophies and medals were awarded. Those that didn't wish to participate watched on with interest, cheering, jeering, and generally creating a merry and joyful atmosphere.

Soar didn't hesitate to participate; competition was in his blood. He entered some of the middle-distance flying events, reckoning himself to possess the exceptional blend of speed and stamina required to shine in these disciplines. He was quite correct, qualifying for finals day after some strong performances. But he was also forced to learn some humility, as he finished sixth out of eight competitors. Being forced to accept that he wasn't the very best hurt Soar, but Sama was extremely proud of his efforts, and it was certainly an exhilarating experience to exhibit his skills in front of a large and appreciative audience. In fact, he received endless praise and congratulation that evening, as the assembled residents sipped cocktails under the twinkling night sky, their immediate surroundings subtly illuminated by a collection of bijou oil lamps.

Everything was to be enjoyed and embraced in moderation. No social pressure and no obligation, but nothing was sacrosanct. The only limitation was the collective imagination of the residents; nothing consensual was ever discouraged, and individual preferences were welcomed and celebrated. The Lost Kingdom performed the impressive contortion of personifying both libertarian and socially conscious qualities. Equally an emphasis on the pursuit of liberty and happiness co-existed with an undeniable community spirit that bordered on collectivism. And yet, as with everything in this realm, the two diametrically opposed, tangentially polarized outlooks somehow fused into one coherent and cohesive whole.

Soar was never obligated to hunt, but he felt intrinsically that it was his responsibility to contribute as much as possible. He didn't go out as much as he had back home, but he was among the most prolific participants. Sometimes the birds would hunt in packs, other times they would venture out individually. They didn't just hunt for meat; sometimes Soar would join convocations of eagles who would forage for fruits, nuts, and even vegetables. They had to fly many miles away from their residence to locate the guava, jujube, and banana plantations that proved to be rich sources of regular pickings.

Although the banana was the ultimate fruit in many ways from Soar's perspective—pleasing flavor, easy to eat, and one that ripened visibly—the guava was not without its charm. Its taste and consistency was somewhat similar to a pear, and if you managed to locate one that was perfectly sweetened, it could be quite delicious. At other times, Soar would corkscrew alarmingly towards the ocean, emerging with multicolored rainbowfish or blue gourami skewered by his razor-sharp talons. And there were rabbits, hares, mice, voles, and other small creatures to be found if one flew far enough.

This was all supplementary to the food stocks of the population, though, as the residents of the Lost Kingdom had long since invested a huge amount of effort in growing their own food. An entire section of the residence was devoted to cultivating crops, with starchy potato fields accompanying nutritious cabbages and carrots. Statuesque trees provided pineapples, avocados, walnuts, and Brazil nuts. They'd even established their own responsibly sourced trout and salmon farms. This was an entirely self-sufficient culture; everything that was used in the Lost Kingdom was either sourced or grown. Excellence permeated everything that occurred in this realm. Not a single straggler, not one creature who hadn't strained every sinew to strive for his or her maximum potential. As a consequence, the parameters of achievement and expectation were that much higher. It wasn't that the residents hoped for a great life, nor that they believed that they could acquire one; they simply expected and demanded it. Soar couldn't help contrasting this abundance mentality with the grim prospect of clinging to survival that was the predominant mindset back in Aquilana.

The prevailing attitude created an ambience in which Soar and Sama's daily discipline and practice became second nature. It was impossible not to feel immense gratitude for everything in their lives, not least for one another. Although his energetic awakening had occurred some time previously, Soar now realized that he hadn't been truly awake. It was only now that he could begin to experience the true potential of his intrinsic connection with the infinite. Energy pulsated through him unremittingly, gloriously. He often felt light, floating like a feather in the air, unconstrained by the considerations of the physical, as if the universe had temporarily sequestered his body weight. Soar realized that he had reached a nirvanic state of bliss and awareness.

He discussed this with Sama, and she confirmed that she had experienced a very similar sensation. Soar even perceived energy pulsing through other objects; the ovate turquoise amazonite glittered in the sporadic sunshine, vibrating soothingly. It was a profound experience anyway, but sharing these moments with Sama made them even more powerful. They'd persevered with their daily discipline and spiritual practices, experiencing moments where they'd been able to connect on this level, but the Lost Kingdom provided them with a more sustained opportunity.

In this ethereal location, Soar felt as if he'd been permanently elevated to a higher plane of consciousness and existence. Once the clouds had been penetrated, one entered a surreal and entirely demarcated land; completely separate from civilization. A permanent cloud cover seemed to shroud the kingdom in mystique, hermetically sealing it from any extraneous influence. At its liveliest, it could be a hive of activity, but every animal residing there understood the necessity of peace and were respectfully silent when this was needed. It was something magical to be surrounded by thousands of souls, yet for the atmosphere to be bleached of even the slightest residue of undesirable sound.

Soar would sit with Sama on the cliffs, and stare into the clouds. Sometimes they were wispy and virtually translucent, and other times thicker and woollier, resembling billows of piped mashed potato. There was nothing. No sound. No cars, no people, no striving, no arguments, no fighting, no guns, no fear. Just unadulterated peace and joy. He would close his eyes and transcend the external reality, reaching a state of Satchitananda— pure bliss. It was mystical and magical, yet it was something that was always within reach. Soar could enter into this quietly euphoric condition virtually at will, and certainly whenever the land fell silent.

The pair of them had become inseparable. Soar retained his independence, but he was acutely conscious that something was conspicuous by its absence when he didn't have Sama by his side. Although they mixed talkatively with the other creatures, Soar also located some secluded areas for some romantic moments. Candlelight had become an important ritual of these amorous trysts; a return to something rawer, simpler, more primal. They would sit beneath the spiky flora of the evergreen conifers, sometimes sharing bread and wine, sometimes deep conversation, and other times no more than furtive moments of intimacy. Everything to express, nothing that needed to be said.

Their bond often provided residual body heat but Soar found that, regardless, he often didn't notice dips in the temperature. As his consciousness became ever more enlightened, so the universe provided ethereal insulation. Indeed, his body was continually teeming with energy, so the world around him resonated with this same universal force.

Such was the penetrating elation that Soar experienced, he found himself flitting between this serene state of joy, and the semi-disbelief that he had found this place, this state of existence, and the perfect partner to share it with. Sometimes Soar felt like an undeserving imposter, but he also recognized that the initial decision that he had made, everything that he had endured, the process of learning he had been through, his growth, perseverance, and determination had led him to this point. And, thus, the realization of his dreams wasn't random. It was entirely natural, having been quite purposefully manifested.

They weren't the only couple in the kingdom. Many other animals had identified, courted, and united with their soulmates in this idyllic setting. Soar and Sama would often socialize with some of the residents and didn't limit this to avian couples. One of their favorite duos was Ella and Gabriel, two camels who were accustomed to trekking vast distances! There was something endearingly unflappable about them; nothing seemed to disturb their Zen-like tranquility.

It was Ella and Gabriel who had explained that the journey to the Lost Kingdom was completely different when tackled in a Westerly direction. Their expedition had been an odyssey across perpetual desert, defined by temperatures that seemed so hostile as to be virtually incendiary. For days they had hauled their weary bodies across sands hot enough to fry eggs, with neither soul nor sign of sustenance in sight. But Ella declared that their chins had never dropped. They had never lost sight of their goal, nor doubted their ability to reach it. They had invested profound trust in the process, not to mention one another, and were immovably confident that they would emerge unscathed from these harshest of conditions.

Soar and Sama both loved the camels. They were talkative but listened with intent as well. In fact, each and every creature that they mixed with was charming and delightful. Everyone had their guard routinely lowered; an innate enthusiasm for sharing was sustained. It was impossible to become intimately familiar with every creature that lived in the kingdom, and yet whenever Soar and Sama encountered someone, they would end up talking the night away, fascinated by the different perspectives on offer. This was simply something that Soar would never have encountered in Aquilana, where outsiders were strictly prohibited. He felt inordinately proud of his growth, of the way that his personality, character, and outlook had slowly unfurled like a maturing lilac.

Love and solidarity seemed to pour from every pore of the kingdom. It was the perfect setting; the ideal way to end this monumental journey of discovery.

15. The Banquet

Not meaning to be dismissive but it had been a spectacularly easy kill, Soar reflected, on his return from a hunting expedition. It was as effortless as a golfer casually beheading an errant dandelion with a five iron. He had descended with rapidity, and yet with a grace that was inaudible, scything the rodent open from the side. Soar said a silent prayer of thanks and gratitude, before devouring the mouse. He had acknowledged that we can become the best version of ourselves, but it must indeed be ourselves that we remain. He had to be his authentic self, and this included hunting!

What had changed was his outlook on the process. Every time he consumed the flesh of another animal, he dutifully thanked the universe with humility. This had become an automatic and heartfelt process. The way that he viewed hunting had evolved. It hadn't quite become a necessary evil; Soar still experienced innate joy as a result of the process. But his outlook was somehow less bloodthirsty; he now viewed hunting as a privilege, not a right.

Ten glorious weeks had passed in the Lost Kingdom, and it truly felt like home. It's funny how you have to travel thousands of miles to arrive home! But Soar and Sama had settled in almost immediately; like trying on tailored trousers, everything fitted perfectly. Soar was sure that Sama felt the same way because they had regular dialogues about their lives, their feelings, and the way that they perceived life in this magical location. Soar had total respect for Sama, fully recognizing her to be his equal in every respect. But this didn't relieve the feelings of protectiveness that he felt towards her. Sama's well-being was more important to him than his own, and there was nothing that he wouldn't be unwilling to sacrifice to make her happy.

As Soar approached the Lost Kingdom, it remained shrouded in clouds, a ringlet of cumulus creating a halo-like effect that crowned the land. Soar made a minor adjustment to his altitude, preparing to sear through the covering. For a few seconds, he was engulfed in a tuft of whiteness, before emerging from the void, the vast territory becoming apparent. Soar could immediately see several elephants engaged in a building project. Antelopes were scuttling and leaping in the distance and six or seven goshawks were circling around playfully. Soar peered across the highlands and felt a sense of inner belonging that was entirely new to him, yet instantly recognizable. It was an affinitive sensation that he had never expected to feel, but it offered an internal comfort that was soothing, like a warming brandy.

Soar and Sama had established blossoming relationships with a multitude of animals. Khalid, a male gazelle, demonstrated beyond all doubt that avian creatures aren't the only form of life that is capable of astounding movement. Khalid was a multiple gold medalist in the Lost Kingdom Games, but this mastery of his craft never betrayed his modest outlook. He regaled Soar and Sama on many evenings with tales of characters that he'd met along the way, and some of the extraordinary sights that he had witnessed.

Adanna was a female hippopotamus, slow in movement, but impenetrable in stature. Her speech was steady and economical, her words measured with the precision of weighing scales. She was fiercely loyal, often reserving Soar and Sama places at banquet tables and other events. And Zikomo was a striking male zebra, possibly the most beautiful of all creatures. He was gallant and driven, fearless in nature, and always motivated to work towards a common goal. Equally, he knew how to enjoy himself, and was an almost ubiquitous presence when wine was flowing. He was courted by many female residents of the Lost Kingdom, but retained a respectful distance, continuing to work on himself before entering into any such intimate relationship.

These creatures merely scratched the surface of the rich tapestry of life that Soar and Sama encountered and became acquainted with. Soar became close to a proboscis monkey by the name of Batara, notable for his striking elongated snout and whimsical attitude to life. There were many other rare and remarkable creatures among the population, including the sharp-horned kudu, and hazel-furred nyala antelope. Soar even met Miya, a king cobra, who was venomous, but harmless in nature, at least to the residents of the Lost Kingdom. Her prowling movements were remarkable, and her lubricious, ringed physique equally wondrous, although remaining slightly alien to both mammalian and avian life.

And Soar and Sama had a special bond with Jake, simply because he'd been the first to greet them when they arrived. He befriended everyone and ensured that the wheels of social interaction were appropriately oiled. He always had a quip, an encouraging remark, and a cheerful disposition regarding life and its many challenges. Overall, a refreshingly diverse mixture of outlooks and personalities existed among the residents; tolerance and empathy were abiding qualities. No one was made to feel excluded; the kingdom was a true melting pot.

A dogged mist hung in the air that evening, refusing to be swayed by the easterly breeze that whistled across the land. But the temperature was agreeable, clement enough for an outdoor meal. A big social event was planned, which would be attended by an array of species. Once upon a time, Soar would have avoided such an occasion, preferring to sulk in the insulating uterus of his bedroom. But his journey had changed him profoundly, and in no more polarizing fashion than in his attitude to sociability. Today, he found that he relished being around hundreds, and even thousands, of other souls. Although this could partly be attributed to the elation that he felt at being surrounded by like-minded creatures, it went beyond this kinship. Soar realized now that he would behave differently in Aquilana. He would be less hostile, he would be more empathic. He would neither bite his tongue nor repress his sincere feelings, but he would sooner darn and stitch together social divides, than act as an irritant and rebel.

Everyone was welcome and appreciated at the dinner; the cuisine on offer would be entirely vegan. This was, Soar would be the first to confess, an underlying reason why he'd scoffed some flesh earlier in the day! But it was, nonetheless, gratifying to be exposed to different cultures and practices, and consuming healthy, nutritious plant-based food was one that he had definitely embraced, albeit not with unerring consistency!

It was also impossible to be glum, or to feel neglected of sustenance, when Sama was around. Her very presence energized Soar. Their relationship had become stronger still over these ten weeks, both in the enduring closeness that was possible in such a nurturing location, and in the nature of communication between them. Saving each other's lives had created the ultimate union between them. They had stared down the barrel of the rifle and come out the other side, thanks only to the actions of one another. They had always been open with each other and these life-changing experiences meant that they had become entirely unrestrained. Nothing need be held back. Soar loved this part of their relationship; any enduring desire that he had to be the strong and silent type had long since dissipated. He wanted to know everything about Sama, and to share all of himself with her.

Between this intoxicating connection and the happiness that he had found in this locale, there was such a diminished need for food that Soar wasn't inclined to throw a tantrum just because steak wasn't on the menu! He could embrace food in its many enticing forms. The more time that he spent here, expanding, evolving, bonding with Sama, growing ever closer to a state of spiritual bliss, Soar found on contemplation that Jake had been entirely correct. Many would seek the Lost Kingdom, but few would leave by choice.

It was evident to Soar that the development and wisdom derived from this journey had matured beyond its initial importance. It had become his *ikigai*, his sense of purpose, his reason for living. It was obvious now that Magna, Eudaimonia, the Master, the walrus, the dolphin, the learning, the challenges, the life lessons, the highs, the lows, the trials and tribulations, all the collective experiences that he had been hoarding all of this time, had been stepping stones to this point.

In short, Soar had reached a state of true self-awareness. His actions, thoughts, and emotions were now precisely aligned with his values and internal standards. Soar would have clashed stormily with anyone who suggested that this was not the case when he set out on this journey. But he knew now that they would have been undeniably correct. He had been far too focused on the standards of others, failing to turn that mirror of inquisition on himself. That was a flaw that this journey had corrected, but he was also aware that it was an ongoing process, and that this would remain so for the remainder of his lifecycle in this realm. Whether the experiences one encountered were positive, negative, inspiring, or terrifying, there was a reason for them all, even if this wasn't immediately apparent. Dark and light were always harmoniously balanced; indeed, one could not exist without the other.

While Soar had been engaging in the process of kneading his thoughts and feelings thoroughly, quite a crowd had gathered for this herbivorous feast. Soar would be the first to admit that he wasn't the most adept with culinary skills; other animals would prepare the food, and he would accept what he was given! So there was always an intervening period between being seated and the arrival of the evening's dishes that was pure anticipation. This was punctuated by delicious aromas wafting over from the preparation area, where an array of gigantic coal-black cooking pots boiled on crackling fires, seething, simmering, sending irresistible scents across the land. Soar always noticed that some of the creatures with particularly acute senses of smell would begin salivating almost as soon as cooking began. Indeed, this very evening, one of the coyotes was already drooling uncontrollably.

It was always a source of fascination to be acquainted with creatures of every conceivable size, shape, and type. Just within his eyeline, within a matter of seconds Soar could see everything from raccoons to rhinos, with horses, deer, and emus somewhere between these extremities. There was a persistent buzz of chatter, with animals crowding around the enormous banquet table in groups of three, four, and more creatures. Some of the more diminutive animals were seated, others would merely use their immense proportions to bend over the table. A few flighted species would even hover above the feeding area, landing intermittently once the huge rectangular serving trays were presented.

The amber sun had been reduced to an ellipse by the horizon, and the atmosphere was steadily veering towards dusk. It was at this point that the lamps would be lit, and a warm yet subtle illumination would be cast over the diners. Soar looked over at Sama, who was deep in conversation with a multi-hued macaw and felt an unmistakable sense of pride. All was right with the world.

It was at this point that the culinary focus of the gathering began to arrive, carried on lengthy metallic receptacles by some of the stronger animals. This was where the bison, camels, and horses came in particularly useful, as they were able to balance large portions of food casually on their backs. Other more dexterous creatures then assisted with the unloading, and soon the lengthy oblong banquet table was stacked with sumptuous dishes.

The identity of the cuisine was always kept under wraps, remaining the preserve of those creatures that handled the preparation. Each of the dishes was neatly labeled, with an ivory-colored card indicating its contents. This evening's menu incorporated:

Pumpkin curry with chickpeas
Vegan jambalaya

Succotash
Veggie shish kebabs
And for dessert:
Zucchini bread with sultanas
Peanut butter cookie bars

An array of extremely wholesome and hugely tempting food was on offer and Sama immediately remarked that the cooks had outdone themselves this time. If the indicator of healthy food is a colourful plate then there could be no doubting the nourishment available. The vivid pumpkin curry was still bubbling as it was served, and it corresponded perfectly with the jambalaya; both dishes were radiant with deep oranges and leafy greens. Succotash was a wonderfully unpretentious dish, its lima beans interspersed with grass-green florets of broccoli. But if there was a *pièce de résistance* of the main course, it was surely the skewered kebabs; quite remarkably rainbow-like, with their crimson bell peppers, golden sweetcorn, and soft, domed mushrooms.

Soar rarely leaned on his sense of smell, but there was such a variety of aromas on offer that even he was able to entrust this less powerful of senses. It was a delectable banquet. The food was expertly spiced and seasoned, ensuring that it was never remotely bland. Alongside the food-stuffed trays were several crystal carafes, all full to the brim with deep burgundy wine. This was all homemade; the settlers had been winemaking for some years now, with the more tropical months being warm enough to support a vineyard. "No hearty meal is truly complete without a good drop," Soar remarked to a neighboring hawk, and the pair of them chinked glasses and wished one another excellent health.

It would have been impossible for Soar to be happier. It was as if someone had encapsulated the concept of glee and bottled it for his liberal consumption. He had everything that he could possibly want in the world—intelligent company, fierce competition and the chance to excel, creativity, intellectual stimulation, a sense of belonging and camaraderie, great food, good wine, freedom, beauty, and an incredible bond with the love of his life. Sama was deep in conversation with a guinea fowl, its speckled body trembling with laughter as they bonded over something amusing. Soar leaned over and told her softly in her ear that he loved her. Sama turned to Soar, smiled warmly, and responded in kind.

Conversation had turned to the process of journeying to the Lost Kingdom. It was fascinating for Soar to absorb the stories of many of the other animals present and he found that he was inclined to listen in respectful silence. The same themes came up repeatedly: striving for something better; wanting to reach the highest level of proficiency possible; feeling that something was missing; craving the freedom from which they somehow felt constrained.

It was soon time for Soar's turn to wax lyrical on his experiences, and he was pleased to note that some of the other creatures were visibly enthralled by some of his tales and toils. As Soar spoke, he even reflected himself on the challenges that he'd endured. When he'd encountered them, he had been so consumed by the moment, or the road ahead, that he'd never properly reflected on the vast accumulation of experiences encountered along the way. It made him feel strong, invulnerable even; indeed, how could he possibly feel anything else with Sama by his side?

The wine was moreish, and Soar was becoming slightly tipsy, his tongue looser than usual. Fortunately, his mood correlated perfectly with the general spirit of the assembled creatures, whose chatter had raised in volume from a subtle buzz to an excited din. Perhaps the imbibing had made some of the animals sentimental, as talk had shifted to the topic of family. This wasn't necessarily Soar's favorite subject, but he also recognized that it was important to avoid brushing it under the carpet. He had felt like an outsider, he had grown up quite alienated, but engaging in a strategy of avoidance simply wasn't healthy. It had to be acknowledged and addressed, so that his feelings could evolve and mature.

Many creatures, in fact, already lived with extended family in the Lost Kingdom. The land wasn't entirely characterized by breaking away; sometimes entire families had decided to seek out this legendary location. Some of the flighted birds with exceptional stamina would also venture home and reacquaint themselves with their folks on an annual or biannual basis, depending on how far away they lived. Others were intending to move their family into the region in the foreseeable future. There were as many different arrangements as there were creatures, but all agreed that, despite their overwhelming need to seek out the Lost Kingdom, their families remained critically important to them. Even Soar could concur with this sentiment, despite his estrangement and troubling relationship with his background and relatives.

The banquet had been the centerpiece of a hearty and joyous evening. Soar had never had the sweetest of tooths, but the peanut butter cookie bars were truly irresistible—spongy and squishy, with a fascinatingly dichotomous combination of sweet and savory qualities.

Yet despite his faintly inebriated state, Soar was still perceptive enough to notice that Sama had become uncharacteristically quiet. She was somehow detached from the proceedings. Nothing so dramatic that anyone else noticed, but Soar knew her better than anyone, and it was evident that her mood had nosedived from an outward happiness to virtual silence. She was withdrawn and distant, not really *with* the congregated creatures in any meaningful sense. Soar didn't want to cause her discomfort in front of this amount of company, but he was also naturally concerned. The most worrying thing was that this mood endured. He kept an eye on Sama for some minutes, and there was no semblance of any change in her demeanor.

It was the first errant stone to create even the slightest ripple in the tranquil pool of their existence in the Lost Kingdom. But it was a stone that Soar, nevertheless, intended to investigate.

16. The Revelation

The modest nest that Soar and Sama had erected for themselves, among the distinctive upswept needles of an *abies squamata* tree, was bathed in the comforting glow of candlelight. Droplets of milky wax were inching their way down the extent of the candle, like beads of sweat, before being subsumed by an ever-expanding molten pool. They'd located the most dazzlingly beautiful *lapis lazuli* crystal one afternoon, and had dutifully hoisted it back to the nest, where it held pride of place. And on cloudless evenings such as this, the discreet illumination would mingle with the glassy, burnished surface, and cast a transcendent cobalt glow across their home.

This ritual of crystal and candlelight had become a fixture in their lives. The *lapis lazuli* is associated with open communication, and thus the couple held some of their deepest inquisitions into each other's souls within this relatively crude cluster of twigs and sprigs. They didn't enjoy the same level of privacy to which Soar was accustomed; many other birds were located amid the branches of neighboring trees and other creatures would sleep amid the shrubbery below. Indeed, it was not unusual for Soar to doze off with the intermittent sound of bronchial snoring penetrating the atmosphere!

Although this setting was typically amenable and life-affirming, on this evening there was an unspoken, but overpowering, sense of tension. Soar was confused by what had prompted Sama's sullenness; Sama wondered if

Soar had noticed. A conspicuous silence permeated the air, Soar staring meaningfully into space, searching for the right words. As he peered across his treasured home, he noticed that the distinctive trunk of the *abies squamata* was exfoliating in several places, its bark peeling in gossamer-thin flakes, like blistering skin.

"Sama, is everything okay?", Soar inquired delicately.

"Sure, why do you ask that?" Sama replied, feigning ignorance of the source of the question.

Soar paused for a few seconds, internally agonizing over the right thing to say, and then realizing that there was no right thing to say.

"Well, darling, you've been rather quiet since we arrived home, and towards the end of the evening, you didn't really seem yourself at all. I was just wondering if you're okay. I don't mean to pry where I'm not wanted, but I thought we could talk about anything and everything."

There was no immediate response, and Soar turned away for a second, gazing at the myriad of twinkling celestial bodies that illuminated the night sky, many light years away, yet feeling close enough to reach out and touch. But when he turned back to face Sama, she had unmistakably welled up, with moisture forming in her tear ducts; her eyes a revealing window to her soul.

"You're right, of course. It was just that something touched me, it affected me, and I tried to swat it away and enjoy the evening, but it brought back a lot of memories, and my mood just deteriorated." Sama was apparently reluctant to meet Soar's eye, staring into space distantly, as if she hoped that fixing her gaze on some indeterminate point would somehow alleviate her pain.

Soar was deeply moved by Sama's tears. Waves of protectiveness washed over him; he felt a profound desire for her to heal.

"Well, you don't have to talk about it, but sometimes it helps," Soar began. "If you can't share it with me then who will you ever share it with? It's not healthy to bottle things up." Soar paused again for effect. "And I know you don't need me to tell you that."

Rather than answer, Sama simply began sobbing uncontrollably. Soar reached over to console her, and nothing was said for some moments. Sama then composed herself and turned to face Soar.

"I'm sorry, Soar. I need to tell you everything. I'm ready to do so, and I owe it to you. You're completely correct. I have brushed this under the carpet, but it's just been my way of dealing with it."

"Whatever it is, Sama, you know that I'm here to support you in any way that I can."

Sama managed a tentative smile in response, and then breathed deeply. "Okay, well the truth is that when we were seated at dinner, everyone was talking about their families, and it took me back to when I was a very young eaglet. I know that I've never really spoken about my family with you, Soar, and there is a reason for that."

Now that Sama mentioned it, Soar realized that every time he had raised the subject of her family, Sama had either changed the subject, or had been somewhat evasive. This hadn't really bothered him at the time, as he hadn't wished to appear cold about leaving his own family, particularly in the early days of their relationship. But it seemed that there was more to this issue than he had originally figured.

"When I was extremely young, my mother left on a hunting trip. I couldn't have been more than a couple of weeks old. I didn't have any brothers or sisters; I had hatched prematurely, and I still remember being surrounded by unhatched eggs in the nest. I never met my father, nor do I know what became of him. My mother never told me. I suspect that he was probably killed before I was born, but I simply never found out."

Soar listened in complete silence, transfixed by her lucid account.

"Anyway, there was no choice, but for my mother to hunt for food. Thankfully, I was the only eaglet around, and I was on the verge of maturation. It was hoped that within a week I would be able to assist my mother with hunting and foraging for food."

Sama stopped once more, biting back some tears, before continuing.

"I can still remember her face as she left the nest, looking at me reassuringly, telling me that she loved me and not to be scared. 'Everything will be okay,' she told me." Sama paused for some moments, and then the register and volume of her voice dropped. "She never came back. I waited from dawn until dusk, through the night, and then until dusk the next day. But there was nothing. I don't know what happened to her, I will never know what happened. She was probably killed as well. I really don't know."

Soar wanted to speak but could see that Sama had more to share, so he maintained his respectful silence.

"By now, I had no choice. I had to fend for myself. I'm sure that you went out on flying expeditions with your parents, and they steadily taught you the ropes." Soar nodded in agreement. "There was no one around to teach me. It was a sink or swim situation." Sama again stared into the distance, searching for solace in the cosmos. "I was terrified. I wanted my mother so badly, but I knew that she wasn't coming back. I didn't know what to do, and there was no one there to tell me. I just had to learn to adapt."

Suddenly, so much made sense. Soar understood the fearlessness of Sama, her unsurpassed flying strength, and her independence. But he didn't have much time to reflect on this; the story continued.

"All I could do was launch myself out of the nest, and hope that I was able to fly. Not to mention locate a source of food. I had no idea what was going to happen. I could have plummeted to the ground like a stone. That would have been the end of me. And I knew little about hunting; I had no idea what to search for. I was a complete rookie. All I had to guide me were my wits and my instinct. These are my earliest memories. One of the first things that I can remember is my mom leaving me, and then never returning…

So I leapt out of the nest, and began flapping my wings in the approximate manner that I'd seen my mother utilize, when she flew with such grace and proficiency. My heart was in my mouth, Soar, I had no faith that I would be able to achieve level flight. I remember frantically flapping my wings; I was like a child writhing around in a paddling pool. Completely lacking in elegance and composure! I know now that I was wafting them far too hard, and that a more rhythmical approach was required. But I thought that, by definition, faster would be better. But luckily, my efforts still kept me upright, and I didn't immediately fall. I was flying! So many emotions coursed through me. I felt exhilarated, relieved, terrified, proud, confused, and uncertain of the future. But I didn't have time to absorb any of this; finding some food rapidly was the priority."

Soar had consumed quite a bit of wine during the banquet, but by now any remnants of inebriation had completely left him with Sama's words.

"Fortunately, I managed to catch a few worms here and there, while I was finding my feet. It was enough to keep me alive, and every day was a learning experience. All I could try to do was get a little better with each experience of flying. There was nothing else to do, no one to speak with, and no one to assist me. I had to stand on my own two feet. Because if I did not then I simply wouldn't survive."

Sama was speaking with a little more verve now, recalling her first baby steps of independence.

"I got a little better each day, and within a few days I was able to fly quite proficiently. Meanwhile, I managed to graduate pretty quickly to some rudimentary hunting, and I was soon able to feast on the meat of a vole for the first time. It gave me extra energy, not to mention confidence, and for the first time I sincerely believed that I would survive."

Soar allowed himself a little smile, feeling empathy towards Sama's predicament, and satisfaction at the way that she'd handled herself. At that moment, as shocked and sad as he was about the profound ordeal that Sama had endured, he had also never been more grateful that he'd connected with her. He cherished her so much, and yet in that moment he also reflected that their paths might so easily have never crossed. This was a clarion call to himself; always capitalize on every meaningful interaction. You never know when it might blossom into a relationship that changes your life.

Sama resumed the story, more composed, but still connecting with the most heartfelt state of sorrow. "I felt that I was going to be okay. But I remained ablaze with emotions. I missed my mother, and I felt completely alone. I had absolutely no sense of belonging. I craved company and connection. I needed someone. But there was no one." Sama had resumed her habit of peering out into the ether, at no point in particular. "Every night, I sat in the nest, gazing into the sky, hoping, praying that somehow there would be a miracle."

Her head drooped visibly. "But there never was one."

Soar didn't know quite what to say and was almost grateful that Sama continued to speak.

"And then there was another problem. I soon realized that the eggs containing my brothers and sisters were about to hatch." Sama stared straight at her talons, as if she dare not raise her head. "I tried my best, but my flying and hunting were nowhere near good enough yet, and I didn't have anyone else to help me." Once again, there were salty tears conspicuous in her regretful eyes. "They all died. I managed to keep a couple of them alive for a few days, but I just couldn't find enough food, and I had to make the very difficult decision of keeping myself alive. I literally had to sacrifice my siblings. Eventually, I couldn't even bring myself to return to the nest, which made me feel terrible. But there was nothing I could do; all I could do was save myself."

This was a sledgehammer blow of such resonance that there was no befitting response. Soar placed his wing on Sama's shoulder, and for some minutes neither spoke a word. There was nothing to say of any validity. Pure silence seemed the only fitting tribute to the lives lost, and the pain that Sama had been living with throughout her existence. Eventually, she turned to Soar, still somewhat sullen, but with an upturn in her expression and bearing.

"Usually, I put all this behind me. I don't dwell on it in everyday life, but it will never leave me completely. It is indelibly etched on my soul. And I had flashbacks when I was shot in the village. I should have gotten out of there on my own, but I just froze. I found myself thinking back to the disappearance of my parents. I always wondered if they were killed that way, as we lived in an area populated by many humans, and hunting with guns was popular. I don't know. I don't hold it against them, but there is always that wariness of humanity within my psyche.

And then this evening brought it up again. It is always there inside me. It will never leave me. Everyone was talking about their families, and maybe it was the alcohol, but I just got a bit overwhelmed. I knew that I had nothing to contribute. I've never had a family. I've never had anyone." She looked at Soar, smiling somewhat sheepishly. "That's why you mean so much to me."

The two eagles embraced for what seemed like an eternity. Soar had never felt closer to Sama, and yet he also had the anomalous sensation of feeling a chasm inside himself; it was as if his innards had been scooped out, like a pulped orange. But he now had a true insight into his partner's character. In particular, he now knew why Sama was shorn of the typical need to feel an identification with one specific place. She had, after all, never experienced the basic attachment that most creatures take for granted. The notion of an affinity with one location was simply foreign to her nature. Although Soar had always been committed to his journey, he had at times been torn by feelings of regret and nostalgia for places and people left behind. Sama had never seemed that way—with very good reason.

"But what I learned from this horrible experience is that life is short and fragile," Sama continued. "And that every day is a gift. It took me a long time to get over this horrible start, but I was determined to make my life a success, and to ensure that this hardship never defined me. And it doesn't define me. Because I'm really happy and always positive about the future."

The couple continued to embrace, and then Soar broke away. He looked earnestly into Sama's eyes and began to speak, mustering all the feeling and sincerity in his heart.

"I want to tell you two things. Firstly, I couldn't be more proud of you. Secondly, I will never leave you. I will always be by your side."

In a moment of tenderness between them, Soar felt overwhelmingly happy and sad all at once, the two polarizing states commingling within him until he was inundated with emotion. He felt gratified that he'd been able to comfort Sama to some extent, and that she'd finally been through this partial catharsis. Of course, Soar wasn't delusional enough to believe that all her internal pain was cured; this would be an ongoing part of her life's work. But at least she had been willing to open up, and this was the beginning of the process.

Conversely, an undeniable sadness rose in Soar's heart knowing that Sama would always feel excluded when discussions on family were raised. She would never, and could never, know how it feels to be part of a family unit, or to have that intrinsic sense of belonging. And then, supplanting that initial sensation of melancholy, was one of guilt. It suddenly became acutely apparent to Soar how lucky he was to have his family. His thoughts inevitably drifted back to them, and, perhaps for the first time, an appropriate recognition in his soul of how much they cared about him.

*   *   *

The flaming sun provided the perfect circadian awakening, its golden beams easing through the cloudy veneer, gently rousing Soar. It immediately offered temperate warmth and comfort, as opposed to blistering heat.

Soar and Sama were wrapped around one another, their bodies inseparable. It was that time of the morning characterized by surreal silence; not a soul moved, nor was there a sound to be heard. Several days had passed since the revelation. The deep discussion had brought them even closer together. Soar felt indescribably connected to Sama, Sama more appreciative of Soar than she had thought possible. They knew that they would be together for eternity, their souls ineradicably conjoined. Whatever sense of belonging Sama had been denied during her early years, she felt it now with Soar. They were inseparable.

This initial meaningful discussion opened the floodgates to many more important and related conversations. Soar and Sama had already agreed that they wanted to start a family and had even entered into dialogue regarding how their children should be raised, as well as the values that they wanted to be inculcated in them, or at least encouraged to adopt. During this passionate debate, it occurred to Soar that Sama was remarkably balanced and astute considering that she'd never had the opportunity to observe any such parental model. He told her this plainly, and she radiated with joy.

Nonetheless, as much as they had made progress, something continued to gnaw incessantly at the back of Soar's mind. And no matter how happy he was in his current situation, in his existing surroundings, it was not something that could be parked, put to one side, or ignored. It was an issue that must be addressed, and the time was right to do so. As a couple, they'd had every important discussion, unturned every stone, established everything important to them going forward. Everything except one thing.

Soar knew he had to raise the subject; indeed, he felt compelled. And yet, he was profoundly torn. The last thing he wanted to do was interrupt the happiness that they felt as a couple, to disrupt the harmonious existence and understanding that they had built together. But Soar knew that this was something that he had to do.

Sama was stirring, straining and stretching as her body roused itself, and once she had negotiated this momentary acknowledgement of her shift in consciousness, Soar observed Sama notice his presence, and the immediate comfort that this instilled in her. They bid each other good morning, with the bare minimum of language, and then lay together for some minutes, relishing the peace, harmony, and unity.

Eventually, they both drifted into their routine awareness, properly awake, reluctant to leave the nest and one another's embrace, but also keen to tackle the day ahead. However, Soar knew that he wanted to resolve this burning issue sooner rather than later.

"Sama, there's something important that I need to discuss with you."

"Of course, my sweet, anything at all."

Soar turned the words he wanted to use over in his head, before deciding on a direct approach.

"There is something we must do, or that I must do, before I settle here, or anywhere else. I have to see my family." Sama nodded immediately and sympathetically. "I'm glad that I came here for so many reasons, I'm proud that I embarked on this journey, and meeting you has enriched my life in a way that I could never express with mere language."

Sama hugged Soar, and they held each other tightly for some seconds.

"But I need to return. There are things left unsaid and undone. I have grown, I have learned a lot about myself, and I understand so much more about life and the world now. I need to go back and reconcile with my family. And I want you to come with me, but if you want to stay here then I will accept that. But this is something that I have to do. And if I have to do it alone then it will hurt, but I will do it alone."

Sama began to answer, but Soar put his finger to her mouth. "There is something else that I need to say to you, and something that I want you to understand. This isn't just about seeing my folks. During my journey, and particularly since I arrived here, something has been churning away inside me. And it goes much deeper than feeling homesick or wanting to return home."

Just as Soar had heeded her story quietly days before, Sama listened silently but intently.

"Everything that I've seen during my journey has made me realize that the majority of eagles, birds, and for that matter other animals, are unaware and unhappy. They are not living their lives purposefully. They are not living abundantly. They are living in a highly diminished energetic space, without ever coming close to their full potential. I know this because I grew up in a place like that.

If one good thing has come out of your early life, Sama, it's that you have found your true self. You had no choice. You weren't influenced by a society, by external values; you had to forge your own identity. Perhaps you don't know this, but that's not always the case. Society can be oppressive. And where I come from, life was all about structure, obligation, and fulfilling your almost pre-determined role. There was no option to fly free; we were always constrained. That's why I left."

Some of their fellow residents had risen by this time and were beginning to congregate beneath the couple. But Soar and Sama remained oblivious to the day's occurrences, instead remaining fiercely focused on their conversation.

"And I know," Soar continued, "that there must be many more eagles like me in Aquilana. Perhaps they aren't quite aware of their innermost feelings, or perhaps they didn't have the courage to speak up. But I want to help them, and I want to help others. I want to share what I've discovered and experienced. And there are a lot of things that I need to say to my family. I want to mend our relationship. And I would be so proud to introduce you to them. But I'll understand if you want to stay here. It's a long way to go, and a big commitment to make."

As soon as it was evident that Soar was finished, Sama smiled warmly. "Come with you? Try to stop me; see how you get on!" Soar beamed in response. "I will come anywhere with you, Soar, because I know you would do the same for me. I want to support you as much as you have supported me. And I can't wait to meet your family. When will we go back?"

Soar gazed far into the distance, the rays of the unhurried morning sun causing him to squint due to its sunken position in the understated, pastel skyline. As he peered, so Soar contemplated the journey ahead, and the commitment that they were making.

"We begin our return today."

17. The Return

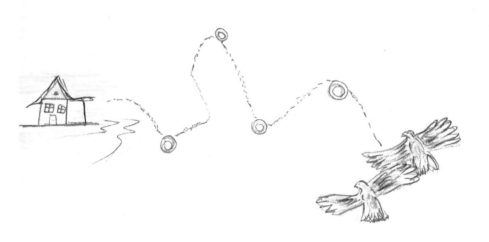

J emima eased open the rickety wooden door. Its whitewashed facade was peeling from years of neglect, and it squeaked jarringly as it opened. Unfortunately, enduring this excruciating sound didn't prove to be particularly worthwhile. There was little in the way of meat stocks; the settlement was running dry in virtually every major indicator of utility.

She sighed, and began to make her weary way back to her husband. It had been a trying time for Aquilana and there wasn't the merest possibility of a blinking light on the horizon. Attempts to rebuild their community had floundered. Promises made by the Elders had failed to materialize. Reassembling and replacing key aspects of infrastructure had proved impossible. There had been a breakdown in the autocratic structure on which they had all relied. People had lost faith in the Elders. In truth, they had probably lost faith in themselves. Some families had fled. Others had stayed. Few were happy. Many were scared.

And, of course, the absence of Soar hung over the family heavily. They thought about him all the time, or at least she did. But they rarely mentioned him. It was too painful to excavate past issues, nor did it offer any assistance in addressing more pressing and immediate problems.

However, they had all done considerable soul-searching in the time since Soar departed on his sojourn. Jemima had to describe it that way; she had to believe that this was a sabbatical, not a permanent desertion.

All of them, even Solomon, had looked deep within their hearts and souls, questioning whether their own attitudes had contributed to Soar's departure. None of them had all the answers, but they concluded that if there was one thing that was lacking it was those fundamental concepts of understanding and appreciation. Everyone wants to feel understood and appreciated, and perhaps this hadn't been conveyed satisfactorily to Soar in Aquilana. "When our paths cross again, it will be different," Jemima had commented during one family heart-to-heart, and there had been not one word of dissent against this sentiment.

As she flew the short distance back to her family, Jemima noticed that the trees were beginning to shed their withered, brittle leaves, as the inevitable cycle of life continued unabated. The harshness of winter was staring them squarely in the face.

* * *

Soar and Sama sailed effortlessly over the immense mountain range. As they gazed across the rugged expanse, the feeling was almost sensual for Soar. Rather than expansive peaks of granite, he instead had the sensation that they were meek undulations, gently caressing him on his path home.

The return had taken some weeks. Soar had long since ceased to gauge life in days, weeks, or other denominations of the calendar, instead choosing to measure it in experiences. Thus, his perception of any passing of time had become no more than approximate. But retracing his steps had, naturally enough, taken quite some time. Even though it was, in this reverse direction, underpinned by the wisdom of experience, and the support of Sama certainly made a major contribution to the process.

There had been fewer unscheduled deferments, and more successful dodging of the most testing conditions, than had been the case during the initial stages of Soar's journey. They hadn't had the time, nor the inclination, to stop off in some of the notable lands that he'd enjoyed on his initial venture, but hopefully there would be the opportunity to do that in the imminent future. The couple had been solely focused on getting back to Aquilana as quickly as possible, and they were armed with the experience and geographical knowledge to do it. Despite some arduous moments, times when the unforgivable nature of the physical world tested their resolve, they were carried through these moments not only by judicious awareness, but also the pure and simple power of love. As long as they were together, neither one of them would ever lose faith for a moment.

As fate would have it, though, they had spent a little time in the village where Sama had nearly met her demise. Given the prevailing weather conditions, it just happened to intersect with their ideal route. Soar was sensitive to the chilling feelings that this might bring to the surface, but Sama was adamant that she wanted to revisit the small community. "Firstly, we know that it's a great place to stock up," Sama had argued. "Secondly, it's where we met, and that overrides any other feelings that I have about the place. Thirdly, I'm not some damsel-in-distress who needs to be protected from things, Soar! I am perfectly capable of dealing with difficult emotions."

Soar had immediately accepted that internally, but Sama still had a fourth point to make. "And, finally, if we're terrified of death, we will never be able to live. I'm not scared of anything. Especially when I'm with you." And so they had spent a couple of well-earned days of rest in the village, once more sending twigs tumbling down the babbling brook, revisiting the beer garden where they'd first laid eyes on one another, and, naturally, spiraling round the church steeple in joyous unison. It had replenished them physically and spiritually, and they were soon on their way once more in an improved state of mind.

And now they were here. On the verge of Aquilana. This was signaled by the parting of the mountains that Soar had witnessed what seemed like a million times, these bulging protuberances separating within his line of vision to reveal the hamlet that he'd once called home. The process created a strange dichotomy between the feeling of awe-inspiring majesty, and the anomalous sensation of these vast landmarks being cozily familiar.

Soar gesticulated to Sama, indicating that Aquilana was within view, and suddenly an emotional pang of recognition began inundating his stomach. He was two months old, barreling over the icy waters in his first solo flight. He was at the summer solstice, when he'd had his first encounter with a female at a communal gathering, the long, lazy, lustrous evening seeming to last forever. He was bitterly arguing with his Preschool teacher. He was disturbing an assiduously arranged pile of autumnal leaves, as he seared through the trees, causing one of his neighbors to curse him. He was circling around playfully with his younger sister, brimming with delight at her rapid development. He was clashing forcefully with his father, and then filled with pride as his father praised his hunting. He was smiling bashfully as his family good-naturedly mocked his singing, all gathered around the piano. He was lonely and isolated, feeling as if no other eagle shared his feelings. Everything came flooding back to him. He was home again.

Soar knew only one way to deal with this febrile mixture of emotion. Silence and deep breaths. He was torn inside, overwhelmed, gasping in air, almost hyperventilating. It was one of those disorienting situations that arise in life, in which half of his body was desperate to do one thing, while the other half wanted him to hurtle rapidly in the opposite direction. His heart and mind were unified in their determination, but his central nervous system was considerably less enthusiastic. But he knew that it was something that he had to do, no matter how conflicted his body was making him feel, no matter the frostiness of the reception awaiting him, and regardless of the potentially undesirable consequences of his actions.

Then as the two eagles began to instinctively reduce their altitude, everything that Soar had experienced began to come back to him. The near-death experiences. Learning to live purposefully. Expressing gratitude for all that is good and embodying that in the way that you interact with the world. Daily meditation. The sessions with the walrus. The magical time spent with the Master. Working through his untimely passing. Evolving his diet. Becoming leaner, fitter, and stronger. The physical challenges that he'd endured. The incredible journey that he'd completed. Coming out of himself, becoming more social, making new friends. All that he had learned about himself. All that he had endured and enjoyed in the world around him. The shift in his mindset. The connection with the infinite. The love in his heart. The lady by his side. He had grown immeasurably. He was a new eagle. He could cope with this. He could deal with what is the only constant in this perpetually evolving universe—change itself!

"Soar, I know this means a lot to you, and I know that you're nervous," Sama began addressing him perceptively, speaking in a soft and elegant tone that contrasted deliciously with her resilient nature. "But I want you to know something before we land. You have to accept souls as they are. People feel fear. People are scared of what's on the inside. Even you are. Even I am. You can't make anyone see things from your perspective, even your own flesh and blood. You can't make them understand. You can only take them to water; you can't make them drink."

"I know," Soar replied with equanimity. "I'm just scared of two things."

"Which are?"

Soar was hesitant to speak, fearing that somehow voicing his fears would make them more real, and create a self-fulfilling prophecy. "Firstly, I suppose that I'm scared of rejection. I love my family a lot, and I know now that I haven't always shown it. I know that I had my fair share of difficulties. I know we had our differences but the fact remains, I had a happy childhood."

He turned to Sama and spoke from the heart. "As we were approaching Aquilana, I just had an array of flashbacks to my youth, and, honestly, there were more good memories than bad. At worst, it was mixed; there was light and dark, as in any life. I don't regret my views, I don't regret leaving on this voyage of discovery, and I don't even regret the way that I felt when I was younger." Soar took a deep breath and continued. "But I've grown, I've become more self-aware, and I can see now that I didn't show nearly enough gratitude for what they did for me. That should be central to who you are. I'm ashamed of that. And I'm really glad that I've experienced everything that has happened to me, including you, because I will never make that same mistake again. I'm just scared that they will reject me."

Sama gazed at Soar with sympathetic, adoring eyes. "Okay, and what's the second fear?"

"I suppose that I'm a bit scared that I will have outgrown them. That we won't be able to relate to each other. And that we'll feel like strangers."

"Right, well, let me deal with the second point first," Sama answered immediately. "If you approach this with the right attitude, which I know you will, then you have nothing to worry about. You're not coming from a place of judgment. You're coming from a place of love. And I'm confident that they will be coming from the same place. So you have nothing to worry about."

Soar began to respond to Sama, but she was already reeling off the answer to his other point. "And regarding them potentially rejecting you, I only know these two things. Firstly, I will be here with you, no matter what, and whatever happens, we'll ride it out together." Soar smiled warmly at this sentiment. "And, secondly, I don't know your folks, but I do know you, and I also know that they made you. And I just cannot believe that people that are capable of molding you are going to do anything else other than welcome you back with open arms."

* * *

Solomon, Jemima, and Carrie hunched around the ceramic teapot, thankful for the warmth that it provided. A decimated shell of their treasured Long-Tail Lodge remained, but there was nothing of substance to keep out the cold. They had clung to their meager possessions, attempting to derive some comfort from them, but their dilapidated home was little more than a depressing reminder of what once stood so proudly. There had been some good times in the warmer climes of summer, even without Soar, but the bite was returning to the night air and Aquilana had never been in worse shape. There was much to ponder.

"This is an awesome cup of tea," Carrie remarked, her sunny disposition never failing her. But her cheery demeanor couldn't disguise the fact that the family were concerned about the future. The physical and organizational structure of Aquilana had essentially collapsed. Because the settlement had always relied on a rigid hierarchy, its residents didn't have the skill sets to adapt. Everything was organized around strictly defined roles, but this approach was useless when confronted with a radically altered, and indeed evolving, situation. Aquilana could break, but not bend.

As plans to rebuild had been revealed as increasingly unrealistic, there had been something of a mutiny. But the residents didn't know how to teach themselves new tricks. They hadn't received a broad education. They hadn't been encouraged to seek their full potential. And they didn't know anything else other than Aquilana. All alternatives had been squashed, so when they needed more radical thinking, there was no one capable of doing it. Eventually, the settlement had splintered—there was no formal organization left at all. It was a completely atomized society; families greeted one another because they'd known each other for many years. They tried to help each other out where they could. There was no hostility, nor nastiness. But what was once a community was now simply individual families looking after their own. It was still Aquilana by name, but by name alone.

It was in this midst of this climate of decline that they faced the unforgiving winter months. They remained a resourceful family, and all three of them had made contributions to their upkeep. No matter how harsh the winter became, they would survive. But their hopes of anything more than survival had dwindled, almost disappeared, like the dying embers of smoldering coal.

As they sat among the wreckage of their home, making chit chat, anything to distract them from contemplating the impending bleakness of the winter months, two figures appeared in the distance, silhouetted against the setting sun. For some moments, they went unnoticed, but then Solomon clocked them in his line of vision. The contours of their bodies gradually expanded as they grew closer, and it became clear that they were headed straight for the family. By this time, Carrie and Jemima were also watching these mysterious figures, who remained shrouded in shadow; dark and unrecognizable.

But then beams of natural light cascaded down on them, finally revealing their identity. One of the figures was Soar! All three of them experienced an emotional epiphany. They were profoundly happy, in a way that exceeded the limiting confines of language. They felt unadulterated joy. It was just so good to see him. They had all wondered if this moment would ever come.

Such was the excitement of this unexpected occurrence, it only barely registered that Soar was accompanied by a handsome female eagle. But his mother was the first to notice this, wondering who this unknown creature might be, her maternal brain already working prodigiously; jumping to conclusions that were, as it turned out, far from inaccurate.

It seemed to take an age for Soar to finally reach them, but when he did the reunion was one of sheer glee. There was no awkwardness, nothing that Soar had built up in his head transpired. Greeting them and being around them again was the most natural thing in the world. He held his mother first, and tears flowed as inevitably as rainfall teems from clouds. In that instance, Soar felt more connected to his family than he ever had previously. For the first time, as emotional as he was, he felt an internal certainty about the path ahead.

Eventually, the sobbing subsided, and it was possible to use language once more. There were so many things to be said, and so much that could have been said, but conversation began with the simplest, yet most heartfelt, words.

"I missed you so much, Soar."

"I missed you too."

Soon enough, they were enquiring about Soar's companion, and he introduced Sama, briefly explaining how they'd met. His family took a liking to Sama immediately; her disarming charm created an almost immediate connection. They gathered around the dining table, and conversation was soon flowing like a robust port. Soar's parents and sister had so many questions for them, and Soar was able to regale them with a few tales from his journey. There was no dwelling on his exit, only jubilation at his return. Questions were flying at Soar from all angles, and, eventually, he had to request for his family to slow down! There would be plenty of time to convey everything in the days to come, and, indeed, there was so much to share.

Both his mother and father were delighted to see Soar with a good spouse, and they went out of their way to make Sama feel welcome. Although she certainly did feel welcomed, those early hours with Soar's family were also something of a quandary. She had the curious sensation of being an outsider among folk who knew one another intimately, while also feeling an unusual, yet undeniable, feeling of comfort with them. And conversely, it was strange to encounter this feeling, to be around a close family, to feel their acceptance, and their love for Soar, precisely because it was a foreign experience for her. She couldn't help reflecting on how she had been denied this in her childhood, and feelings related to this inevitably surfaced. Indeed, it wasn't just Soar who found this reunion emotional.

It was sad, though, for Soar to see the old place in this disheveled state. He had left so soon after the storm that its impact hadn't really sunk in. There were so many conflicting feelings surging through his mind and body at that time that it had been impossible to process all of them. He had almost expected to return and witness everything having gone back to normal, as he remembered it from his childhood. But that was far from being the case. Few buildings remained, and the population had significantly diminished. When he asked his parents about this, they were evasive, but it seemed likely that many eagles had deserted the community, or possibly even perished.

Nonetheless, the friendly atmosphere raised spirits, seeming to warm the air around them. Soar's mother was soon, inevitably, busying herself in the kitchen, arranging something from the food that was available. The remaining four eagles continued conversing in the meantime, as Soar revealed a few more of his experiences. It became increasingly obvious as they spoke that his father was less severe and had mellowed significantly. He was shorn of cynicism and seemed genuinely interested in everything that Soar had to say, even when it veered into more esoteric territory. It seemed that time had softened his father, like frozen ice cream slowly melting on a summer afternoon.

Dinner was soon being presented—legs of lamb served with shallot gravy. Soar glowed with pride that his mother could prepare food of such quality, remaining blissfully unaware that their food stocks were running dangerously low. As they ate, Soar and Sama explained that their diets had become far more diverse and adventurous in recent months.

"You mean that you don't eat meat half the time?" his mother exclaimed. "I don't even know my own son any more!" She looked at Soar and grinned. "I hope my meager cooking is good enough for your sophisticated palette!" she teased.

"Well, you don't see us leaving anything, do you?" Soar retorted lovingly.

After they'd eaten, the family retired to the sitting room, or what remained of it, and continued their discussion. Soar and Sama naturally became intimately entwined with one another, and it was obvious to everyone that he had found true happiness. Soar continued to charm his family with tales from his journey, and the stories were so rich and vivid that he never needed to become evangelical; the magnitude of what he had experienced was immediately obvious.

The interaction between all four of his family members had become somehow warmer in Soar's absence. Although the presence of Sama perhaps played a role in this, and they were all on their best behavior, there was also no doubt that they now meshed with one another. Soar had quite simply matured; he now knew how to traverse the tightrope between being true to himself, and diplomatic towards the feelings of others. Their period of separation had caused everyone to examine their own attitudes, as well as to fully appreciate each other, and the resulting interaction was less sharp, less confrontational, and all the more loving and supportive as a result.

Soar's growth did not go unnoticed, and his father also observed his physical development, remarking on this glowingly. His parents could see how happy Soar was with Sama, and how much he had developed as an eagle. This was an entirely new Soar; a polished diamond, whose serrated edges had been smoothed off. Meanwhile, the foundation of his strengths and qualities had been used systematically to build himself into an impressive specimen. He still spoke with passion, but now also listened patiently. He still soared through the sky, but now his energy was more focused and controlled. His views were as piercing and distinctive as ever. But now they were delivered without resentment, with an understanding that finding common ground was more important than asserting one's rightness and righteousness.

Suddenly, Sama arose, excusing herself, declaring that she'd like to spend a little time acquainting herself with the surrounding area. There was some protest at this decision, with Soar's mother pointing out that the sky was pitch black. "Oh, that's okay," Sama replied magnanimously. "It is a beautiful clear evening, and there is a full moon. I can see just fine! And I'm itching to check out the region. I'll be back soon enough, rest assured, and I promise you that I can look after myself!" She gave Soar a reassuring squeeze before swooping off into the distance. She was the perfect partner—conscientious enough to recognize that the family needed space; the opportunity to talk without her presence restricting them to forced politeness. Already, before she had even passed out of sight, Sama marveled at the ghostly, shimmering reflection that the moon cast across the inky river, the column of illumination oscillating in the most marginal fashion on this virtually motionless autumnal evening.

"Sama is wonderful, son," his father commented warmly.

"I know. I feel like the luckiest eagle alive every time I wake up next to her."

Soar's mother began to concur with his father, but before she could voice this sentiment, Soar interrupted.

"Listen, there are some important things that I want to discuss with you, and some things that I want to say to you. He turned to his sister. "And you, Carrie, too."

"Go on, Soar, we're listening," his mother replied.

"I have a lot of things to say, and I don't quite know how to say them. I don't know what order to say them in, how to explain them properly, or how to make you understand. But I just want you to listen until I've finished, no matter how much you want to speak! Is that okay?"

Solomon, Jemima, and Carrie all indicated their agreement.

Soar paused for some seconds, briefly becoming conscious of the metronomic clock ticking in the background. He began to speak slowly and carefully, choosing each word diligently. "Okay, well, there are two things that I want to begin with. Growing up was really hard for me, just because of who I am. I didn't choose to be who I am. Fate chose me. And I honestly had to get away from here to find myself. But now I have, and I've never been happier or more comfortable with myself."

"On the other hand, I want you to know that, although I didn't agree with a lot of things that happened when I was younger, now that I've seen and experienced so much, I have realized that you were correct about many things, you knew lots of things that I did not, and I wasn't right about everything. Not only wasn't I right about everything, but I also didn't express myself in the way that I should have done on many occasions, and at times my behavior was, at best, juvenile. And I want to say sorry for that, and sorry for not listening more. I've learned that skill now."

Soar could feel emotion coursing through his body. He had turned these issues over in his head countless times, but that didn't make voicing this any easier. "I know that I was unruly from a young age, sometimes unduly so. But I also think sometimes that it was justified. I can't live a buttoned-down life. It makes me feel trapped. It goes against my nature and what I believe in. I should have tried harder to express this to you calmly, but I guess that I didn't do the best job."

As he spoke, he was struggling to look at his family, particularly his parents, hoping that his words were being received favorably. "And now that I've been on this journey of discovery, I know that there is so much to learn, so much to experience, so much to see beyond the confines of this region. That is why I've become the eagle that you see before you. I know that you will have noticed the change in me. That's all because of the growth that has occurred naturally in this vast world of opportunity."

Soar swallowed, gulping back his nerves, and continued. "And there's one last thing that I want to say. And it's important." Soar paused again for effect. "I'm not staying. Not for very long. I can't stay here. Not now. In fact, I only came back here for one reason." Soar finally glanced up, and earnestly looked his father, mother, and sister in the eye, one after the other.

"To convince you all to come with me."

18. The End of the Beginning

It was nearly noon as Sama began heading back to Aquilana; the time of day indicated by the lofty position of the lemonish sun. It was that time of year when the degree of radiance that the sunlight provided was unpredictable, but this seemed to be one of the less brisk wintry days. This relative warmth pleased Sama as she navigated back to Soar and his family.

Having barely slept overnight, Sama had thoroughly investigated the surrounding area, and thus her internal compass was already fully attuned to the idiosyncrasies of the region. It was not that she was unable to rest, more that she didn't wish to miss the opportunity to explore the breathtaking natural beauty of this locale. Who knew when they would be here again? Life is unpredictable, and it's important to squeeze every conceivable drop of juice from each day. We never know how many days we have ahead of us, so none should be taken for granted. Sama had learned that lesson at an age when few consider it.

From a distance, the mountains on the horizon resembled giant Brazil nuts, with their rugged and ridged appearance. Sama noted just how steep and slanted they were and considered the difficulty of scaling them. Being flightless is unimaginable, she reflected. It was perhaps this prospect that had scared her as much as death, when the searing bullet had damaged her wing. To be rendered incapable of flight would be unbearable, not to mention the inevitable segregation from other birds.

As she closed in on her destination, she observed several lambs dancing merrily in the fields below, their fluffy coats as pure as the driven snow. "Pure in color, pure by nature," Sama thought. As much as she had successfully enjoyed her brief sojourn, it hadn't been enough to completely distract her from the matter at hand. She was very concerned for Soar. She was worried about what his family would say, and indeed what he might say to his family. The consequences of this were quite unclear, and she recognized that there was a huge amount of uncertainty surrounding the whole thing. All she could do was deliver on the promise that she would be there to support Soar whatever happened, and nurse him through whatever distressing feelings he might encounter.

Sama was turning this over in her head repeatedly as she approached the landing area for Aquilana, pondering what the future held for them. It was the right thing to do to give them their space, but that didn't make the wait to reunite with Soar any less agonizing! Such was the degree of her distraction that she didn't even notice the group of eagles that were congregating alongside the Byzantine lamps. There were dozens of eagles, all gazing up attentively at her, as she began her descent. Sama was taken aback by this unexpected sight, so much so that she didn't even clock Soar at first. But then his eager waving registered with her, and, sure enough, there were his parents and sister alongside him, smiling encouragingly. A promising sign!

Landing proved to be tricky, simply because there was less space than usual, but Sama was soon picking her way through the crowd to greet her partner.

"Soar! It's great to see you!" Sama turned to Soar's family. "Hi everyone! How are we doing today?!"

Solomon, Jemima, and Carrie all indicated that they were great, before excusing themselves so that Soar and Sama could catch up. They drifted off to speak with a neighbour and were soon in animated conversation.

"Hey, sorry I didn't come back last night," Sama began. "You guys needed some space. I wanted you to talk everything over without me getting in the way."

"Well, you're nothing if not full of surprises!", Soar observed.

"You should know that by now…"

"Before you go any further, I want you to know that everything's great, and everything's going to be great. Let me explain all that's happened while you were away."

*   *   *

When Soar had put the proposition to his parents and sister, there was no initial acceptance. In fact, they shifted around uncomfortably, as perhaps would be the natural reaction to being told that they should abandon their home of many years.

But something perceptible had shifted in them. They were ready to be persuaded. Considering everything that they'd endured, the scales that governed the decision were finely balanced, and even tilting slightly in Soar's direction. They just needed to be convinced.

"I understand how you feel. But it's not a case of abandoning Aquilana. No one is forced to stay here unless they choose to do so. There are millions of eagles out there, plus countless other creatures. There is so much to learn and experience. You know that from my stories. You're not even scratching the surface of your potential here, let alone life itself. I want you to come so much. And I know that it would make you happy."

Soar was amazed that there was no interruption at this point, and so, emboldened by this at least neutral reception, he continued.

"Also, my plan is for it to be more than just us four and Sama. I want to try to bring some of the other residents with us. I want to help other eagles, and for that matter other animals as well. I want everyone to know that there are some extraordinary places beyond the immediate confines of Aquilana."

Each of his family members continued to listen attentively to Soar. They could see how much he had developed; his qualities shone through in both his words and manner.

"And there's one last thing that I want to say to you."

Soar spoke deliberately, his voice dropping in volume slightly. This was not pretentious, but rather a reflection of the gravity of his words. He explained everything that had happened to Sama, her early life, her struggles, and the fortitude that she had demonstrated to achieve a situation of equilibrium in life. Then, without dwelling on the near-death experience too much, Soar also briefly recounted the sobering fact that she had saved his life. And that he wouldn't be here without her.

"And, as tough as she is, and Sama is way too strong to ever admit this, she needs a family. I know that she only met you today, but she needs you as much as I do."

His parents had listened attentively to every word and Carrie shed a tear when Soar recounted the tragedy of Sama's early life. And when he finished, they were quite magnanimous in their response. They conceded that Aquilana had never really recovered, and that actually Soar had been correct in many of his observations.

"It was so hard to let go, son," his father began, "but the reality is, and I've discussed this with your mother, we should have joined you when you left. It was the right time to make a new start." Solomon leant forward in his chair meaningfully. "But I'm glad that we didn't make that choice because you might never have met Sama, and that was something that was destined to happen. We can see the good that she does for you, and the good that is in her, and we've never seen you this happy and fulfilled."

His mother interjected. "So there have been some horrible times while you've been away, but we know it was for the best. And that's all we want for you—the best. That's all we've ever wanted." Before Soar could express his elation, there was another surprise. "And I don't know how your father or sister feel, but I feel quite confident that I speak for all of us when I say that I want to come with you. But it has to be a family decision," Jemima said.

Carrie quickly indicated her agreement. "I'm itching for a big adventure; I can't wait!"

This merely left the patriarch of the family to concur. Solomon mused on the prospect for some moments, his conservative nature seemingly engaged in a duel to the death with the reality of the situation. Then suddenly he spoke with an uncharacteristic abandon. "Oh, what the hell! Let's go for it!"

Soar immediately shot from his chair, hugging his father, and soon all four of them were gathered around one another, with a closeness and camaraderie that made Soar's heart leap with joy.

"No, Soar. What we'll do is get up at the crack of dawn, seek out everyone who lives here, and tell them that we're going to have a meeting first thing in the morning. You can speak before all that attend and tell them what you told us. I want you to address Constantine, the village Elders, and everyone who lives here. And if they want to come with us, wonderful, and if they don't want to come, that's their choice."

Soar was not an experienced public speaker, and as he pictured himself orating before dozens of unblinking, intimidating eyes, the concept wasn't a particularly appealing one. But his mother reassured him: "You'll be absolutely fine. We all believe in you. I'm sure that everyone will be willing to listen to you. We're not in a good state. If we can see that, I'm sure others will as well." And he recognized that although this might not be an appealing prospect, it was another one of those things that he simply had to do.

So the very next day, Soar found himself in front of more eagles than he would care to count. His family had done a sterling job in rousing virtually every resident, but now the reality of what was required from him had become undeniably real. In that moment, Soar recognized that his life had come full circle. He had begun as the outsider, the ostracized, skeptically listening as he was forced to absorb the words of others. And now it was his turn to convince an audience of the worth of his words. Soar was self-aware enough now to recognize that he had no ethical right to refuse this opportunity, as it was precisely a platform of this nature that he had desired when he had felt marginalized. All of the feelings he had of being sublimated into an unfulfilling role, his views dismissed, his concerns attacked and ridiculed, returned to him vividly. He pictured the moment that he had decided to leave Aquilana; it appeared graphically before him with startling lucidity, as if he could see through time. All of his journey had been leading to this moment. He had asked for this. And if he couldn't grasp this opportunity when it was in front of him, he was a coward; a mere fraction of the eagle that he believed himself to be.

Standing on a makeshift podium composed of a few discarded logs, Soar breathed deeply and purposefully in an attempt to calm his nerves, scanning the audience as he did so. There were hundreds of familiar eyes gazing up at him in anticipation. Then suddenly Soar spotted Constantine among them. In fact, a few of the Elders were present. This initially made Soar feel tense, but he noted that the face of his former nemesis was set in a neutral expression. He was at least prepared to listen. Soar steeled himself. He had no speech prepared, nothing to follow but his gut instinct. All he could do was speak from the heart.

"Ladies and gentlemen, thank you for heeding my call, and assembling here this morning. I know that I have been absent from Aquilana for some time, but I wanted to share something with you all. I've been on an incredible journey and have witnessed amazing places. I have eaten sumptuous food that I didn't even know existed. I've met inspirational characters right across the animal kingdom. And I've learnt so much about life and myself. I connected with powers that are unimaginable, and equally difficult to describe! I challenged myself so much. I grew so much. But, above all else, I developed so much empathy for other sentient creatures. And that includes you."

Soar noticed that his audience remained silent and watchful, apparently interested in his words. This encouraged him to continue boldly.

"I didn't have enough empathy before. I know that now. I also know that I could be an irritant. But I want to make amends for that and invite you all to the opportunity of a lifetime." Soar's eyes scanned the crowd for dissent as he spoke. "I know what all of you are capable of doing and achieving. You don't need to limit yourselves. I want you all to live a life of ambition and abundance. I want you to be able to experience the things that I have experienced, to see the things that I have seen. I don't deserve this more than you; every one of you deserves it just as much as me."

"There is a staggering array of diverse beauty out there. Out in the big wide world beyond these confines. There are lands that will take your breath away. Climates of every type imaginable. You can wake up warmed by tropical beauty every day or surrounded by a shimmering ice palace. There is a bounty of food that goes way beyond anything that I could have imagined. Simply by changing my diet and exercising diligently, I've become leaner, fitter, stronger, and a better flier. The more that I've tested my physical and mental limits, the more I've realized that I can extend those limits beyond anything that I believed possible."

"I know that many of you will always love Aquilana. And I'm not here to bash our home. But we have been, and I've always said this, too suspicious of outsiders. It has been one of my greatest lessons and experiences to mix with other creatures, embrace other cultures, to recognize that I don't know or understand everything, and never will. Just in this way alone, I have grown beyond all recognition. I have become a better eagle, a better avian being, than when I left. I hope that you can all see that."

People were still listening, and Soar's nerves had largely dissipated. He had grasped the nettle like a baton, and now he was running with it.

"We have had a great home here in many ways, but it was one that I felt limited me. I don't say that because I believe that I'm anything special; I believe that it applies to every one of you as well. I want you to experience the joy of living purposefully, with true freedom, and no ceiling on what you can see, experience, and achieve. And when you're truly ready, you can even have spiritual experiences that go way beyond the perimeters of your five senses."

"I know that this is a lot to take in now. I don't want to say too much or give you too much to digest. I just want you to know that there is a better life for you out there. If you're willing to challenge yourself. If you're willing to step outside of your comfort zone. If you're willing to step beyond the cozy familiarity of Aquilana. I believe that this is the ideal time, and not because Aquilana may be struggling a little, or because you've been through a lot of trauma." Soar surveyed the audience, monitoring their reactions as he spoke. "But because you cannot waste a single day of your life, living in a way that is reductive, restrictive, and restraining you from realizing your true potential."

"I want you all to come with me on a journey of discovery. I want you to leave Aquilana. I want you to believe in your heart that the whole planet is your home. And that you can do anything and go anywhere that you wish. I set off from Aquilana several months ago with the simple notion that I felt there was more to see and do. I thank the universe that I made that decision. There were challenges, immense challenges, along the way, but at the end of that journey of growth, I have everything that I ever wanted, and more than I could even imagine."

Soar looked up, surveying the audience once more. Out of the corner of his eye, he spotted his mother, who was crying softly.

"I want every single one of you to have that opportunity as well. And the only way to do that is to throw off the shackles of this place, and the limiting mentality associated with it. So, I hope that you will all join me."

As soon as it became clear that Soar had finished speaking, he received a heartfelt ovation. His words were encouraging and energizing at a time when Aquilana was at its lowest. The assembled eagles had craved something of substance to cheer them; suddenly they were being promised a dish that far exceeded mere crumbs of comfort.

Soar was soon being slapped on the back and commended for his words. They had struck a chord with a community of eagles that were ready for change. It was not merely his oration that had captured their hearts; many of the eagles present had noticed the admirable growth in him. Soar had been a prominent figure in Aquilana before leaving, and thus virtually all residents were well acquainted with him. This was, unquestionably, a new Soar; more mature, healthier, wiser, and, quite frankly, rather impressive.

Within a matter of minutes, Soar was receiving expressions of interest from eagles that spanned every conceivable demographic. Some of the eldest residents, who had lived in Aquilana for many years, and had known nothing else, were keen to join him. Some were skeptical, some were torn, and others expressed the sentiment that they simply didn't want to leave.

As the assembled creatures thronged around Soar, eventually the inevitable happened. He felt a powerful wing tap him on the shoulder, turned to respond, and came face-to-face with Constantine. Soar's heart began beating palpably. But before he had even spoken a word, this once severe figure already seemed somehow softer, as if the harsh realities of life had tenderized him.

"That was a very compelling speech, Soar. I didn't realize that you were such an accomplished public speaker."

"Neither did I!", Soar joked, attempting to lighten the mood.

"Listen, I owe you an apology. I shouldn't have spoken to you the way that I did before you left. It was rude and unnecessary." Constantine's wizened features morphed into a smile. "I'm glad that you came back, even if it's just for a brief visit."

"That's okay. I'm sorry too. Let's be honest, I was a considerable pain in the ass!"

The two eagles chucked in unison. "I wouldn't disagree with that observation! But you were also correct about many things, and I was too stupid or stubborn to see it. And I was probably too pig-headed to admit that you might be right, and I might be wrong."

"Well, maybe we were more alike than we realized!"

Constantine nodded solemnly, as a wry expression played upon his face. There was no time for a long conversation, as Soar was literally surrounded by dozens of eager residents. But the two eagles that had clashed so frequently over the years did find enough time to make their peace. They would perhaps never be the best of friends, but they were now much closer to this than enemies.

Soar was fully prepared for Constantine to accompany him, his family, and anyone else from Aquilana who was ready to take a voyage into the unknown. But the Elder politely declined. "My family grew up here, and their family before them, and their family before them. I belong here." The patriarch looked Soar sincerely in the eye. "But I wish you well, young eagle, and I want you to remember these words. If you ever return to these parts, as long as there is breath in my lungs, I can guarantee that you will receive the warmest welcome."

After so many years of antipathy, the two eagles parted amicably. Eventually, after some swift organization and head-counting, of the approximately three-hundred eagles present, nearly two-thirds stated that they would journey with Soar and his family. There was a consensus of appreciation for what Soar had done, and the general mood of receptiveness was hugely gratifying for him. But what was even more gratifying was a revelation that surpassed even the overarching sentiment of positivity. As Soar spoke with his fellow residents, their warmth towards him made him understand something that he had somehow never realized previously.

He was respected and loved in Aquilana. And always had been.

So that's how it came to be that this band of buoyant eagles were massed together, ready to desert their home, and fly off into the blue yonder. His parents were initially slightly concerned about Sama's non-appearance, but Soar reassured them that she was merely acutely sensitive to the needs of others, and that he had no doubt that she would reappear at the perfect moment. Which, of course, she did.

Soar was beyond excited. He couldn't wait to show his family Eudaimonia, Magna, and whatever other majestic and remarkable lands they happened upon in this always unpredictable world of unending possibility. Not everyone would make it as far as the Lost Kingdom; each creature's journey is its own. But Soar knew exactly where Sama and himself were headed. He was already thinking back to last year's games — sixth place was never going to be good enough for Soar. Next year, he'd show them!

Soar was flanked on either side by his family and his soulmate. His father placed his wing lovingly on Soar's shoulder and expressed his excitement and gratitude. "I'm proud of you, son," he said with touching sincerity. In response, Soar merely beamed.

The band of fearless eagles set off on their journey, infused with a feeling of hope and expectation that echoed across the universe. For the first time in his life, as the Master had said, Soar knew that his potential was limitless. He felt irresistible, indestructible, beyond infinite. It was daylight, but the joyful vibrations in his heart chakra were so potent that they could still have illuminated the sky like fireworks. There was an energy, an optimism, an awestruck feeling tangible among those present that was truly inspiring, and Soar could only wonder at the cosmic potential of this aspiring collective.

This wasn't the end; it was just the end of the beginning.

Acknowledgements

A big thank you to all the amazing people who have assisted in the development of this book. Firstly, we appreciate the invaluable contributions made by Lauren Squillino as the editor and cover designer of Soar.

Ketan Kulkarni

This book could not have been written without the unconditional love, support, inspiration, and encouragement of my significantly better half, Saty. My children, Reeva, Risha, and Neil also ensure that I experience and understand the fathomless equations of love, gratitude, and giving without expectations.

My family nourished me in their loving environment, providing a rich experience by imparting invaluable life lessons and character building. My close friends provide me with mentorship, guidance, encouragement, appreciation, and even reprimand me as needed. They are my infallible safety net.

I am enormously indebted to my hundreds of teachers, coaches, and mentors, from kindergarten to the present day. They are far too many to list here, but all of them are/were amazing! Furthermore, my large circle of friends further enriches my lived experience.

I want to extend a special gratitude to my friends, colleagues, and co-authors, Francis Yoo and Christopher Morris, for their deep and whole presence and inspiration.

And a special thank you to *Padmashri Dr. Vijaykumar Shah* for his vision, encouragement, enthusiasm, guidance, and support.

Christopher Morris

Although I can never convey this to her, I would like to thank my dog Keiko, who taught me so many of the lessons contained within this book that it could not have been written without her—even though she frequently tried to interrupt the process!

I would also like to thank everyone who has ever believed in me or offered any form of support. I would also like to express my gratitude for the abundance of this world, all the good fortune that I have had, and the extremely fortunate way that I am able to live my life today. Each day is a gift, and I give thanks for every day that I wake up still breathing.

Francis Yoo

First, my deep thanks to my co-authors Ketan and Chris, whose contributions to this book far outweigh mine. The relationship and teamwork we have developed gives me both peace and excitement.

Second, I thank all the people presently in my life on a regular basis, that give me comfort and challenge in different dimensions of my life today: Mary Bayno DO, my fellow OMM department faculty members at TouroCOM Harlem, Craig Wells DO, Lauren Davis DO, Tao Semko, the crew at Hi-Collar, おぎの先生, Joshua Kim, Julian Kim, Wesley Han, Rev Chongho James Kim, Kathryn Staley, the LGA crew, Amelia Bueche DO and the Coaching for Institutions crew.

Thank you to my mother and father who continually care for me and about me, annoy and bug me, and make sure I always eat delicious food when I am with them.

Thank you, Health, Essence, Presence.

覚悟, 経験値.

We would also like to thank John Graham-Pole and Dorothy Lander, our publishers at HARP, The People's Press, for their wisdom, patience, feedback, encouragement, and support.

About the Authors

Ketan Kulkarni is a multiple international award-winning physician, clinician-researcher, passionate entrepreneur, finance and career coach, avid learner, traveler, photographer, artist, art enthusiast and antiques collector, and music buff. He has a huge interest in Ancient Wisdom, history, spirituality, and ancient knowledge. Ketan has been featured nationally and internationally in several magazines, media, interviews, and podcasts. He was recently conferred an honorary PhD in humanities by the Open International University of Complementary Medicine.

Christopher Morris has worked on over 50 books as an author, ghostwriter, and editor, across an array of subjects, including several bestsellers. His journalistic writing has also featured in many notable publications, including the New York Times, the Sunday Telegraph, the Financial Times, Newsweek, Yahoo, the Times Educational Supplement, and Seeking Alpha. When not reading or writing, Christopher enjoys sport, music, travelling, dining in restaurants, and walking his dog in the countryside.

Francis Yoo is a practicing Osteopath at his private Osteopathic Medical practice, Whole Presence Osteopathy, in New York City, electric guitarist, sushi enthusiast, video gamer, scholar and educator. He is a Cultivation Coach who draws upon a variety of experiences as a certified Myers-Briggs Type Indicator practitioner, Riso-Hudson certified Enneagram Teacher, faculty member for Glenn Morris' Kundalini Awakening Process to help himself and others cultivate Wholeness, Presence, and palpable personal development.

For further information or communication contact:

Dr Ketan Kulkarni
www.savvyphysician.ca

Dr. Francis Yoo (SOUL Coach):
www.DrFrancisYoo.com

Christopher Morris
https://christopherpaulmorris.com/

Book related and media inquiries:

legendaryquestpro@gmail.com
www.thelegendaryquest.pro

Printed in the USA
CPSIA information can be obtained
at www.ICGtesting.com
LVHW010550240124
769435LV00039B/439